RECLAIMING KATE

MYSTIC FALLS
BOOK FOUR

MARY WARREN

To those who left their dreams behind, it's never forget too late to reclaim them. It's never too late to live the life you want.

FOREWORD

Hello Reader,

I'm happy to be sharing Kate's story with all of you. Please be aware that in this story Kate is dealing with the past trauma of being in an abusive relationship. Please check the content warning to make sure you are safe reading this story. If you or anyone you know needs help please call the National Domestic Abuse Hotline at 800-799-7233 or visit https://www.thehotline.org/

Content Warning - Past Domestic Violence, Description of Domestic Violence, Confronting Abuser, Mention of Past Suicidal Ideation, Minor Anti-fatness, Injury/Hospital (not related to domestic violence), Graphic Sexual Content

CHAPTER 1

Kate

It was January in Mystic Falls, and that meant one thing.

Hockey.

Kate watched from the bookstore's window as the town square being transformed into an ice rink for the winter festival. Winterfest not only turned the town square into a skating winter wonderland, but it was a homecoming for the town and their hockey team. It had always been one of her favorite town festivals growing up because Kate McPhee was from THE hockey family in Mystic Falls.

Her dad was the town's hockey coach. Not only that, but it was her father's sixtieth birthday. So this year, it was even more of a big deal. Saturday morning there would be a scrimmage with a bunch of his old players over the years, including all her brothers. Then, there would be a birthday party that afternoon, then hopefully life would go back to normal. Kate loved her dad and was happy the town was celebrating him in this way, but she had a complicated relationship with hockey.

Her whole family had made hockey their lives. All three of her brothers had gone on to have careers in hockey; the oldest was a coach at the college level, the youngest was a sports agent, and her twin brother played for the Glendale Magic. She used to love the game growing up, but that love was gone. Now she just tried not to resent it, but this week was going to make that especially hard.

The bell over the bookstore's door sounded and Kate turned to see Bridget walking in from next door. This charming Scottish woman ran the magic shop next to the bookstore. She had only been in Mystic Falls for a little over a year, but she was already becoming a big part of their little town. She kept life interesting, that was for sure.

"Good mornin' Kate," Bridget said as she made herself a cup of tea at the counter. "Looks like they're putting that ice rink back up in the town square again."

"It is that time of year. The Winter Festival should be in full swing this afternoon. And with my dad's birthday party, it's going to be a crazy weekend."

"Are ye going to get on the ice?" Bridget asked with a smile.

"Yeah, I'll probably skate. I always loved skating around the gazebo. I actually really missed it while I was away from Mystic Falls." After college, Kate had moved in with her boyfriend and stayed with him in Indiana. They broke up over a year ago, and Kate found herself back in Mystic Falls working at their local bookstore. It was a cute little store. Kate had started some social media accounts for it and was really getting some buzz. She had even opened an online shop that was pretty successful. Mystic Falls was a good place to get back on your feet, but this weekend was going to be tough. It would be hockey...all hockey.

"The square certainly does look pretty this morning," Bridget said, joining her at the window.

Kate just nodded. "Well, I need to get some of these new releases photographed and shelved, so if you'll excuse me."

"Of course. I might need to venture out into the cold and see some of the fine-looking men. I think I see one ye might like out there."

"I highly doubt that," she said as she turned to go into the backroom. As she made her way, she heard the bell sound again and she assumed Bridget was leaving.

"Oh, well hello. Aren't ye a handsome lad?"

Kate turned back out to see a tall, muscular man with a well-kept beard and a head of red hair.

"Here's one of the handsome lads for ya now, Kate, my dear," said Bridget grinning ear to ear.

"Hey KitKat," greeted the ginger haired man.

"It seems you are acquainted already?"

"That we are, have been for our whole lives," Kate said with a smile.

"Longer than our whole lives," he answered with a warm smile all his own.

"Bridget, this is my brother, Conner."

"Twin brother," he corrected. "Nice to meet you," he said and stuck out a hand to greet Bridget.

"You sure are a handsome lad," she said with a mischievous smile.

"Thank you. Make sure you come to the hockey game tomorrow," he said as he flashed her a smile.

"If there'll be more men who look like ye, I wouldn't miss it. Ye all make me feel like I'm back home in Scotland."

"Well, just wait until you meet my brothers," he said.

"I'm looking forward to it," she said, giving his hand a pat. "I'm off Kate, I'll see you soon, I'm sure."

"Goodbye, Bridget."

Conner walked over to his sister and gave her a hug. It would be hard to tell they were twins. He was tall and chiseled and friendly looking. She was shorter and rounder and...less friendly looking. Where Conner had an inviting smile, Kate had a pretty severe case of Resting Bitch Face. She liked it that way, it kept all the unwanted small talk at bay. The only thing that pointed to their relation was the mess of red curls that sat on top of both their heads.

"How ya doing KitKat? I missed you during the holidays this year. I was bummed that I couldn't make it home."

"It was just another McPhee family Christmas. Too loud, too much food, and too many McPhees, and still pretty wonderful."

"I bet, I'm glad I could make it home for this. I think it is going to be a pretty great event. In fact, I was just looking over the roster for the scrimmage. There are so many people who are coming to play, and a couple of the high school kids too. It should be good...but...we are short on one crucial part." He looked at her with pleading eyes.

She took the roster from him and looked at the teams. She saw all of her brothers on the list, a couple town favorites like Sam Smith, DeMarcus Jones, Lucas Fipp, and many other names she recognized. And then she saw the name Wes Darling.

"Wes Darling? You brought your teammate? Is he as cocky as he appears on the ice?"

"Nah, that's all for the ice. He's a pretty great guy."

She just nodded as she continued to look at the list.

"Do you see the problem with the teams?" he asked.

"I do," she said, but left it there.

"I am prepared to beg," he said. "And it won't be pretty, so you might as well say yes right now."

"No. Conner, I haven't played since college."

"Come on, you know you still got it, and we need another goalie."

She shook her head. She couldn't do it; she could not get back in front of that net. "Just make Patrick do it. He knows how to play goalie."

"Come on KitKat, knowing how to play goalie is different than BEING a goalie. You know that."

"Conner, no."

"Come on, you know how happy it would make dad to watch all four of us out there again. When is the next time all four of us will be home like this? I know after college you were done with hockey, and I get it...kind of. But come on, for dad."

That wasn't playing fair. She had only been on skates a handful of times since college, and she hadn't held a stick or put on her pads since the last game her senior year. Could she even still do it?

But Conner knew how to hit her where it hurt. He knew full well that she wouldn't be able to say no to her dad. And she did know what it would mean to him to see all his kids out on the ice one last time, and if she was honest, she didn't know when that would happen again. They were all getting so busy and coming home less often. It had been a long time since they had all been together like this. Patrick and his family live in Ohio where he coached. Dylan lived in the city as a sports agent, he traveled a lot. And then of course Conner plays professionally so for ten months out of the year he is at the mercy of the league.

"Conner, I'm probably not even that good anymore," she said, desperately trying to find a way out of it.

"We both know that's a lie. You may not be at the top of your game anymore, but you can still play well enough to play here."

She just looked at him.

"Look, I know you don't play anymore, but it has been so long since Patrick, Dylan and I have all been in town at once. AND it's dad's birthday. It would mean so much to him."

"Let me think about it."

"We kind of got to finalize the roster -" She shot him a glare. "Okay, you think about it and tell me later tonight."

"Deal. Now why don't you go out there and help get the rink up and going. The ice looked almost ready when I came in this morning." They both looked out the window and sure enough it was coming together. "I'll be out there for the opening at three. I'll let you know then."

"Okay, see you out there. Just so you know, I already dug out your old skates and pads. You just have to show up. I even have your skates in my car right now. I know you like skating the square."

"Bring me my skates and go away. I'll consider it."

"It'll be fun to be back on the ice with you, just like old times," he said with a grin.

"You are pushing your luck," she said with a smirk.

"Okay, I'm outta here. I'll drop your skates off. Then Wes and I are going to the school to lead a hockey workshop for the kids. I'll see you at the kickoff for the winter festival and for dad's announcement."

"See ya then," she said as he left.

Kate took a deep breath. She should've known this would happen this weekend. She searched her mind for reasons to say no, but she knew she would be playing. The only person she would consider it for was her father, but it would be nice to get back on the ice with her brothers. She had grown up on the ice with them, so one last time for her dad and her brothers. She could do it...she hoped.

CHAPTER 2

WES

"Hey! Great skate everyone! I know you guys are going to dominate that state championship. I don't remember the last time I've seen a group of kids this talented," Wes said with a big smile stretched across his face.

"Yeah, I'm looking forward to tomorrow morning," Conner said.

"Alright guys, hit the showers. I'll see you all at the festival in a couple hours," Gus McPhee said.

The players all skated off the ice in a chorus of "Thanks, Coach."

"You got a good group of kids this year, Dad. You guys have a shot at the championship."

"It's looking that way, but anything can happen. It would be nice to win though. We haven't won the state title since your senior year. You and Dylan skated really well that year."

"Yeah, that's probably why Patrick won't let us play on the same scrimmage team."

"That's not surprising," said the older man.

Wes had taken a liking to Mr. McPhee, who had of course told him to call him Gus. He liked him even more after watching him with the players. Hockey had been Wes's entire life since he was ten. Coaches were father figures to him, and he could tell Gus was one of the best.

"Can I look at the lineup for the scrimmage?" asked Gus.

"Yeah, I got it right here." All three of the men skated off the ice and to the bench where Conner had his phone. Gus adjusted his glasses and took the phone from him. "It looks pretty good. Looks like you spread out the talent pretty evenly, a lot of good names on this list. I can't help but notice we are short a goalie."

"I'm working on it," Conner said, giving his father a knowing smile.

"Don't get your hopes up," Gus said.

"Oh, my hopes are up. I'm gonna make it happen."

"I'll believe that when I see it. But let's get going. Your mother is home and fussing about the weekend. I want you boys to help her in any way she needs."

"We will," Conner said as he sat down to take his skates off.

"You too, young man. When you're in our house, you're a McPhee," he said as he clasped Wes on the shoulders.

"Of course, I'm happy to be an honorary McPhee for the weekend," he said with a smile.

"Good, I'll see you all later. I'm gonna go talk to the boys before they clear out," he said as he disappeared into the locker room.

Wes sat down next to Conner and started taking off his skates.

"So, what's next?" Wes asked. He was someone who had trouble sitting still, which served him well in his career as a professional hockey player.

He'd been traded to the Magic two years ago, and he was happy with that trade. Hockey had always been a surrogate family for him. When he was originally drafted to Florida, he knew the team's reputation, and his gut told him it was a bad decision, but what could he do? He had no idea how bad it would get. After two years there some serious stuff went down, and he was traded early to the Magic.

It was just what he was looking for. It had a great staff that fostered relationships on and off the ice. His teammates were all wonderful, but he and Conner really connected on the ice. Conner was the team captain. He was a steady, solid center. Wes was a showboat on the ice, but he had the points to back it up. He was fast and could always find his window to be the top scorer on the team. Especially with Conner feeding him puck after puck. He hoped to be here for the rest of his career, he just needed to keep playing like he did and become a franchise player.

"I think they're about to start the festival. I said we would be there to sign some autographs and skate for a bit. Wanna head over there?" He asked as he slipped his shoes on.

"Yeah, that sounds great."

They got their coats on and headed out the door. Wes thought this little town had something special. He had grown up in a rough spot in Detroit. It was a pretty hopeless place until his coach spotted him playing street hockey with some friends. He brought him to the skating center, got him all signed up, and the rest was hockey history. He had never really been to a town like Mystic Falls, but could tell, this place had good vibes. Any town that puts up a rink around their town square every year couldn't be that bad.

"I'm gonna go and see where they want us for autographs. Why don't you head over and check it out?"

"Sounds good." As he made his way closer to the square something caught his eye.

Next to the square was a store that seemed to be glowing. He walked over and found a cozy little shop full of herbs and crystals. This wasn't usually his thing, but he was curious. He opened the door and a bell tinkled over his head. He took in the space as a feeling came over him that he couldn't quite place. It was warm and inviting. All the light came from a couple lamps and some candles and the whole place just seemed to glow. It had an ethereal quality to it, the peace that settled in him wasn't a feeling he was used to.

"Well, hello. Aren't ye a handsome lad? Ye must be in town with Conner McPhee," she said with a knowing glint in her eye.

Wes had never seen anyone quite like her before. She was a short round woman with wild red hair streaked with gray and a thick Scottish brogue.

"I am. I'm Wes Darling," he said with his self-assured smile.

She looked at him for a moment longer than felt necessary and she seemed to be assessing him. "Have you ever had your tarot cards read before?"

"I can't say I've had the pleasure," he said.

"Come. Sit. It's on the house." She went and sat at the small table in the middle of the store and gestured for him to join her.

'Why the hell not' he thought and joined her.

"Cut the cards and let's see what they have to say."

He cut the well-worn deck of tarot cards she placed in front of him. As he split the cards, he felt a tiny jolt of electricity. He didn't really believe in any of this stuff, but he didn't rule it out either. There was so much in life that was unexplainable. Some people, like this woman before him, were one of those things he stopped trying to explain a while ago. Hockey players were a superstitious group, believing in tarot cards and magic wasn't a huge jump.

"Are you ready?"

"Let's do this," he said with a grin.

"The first card is a symbol of your past," she said as she

flipped over the first card. "The Five of Wands," she said, carefully evaluating the card, then her eyes came up to him. "It would appear that you are coming out of a period of conflict and hardship. A clash of egos or a power trip, and if I had to wager, I would say you were put in a tough situation."

He nodded. That would easily describe his time in Florida. Hardship and conflict were putting it nicely. But luckily that was behind him and his new team in Glendale was a much better fit.

"This next card will give some insight into your present situation," she said as she flipped over the next card. "The Chariot," she said, giving him a proud smile. "It seems you've overcome whatever happened and are now in a pretty solid place in your career. Clearly you are a confident young man, and you just keep moving forward. Good for you. Your self-assured nature will work well for you. Now this next card is what the stars hold for you. Are you ready?"

"Flip it on over," he said with a cocky grin.

"Lad, the world is at your feet," she said with a smile as she revealed the final card: The World. "All of your wildest dreams will come true. And I would wager that even being a successful professional athlete you are still waiting for something. Am I right?"

He thought about it. I mean, who wasn't waiting for something? He did have the career he wanted, and he knew the cup would be coming to them soon. The only thing he hadn't had the time to find was love. He had never really taken the time, but he was starting to think it might be time. That was a new thought for him. As he settled down into life playing for the Magic, he found himself wishing he had someone to call on those long road trips, and someone who was excited to see him when he came home.

"There is something isn't there?" she asked.

"I mean maybe. I'd love to have a partner in all of this.

That is the one missing piece I've never really had the chance to find."

"Well, lad, keep your eyes open. You might just find what you are looking for right here in Mystic Falls," she said with a twinkle in her eye filled with pure magic. "And if you do, remember to be patient, and trust your instincts. I can tell you are someone who already does that."

He nodded. "I am. I'll keep my eyes open. Thanks. Are you sure I can't pay you?"

"It's on the house," she said with a warm smile.

"Well, for your time," he said, leaving a large bill on the counter. He turned to leave but turned back "Thanks again."

"Enjoy the winter festival," she said with a knowing nod.

When he made his way back outside, he saw some people were already skating around the town's center. He made his way over to a bench to slip his skates on. On his way there, he noticed someone sitting on a bench. All he could see was a mess of red curls because her nose was buried in a book, but he did take note of the skates next to her. And he was not above using his excellent skating skills to impress cute girls.

"Is this seat taken?" he asked her with the most charming smile he could muster.

"Nope," she said, barely looking up from her book. But she scooted over to give him more space.

"Hi," he said. His friendliness would take more than that to be deterred. "I'm Wes."

"I know who you are," she said, finally looking up at him. Her hazel eyes were so sharp, but Wes couldn't help but gaze into them. There was something about her. She had this wild red hair, but everything else about her seemed to be contained and deliberate. Her nose was red from the cold, but he could still see the smattering of freckles dotting across her nose and he couldn't help but smile.

"Are you going to skate?"

"I'm thinking about it," she said, looking over at him. She was unsure of something, if Wes had to wager, he would bet she was nervous to skate. Many people were nervous about falling on the ice. He could help with that.

"Let me help," he said with a grin as he ran his hand through his blonde hair. She looked at him and gave a small smile and Wes's heart swelled. He was going to enjoy this.

"Have you skated much before?" he asked.

"A time or two," she said quietly.

"Well, let's get these on and get out there. I won't let you fall," he said, scooting just a little closer to her. He started to slip his own skates on as she did the same. "Let's get those laces nice and tight," he said, bending down to help her. He was not above using his hockey skills to flirt either. As he tightened her laces, she slipped her book into her bag.

He stood up and held out a hand. "Are you ready?" he asked.

"Ready as I'll ever be," she said with a look on her face he couldn't quite place. Wes took her hand. Even through her mitten, a spark danced between them. He looked at her and wondered if she felt that too. Was the rosiness on her cheeks from the cold, or was she suddenly feeling as hot as he was? He gently led her out onto the ice. He steadied himself, ready to catch her if she fell, but she seemed to be steady enough. "Gentle pushes until you get the feel of the ice," he said, still holding onto her hand.

She looked up at him and smiled. He still couldn't quite read her expression. It was like she had a secret. But she was smiling, and that had to be good, right?

"You're a natural," he said.

"Thanks," she said with a little chuckle. They skated a full lap with her hand in his. Once they were back to the bench, he turned to face her and took both of her hands. "Wanna try it a little faster?"

"Show me whatcha got," she said with a grin.

He began to skate backwards with more speed, pulling her along. The wind blew his hair into his eyes, and he shook his head so he would be able to watch her. The added speed was causing her hair to blow those beautiful red curls out of her face, her smile and her red round cheeks made him happy. For the first time he felt like he got an unguarded smile from her, and it filled him with as much pride as an overtime goal.

"What's your name?" he asked, as he easily maneuvered them on the ice.

"I'm Kate."

Kate. Why did that sound like it should mean something to him?

Just then he saw Conner barreling towards them and turned to stop spraying them with ice. Wes was surprised by that behavior. Conner was usually polite, but that sure wasn't.

"Hey, watch it," Wes said, feeling protective over the woman he was skating with.

"I'll race you, KitKat," he said.

"You're on." And before Conner could catch up, the timid girl he had been helping across the ice took off around the ring and Conner had to catch up with her. Wes watched in awe. Conner was fast, not as fast as him of course, but still fast, nonetheless. Then it hit him why the name Kate sounded familiar. Conner's twin sister Katie.

Well damn.

Hitting on his teammate's sister was a lot more complicated than he had planned on, but he might not care. Watching her skate like that made him happy. There was something about this woman he couldn't put his finger on. All he knew was he wanted to know her better.

They made their way back around to him, and Kate was smiling up at him.

"Someone was putting on an act," he said with a shake of his head. She clearly had been playing with him.

"Hey, I never said I couldn't skate. You just assumed," she said with a big smile.

"I guess you're right about that. So, you're Conner's sister?"

"Yeah, I'm Kate McPhee. It's nice to meet you. I'm glad to see you aren't the cocky asshole I assumed you were from the couple games I caught."

"Nah, that's an act for the ice. It pisses people off real good," he said with a laugh.

"Yeah, he gets under the defensemen's skin like no one's business. Last week, a goalie even tried to hit him," Conner said.

"Yeah, they'd have to catch me first. It's a fine line between running your mouth and having the skills to back it up," Wes said with a grin.

"So maybe you are as cocky as I thought you were," she said with a raised eyebrow.

"Maybe a little cocky," he admitted and winked at her.

She scowled at him, and he didn't know why, but he loved it even more than her smiles. He was going to have to tread lightly with her, but he was very interested in seeing where things went. He had never felt the sort of instant attraction before, even through all the wintery layers they were all wearing, he just couldn't stop looking at her.

The lights that had been strung up over the makeshift rink around the gazebo kicked on and a microphone screeched to life at the gazebo. Wes watched as an older man stepped up to the gazebo and adjusted the microphone. Everyone cleared the ice for the announcement.

"Hello. I would like to welcome everyone to the twentieth annual winter festival. We have some fun planned for you all. We'll have live music, and of course, some hot cider and yummy baked goods provided by Smith's Orchard. We also have Mystic Fall's very own Conner McPhee here with us this weekend, and he brought his teammate, Wes Darling with him." the man gestured over to them on the ice and they both waved.

"Y'all have no doubt been watching the amazing season they're having. They'll be signing some autographs over in one of the booths later tonight. But let's welcome the real stars of the show, The Fighting Foxes!" he called out and the high schoolers he had been training with earlier that afternoon took the ice. "They're looking great for the state championships. Let's all give it up for their fearless leader, Gus McPhee."

As Gus stepped into the gazebo, they were joined by two men. One with strawberry blond hair a little shorter than Conner, the other slightly taller than Conner with auburn hair. They were the McPhee brothers, and soon they were accompanied by a short woman with her graying red hair piled neatly in a bun on her head. She was short, plump, and glowing with pride. The whole McPhee family was watching Gus on the stage.

"Wes, this is Patrick, and my mother, Nancy," said Conner. "I think you've met Dylan." He had met him before. Dylan was an agent for a couple of the Magic players.

Wes went to shake his mother's hand.

"I'm a hugger. I hope that's okay?" asked the little woman holding open her arms. Wes smiled and went in for a hug. She hugged him tightly as her hair tickled his face. "I'm so glad you came with Conner this weekend."

"Thank you for having me, ma'am," he said.

"Please, call me Nancy. I'm just so glad to have all my

chickees home at one time," she said as she squeezed Conner and Patrick's hands.

They all watched on as Gus took the stage. "Hello Mystic Falls. Thank you for coming to my favorite festival, and this year is a big one. We are celebrating the Mystic Falls hockey team and we are here to wish them luck when they take on the Albany Warriors next weekend, and let me tell you, they don't stand a chance!"

The crowd cheered. "Let's give it up for the Fighting Foxes!" Gus exclaimed. Then the whole team took the ice and skated a lap.

The entire crowd erupted into cheers and Wes watched as Nancy beamed up at Gus on the stage. When Wes looked back around him, he saw that Patrick had been joined by his wife and their three beautiful children. This moment was right out of a movie. It wasn't something he ever grew up with. The moment pulled at his heartstrings; he looked over to Kate to find her smiling up at the stage. When she caught him looking at her, he quickly looked away. Perhaps the warmth of this moment had messed with his game a bit. It all felt so genuine. He couldn't help but feel like an outsider, but he would love to be an insider to a family like this. He looked back at Kate who was still watching him. She gave a small smile and turned away. This was going to be an interesting weekend.

As the night went on, Wes and Conner made their way over to the booth they were assigned and took pictures and signed autographs. While they were busy, his eyes kept finding Kate on the ice. She was good on skates. She was skating around with her niece who looked to be about four. She was holding her hand and slightly bent over, Wes couldn't help but notice her ass as she skated by. It was juicy perfection. He wanted to know what the rest of her looked like under her puffy coat. His thoughts were turning dangerous to be standing beside her brother who was also his teammate and captain.

"Hey, would you mind if I asked your sister out?"

Better just to come out with it, he decided. If it was a problem for him, he would have to pass. He couldn't mess up their chemistry so close to playoffs.

"You wanna ask my sister out?" Conner asked, looking at him with both eyebrows raised.

"I was thinking about it. She seems really nice," he said, trying to be as earnest as possible.

"Nice," he repeated. "I don't think anyone has ever called her nice before. That's fine with me. I have no say in who she dates. But I will say good luck. She's a tough cookie," he said.

"Good to know." Wes watched her make another lap around the gazebo. With that out of the way, it was time to up his game.

Bring on the full Darling charm.

CHAPTER 3

WES

After skating last night, Wes hadn't found any time to talk to Kate again. By the time he finished up with pictures and autographs, she had already headed back home. He was staying at the McPhee's. It was a full house. It was him and Conner, plus Conner's two brothers, his brother's wife, and their three children. He was actually sharing bunk beds with Conner.

"I can't believe we got stuck here," Conner grumbled beneath him. "I should have thought about it and booked a room at the inn, but it's booked full up now. I checked." He stretched his neck while getting out of the bottom bunk.

"It's cool. I don't mind. I've never been around a family like this. It's fun," Wes said, hopping down off the top bunk.

"It's a mad house is what it is," Conner grumbled as the sound of the kids screaming downstairs traveled into the room.

"Breakfast!" Nancy McPhee called.

"So maybe it's not all bad," Conner smirked. "Let's go eat."

Wes pulled on his hoodie and the two of them headed downstairs. Nancy was standing at the foot of the stairs.

"Dylan, food's going to get cold," she called up as Wes and Conner came down. He turned the corner and saw the spread of food set out. Patrick was already there, filling a plate for his little girl as her two older brothers raced around.

"Owen! Stop running!" Patrick shouted. "Did you want gravy on your biscuit, sweetheart, or do you just want it plain?" he patiently asked the little girl.

"How did you sleep last night?" Nancy asked. "I'm sorry I had to put you two up in the old bunk beds, but we have a full house."

"Oh no, I slept great. This all looks delicious." Wes said.

"Well help yourself. I think we're all heading over to the rink in an hour and a half. The game starts at ten."

"Is Kate coming over for breakfast?" he asked her. Conner gave him a knowing glance.

"No, I think she is meeting us over at the rink later. Which is a shame because I made her favorite. Chocolate chip pancakes," she said, grinning at Wes. "Owen, why don't you get some breakfast and stop running?" Nancy said and then disappeared to corral her grandson.

After breakfast, they made their way over to the high school. Wes and Conner pulled up to the rink and a calm came over him. He had enjoyed his time at the McPhee house, but he wasn't used to being around that many people. The rink he was used to. And the rink before everyone else arrived was peaceful. Conner was in the office getting some of the final pieces for the scrimmage put together. So, it was just him in the locker room putting on his gear and lacing up his skates.

The hockey player's meditation.

As he walked over to the ice, he took a deep breath. He never got tired of the smell of the ice. It smelled like home to him. Hockey had been his saving grace growing up, his calm in the storm. No matter what was happening in his life, it all went away when he stepped on the ice.

While this place was no Madison Square Garden or any of the other amazing places he had played in his career, it did remind him of the rink he grew up in when he played AAA in Minnesota. It was chalk full of nostalgia. He remembered how the other guys on the team would have their girlfriends come and watch them play, but he never had a girlfriend in high school. He was all hockey all the time, and that had served him well being the number one draft pick right out of high school.

As he skated onto the ice in the empty rink, he felt that familiar peace wash over him. As he made some quick laps around, he thought about Kate in the stands watching him. Yes, he was aware she would be here to watch her community and her brothers, but he liked the idea of her being there to watch him too.

Conner skated out on the ice to join him. "Everything is all set. I think the teams are pretty evenly matched. We're on different teams clearly, but you have Dylan on your team. He's fast and a good shooter. You also have Sam Smith. I'll point him out. He played with Patrick. He's a steady center so you should be good there too."

"So how are we playing? You gonna go all out?" he asked with a grin.

"No, but you'd be surprised how these games go. They have a league here, so most of these guys are still playing. I'm sure you can gauge it, just don't show off TOO much," he said with a knowing look.

"I have to show off a little...but I will keep it to a minimum."

The players started coming on the ice and Wes started greeting his teammates and warming up with them. Conner was right, the team was pretty good. This was going to be a fun game. He was helping DeMarcus, who was the captain of the high school team, with one of the spin shots over at his team's net, but he kept watching the stands for Kate. She wasn't there yet. He went over to Conner who was talking to the goalie for his team to find out when they were going to get started.

"Hey, it looks like everyone is warmed up. When are we getting started?"

At that moment, Gus McPhee came over the loudspeaker, drawing his attention. "Alright players, make your way over to your team benches and we are just about to get started." The teams made their way over as the refs took to the ice. Gus and Patrick were coaching the teams.

"Alright green team let's do this," said Gus. "We have the better team. We have the quicker team. Sam, get the puck to either Dylan or Wes, both of them will know what to do. We got the best goalie in town on our team this year," he said with a wink to Dylan and a pat on the goalies back. "Let's do this, Go Foxes on three" They all put in their hands and then headed out for face off.

When they were finished Wes scanned the crowd one last time for Kate.

"Looking for anyone in particular?" a feminine voice asked.

He turned and saw he was talking to the goalie for their team. Kate McPhee. His brain stopped.

"Hey," Conner called to him as they were all waiting for him at center ice. He tried to shake it off, but his entire world was flipping upside down. Kate McPhee played hockey.

Gus had been right about the goalie. Kate was good. She hadn't let in a goal yet. Wes couldn't help but smile. Conner was getting a little worked up, but she kept blocking his shots. Just then the puck bounced off his stick. It literally bounced off his stick because he wasn't paying any attention, he was still in awe of their goalie.

"You good?" Conner asked as he skated by.

"What?"

Conner just tilted his head as his words finally registered. "Yeah, I'm fine." He tried to shake it, but he had never been this distracted on the ice before.

They were at the top of the third period and the score was 2-0. Conner was looking to score. Wes thought he just couldn't fathom a shutout. He was starting to play hard. He was going to the net hard every time he could, and Kate seemed to be able to read his every move. It was entertaining to say the least. He skated to the net hard and stopped just short of a collision spraying the goalie with ice. In the NHL, that would have been a penalty. This was getting a little out of hand.

"Hey, take it easy man," Wes said as he skated by Conner, but Conner just ignored him.

Conner got the puck on a breakaway and was headed down the ice fast. It was just him and the goalie. Conner stopped and with a wicked wrister sent the puck top shelf and the crowd went wild. He watched as Kate got a little flustered and hit her stick on the post. Wes skated over to her and gave her a small smile. "You're doing great. Professional goalies couldn't have stopped that one."

She just glared at him. Okay, so she was as competitive as he was. This was getting more interesting by the minute.

The game was almost over, and the score was 5-1. Wes had finally got his head on the game, and he may have been showing off a bit more than he expected to, but he couldn't seem to help himself with Kate on the ice with him. Wes could see Conner starting to work for it again. He got another break away, but Dylan caught up to him this time and was making him work for it. As he went back for his shot, Dylan went for the puck but took Conner's skate out a bit. Conner lost his footing, but quickly recovered and drove it hard to the net. He followed the puck right into the net landing on the goalie.

Wes skated over to her. He was pissed. "Seriously, Conner, chill out a bit. This is supposed to be a fun game," said Wes.

But at that moment, Kate came skating for Conner and shoved him square in the chest and he fell back on his ass. She ripped off her helmet and a mess of red curls came out as she did. "What the fuck, Conner! You seriously need to chill out! You are in the NHL and I haven't played in years. Can you calm the fuck down please?!"

Conner stood up and skated to her. "I go as hard as you go, Kit Kat," he said grinning at her from ear to ear.

Wes's brain stopped functioning. Kate McPhee was a kick ass goalie who stopped almost everything Conner had to throw at her. Not only that, but she was feisty as hell. He knew right then...he was going to marry that girl someday.

He watched in awe as she put her helmet back on and skated back to the net. His body still frozen and his mouth hanging open as he watched. The only thing he was aware of was a sharp sudden pain. That pain was him getting a hard on in his cup. He bent over and blew out a breath, trying to get himself under control. He had wanted her when he thought she was a beautiful shy little book nerd, but knowing the shy little book nerd could play with such fire did something to him.

Kate McPhee. That was what his whole world revolved around now, there was no getting around that. Now he just had to find a way to get to know her a little better.

CHAPTER 4

KATE

Kate was home and taking a hot shower. She was going to feel like garbage in the morning. She hadn't played like that in years. It was a surreal experience putting on the old goalie pads. Even though it had been years since she was in front of the net, it all came back to her. The ice still felt like home. Her body still remembered how to move, she remembered how to track the shots. It was all still there.

She donned those pads almost every day in grade school through college, but when she left the sport after college, she needed to leave it all behind, a clean break. A clean break wasn't a possibility for her though, not when her family breathed hockey. Which was probably why she had been pulling back from her family since then as well.

If she was honest with herself, it might have more to do with the boyfriend she moved in with after she had graduated. He never understood her love of the game and when she left the sport after her last game her senior year, she had thought he was being supportive. That support turned into control quickly, but that was behind her. Now she was just trying to see who she was. Hockey had defined her, then she had let a man define her, now nothing defined her but the bookstore.

She loved working at the bookstore in town, loved bringing it from a dusty old bookstore to a vibrant spot in the community. She started a book club with the purpose of diversifying your bookshelf. The store also hosted drag story hours, and the local high school Queer Spaces club. It was a safe space and bringing Mystic Falls into the present day. Kate had been surprised at the way Mystic Falls had welcomed all the changes and new ideas she had brought. Not all small towns were welcoming, but Mystic Falls was.

Kate had to be at her parents' house in an hour to celebrate her father's sixtieth birthday. She needed to find a way to center herself before she left. She managed to keep hockey talk at bay for the past couple years, but then Conner came in playing the 'do it for dad' card and how could she say no to that? She had the best dad in the world. Of course, she would do this for him, but it didn't make it any easier.

So, she popped some ibuprofen, stretched her already sore muscles and got ready to head over.

When she pulled up, the party was already in full swing. She had to park on the next block over because there were so many cars. When she entered the house there was a big banner hanging up that the grandkids had made, the kitchen was a buffet of food, and people everywhere. She hung her coat up in the closet and the chaos started.

"Katie!" cried one of her aunts.

"Aunt Tillie, hello." Her words were muffled when she was pulled into a perfumy hug. Tillie always wore too much perfume.

"How are you doing, dear? Are you still working at the bookstore?"

"Yep, just got the online bookstore up and running. It has
–"

"Oh, that's nice. It was so good to see you out on the ice
this morning. It's been too long."

Kate suppressed a sigh. It was going to be a long day of
this. She needed a beer. She squeezed her way through to the
kitchen; her mother was in there setting out some more
food.

"Do you need any help?" Kate asked.

"Yes, would you mind checking the coolers and making
sure there is still plenty of soda and beer?"

"I can do that. I was just on my way to get a beer anyway.
Where's dad?"

"I think he is in the garage watching the game. There are
extra sodas and beers there to restock the coolers," she said
as she set out some bacon wrapped cocktail weenies on a
plate.

"Okay, I'm on it." She made her way to the attached
garage that her dad had decked out to be his man cave. He
didn't use the basement because he couldn't smoke his pipe
inside. Somehow, he managed to stay warm out here in the
upstate New York winters.

She was almost to the red cooler, which was the beer
cooler, when she was stopped by another aunt. Bombarded
by the same overwhelming hug and hockey talk. This was
going to be a long day.

She finally made it to the garage and checked the coolers,
sodas were stocked. She checked the beer cooler, added a few
more, and took one for herself. As she opened the door a
goal must have been scored because the whole place erupted
with cheers. Gus looked over at her with a big smile on his
face.

"So, I see the Rangers are up," she said to her dad.

"They are...they might move up a spot today, but the Magic are right behind them. Right, Conner?"

"That's right, Dad."

He got up from the couch and came over to Kate. "I just wanted to thank you, Katie. I know you don't play anymore, but to have all my kids out on the ice one last time was very special..." he choked on the last word with tears in his eyes. He pulled her into a hug. This hug was one she didn't mind. "Thank you, Katie," he whispered in her ear.

"You're welcome, Daddy," she said, hugging him right back. This moment made it worth it. He was the only reason she was back in front of that net. She recalled a conversation they'd had after her decision not to go out for the national team. He seemed so confused. He was an amazing dad and coach, but he had just assumed she would keep going. But for women after college, opportunities dried up and Jason had been there loudly voicing his opinion on her next career steps, and that was not hockey. But she had to stop herself before she spiraled down that train of thought.

"Only for you Dad," she said coming out of the hug. "Too bad Conner's still a puck hogging ass on the ice," she said, punching her brother in the arm.

"Only when I play against you and Dylan," he said with a smirk. She would argue, but he was right. He was an incredible team player when it counted, he always had been. That was something their dad had instilled in all of them. Always put the team first. But when they played with each other, they played dirty.

Kate scanned the garage and didn't see Wes. She had assumed he would be in here watching the game with everyone. She wanted to find him and give him shit. They hadn't really had a chance to chat since they had skated together on the ice, and he had tried to help her like she had never skated before. It was cute, but seriously, how could he think a McPhee wouldn't know how to skate?

"How ya holding up, KitKat?" asked Conner as he joined her behind the couch.

"Good," she said with a sigh.

"Sore?" he asked with an irritating smirk.

"Fuck off," she said with a smile. Her and Conner gave each other lots of shit, but he was still her twin after all. He got her on a level not many other people did. He didn't really know everything that had gone down in Indiana when she left hockey, or in Glendale for that matter when her toxic relationship had combusted, but he didn't press her too much. She liked that.

"You still got it though," he said as he nudged her shoulder.

He was right. Kate had been a little worried she would let too many pucks in, but that muscle memory and ability to let it all go once she was on the ice was still there.

"That's gotta feel good, right?" he shot her a knowing glance.

"What feels good is you still can't score on me," she said with a grin. "Where's Wes? I kind of assumed he'd be with you."

Conner looked around, "I don't know where he is. He's here somewhere."

"Hey Conner, come here," called one of their cousins. He gave her one last nudge. "Elbow Room tonight?"

Kate nodded and Conner turned and left. She made her way through the house, stopping to talk to family members and people from the town who had come to celebrate his birthday, but this was all too much. Too many people and too many questions she didn't want to answer. She couldn't leave yet though, so she decided to head down to the basement.

The younger cousins and her nephews would be less likely to want to discuss her life, so that option seemed safer.

As soon as she opened the door to the basement stairs, she heard the screams and laughter. Between the spikes of laughter, she heard the ping pong table. Another sport she could dominate, and if she could get any of these suckers to take her on at the foosball table she would dominate there too. She chuckled to herself, getting back on the ice this morning had awoken her competitive side. All McPhee's were competitive, and Kate was no different.

When she turned the corner, she couldn't help but smile. There—dominating the ping pong table, was Wes. She should have known he would be where the kids were, that seemed fitting.

"Hey! Kate! After I'm done destroying Nate here, would you like to lose next?" he asked with that cocky grin of his.

"She's good. I'd watch yourself," warned Nate, her four-teen-year-old cousin.

"I called the next game!" protested Owen.

"That's right, you did, little guy. Why don't you take over for me? I think I could use a break," he said as he ruffled Owen's dark hair. Owen took the paddle from him, and the ping pong game commenced. Wes walked over to one of the quieter corners of the basement and sat on one of the bar stools and pulled one out for Kate.

As she sat, he said, "So I feel pretty foolish about the skating rink yesterday."

"Oh yeah, and why is that?" she asked in feigned innocence.

"You know why. Why did you let me think you couldn't skate?"

She chuckled, "Because it was funny. Did you really assume I wouldn't know how to skate? You know my brother."

"To be fair, I didn't know you were Conner's sister when I sat down next to you."

This surprised her. She had assumed he was talking to her because he knew she was Conner's sister. Why else would he have sat down next to a random girl reading a book on a bench?

"Are you serious? You didn't know I was Conner's sister? Why did you stop and talk to me then?"

"Because I saw a beautiful woman sitting by an ice rink, skates beside her, I thought I could help...clearly I was wrong," he said to her with a big smile on his face.

Kate wasn't sure why that smile called to her. He was a quintessential hockey player with chin length floppy hair and the style to prove it. Kate had grown up around boys just like him. She'd been in way too many locker rooms and heard the way they talked. That's only one reason she didn't date them, but there was something about him she couldn't stop looking at. And smiling at. He was a fan favorite for a reason. Guys loved his trick style of play, and his smile made him a favorite among the ladies. Even Kate had to admit he had a nice smile.

"I knew I was wrong the second you and Conner took off, but I had no idea just how wrong I was until this morning. You're really good."

"Thanks," she answered back quietly. She wasn't sure why that felt so nice. She was good. She knew it. But it still felt nice having someone like Wes Darling tell you that you're good. She could stop Conner's shots all day long, but she wouldn't have been able to stop some of his goals. While she didn't watch many of her brother's games, in the ones she had caught, Wes had been incredible.

"Where did you learn to play like that?"

"I grew up in this family...We play hockey. I also played a little in college," she said as she took a sip from her beer.

"Where did you go to college?"

"Notre Dame."

"Isn't that where your brother went?"

"That's where all McPhee's go," she said. "It's okay though, they have a good English Department."

"English major huh? That explains the book?"

"Non-English majors enjoy reading as well," she shot back at him.

"I know, I was just saying. What do you do now?"

"I work at a Mystic Falls Books."

"Something non-English majors can do too," he said with that ridiculous cute smile of his. "What are you up to later tonight?"

"Why?" she asked.

"I wanted to see if I could take you out to dinner," he said

"I don't date hockey players," she said plainly.

"Awww, come on," he said with a look in his eyes that shot right through her. She felt chills and had the ridiculous urge to kiss him. On pure instinct she licked her lips. It wasn't lost on him, and he raised an eyebrow.

"How about this? It's not a date. Just keep me company while I go eat at the diner in town, so I can get a quiet moment away from all this," he said.

"Hey Wes! Come play with me!" called one of the kids and pulled on his sleeve.

"I'll be right there, buddy," he said with a warm patient smile.

"You seem to be handling the McPhee Madness pretty well by yourself," she said.

"Yeah, your family is great. I'll play you for it?" he said with a mischievous smirk.

"Excuse me?"

"I win, you go out to dinner with me. You win...you go out to dinner with me another time," he grinned at her.

Something about being back on the ice and being back in this house with everyone made her unable to pass up his challenge. She would win, but in the worst-case scenario, she would go out for a friendly dinner with someone who seemed like a pretty good guy. What did she have to lose?

"You're on. What are we playing?"

"Take your pick," he said, gesturing to the room. The basement was full of options: pool table, ping pong table, darts, and a foosball table. Not to mention the video games.

"Foosball," she said. An easy choice. She dominated the foosball table. She could have picked darts, but he deserved a fighting chance.

"Foosball...interesting choice," he said flatly. She was almost regretting her choice.

"Let's do this," she said as she made her way over to the table.

"You're sure?" he asked.

"You're going down," she said to him playfully.

A chorus of 'oooooh' erupted from the kids as they all gathered around the table to watch. They started to play, and she got the first point easily. She gave him a grin. "Guess we'll have to have that dinner another time then," she said.

He raised an eyebrow and with a few quick turns of the handle he had a goal. "We'll see about that," he quipped back at her.

Then the game started in earnest. She was surprised how good he was. This wasn't going to be as easy as she thought. As the game went on, she realized she was going to lose. When he was one point away from winning, she realized she wasn't all that upset to be losing. Dinner with him might not be terrible. But then the tides of the game seemed to turn, and she got a few in. They were now tied up. Was he letting her win?

"Tied up," he said. "Before we finish this, I just wanted to check in. You still good with the bet?"

"Yeah," she said, biting back the smile trying to spread across her face. He may still be a hockey boy, but he seemed like one of the good ones at least. "Now, let's get this over with so I can beat you."

He cocked his eyebrow as the ball dropped into play. In two hits he got the ball in and just grinned at her.

"Smokey's Bar and Grille. I'll pick you up at six."

"It's a date," he grinned back at her.

"It's not a date," she said as she turned to go back upstairs.

CHAPTER 5

KATE

Kate made it home from the party around five. She had mixed feelings about going out to dinner with Wes. He seemed like a nice enough guy, and he had offered her an out, but she wasn't sure why she didn't take it. It probably had something to do with the fact that she was attracted to him. She wished she wasn't. She didn't date hockey players, and he wasn't her type at all. The only serious relationship she had been in was in college.

Her senior year, she started dating her TA, Jason. While that was probably not a great decision, they were together for a long time. He was exactly what you thought of when you thought of a PhD student in English. He was studying the great American writers. She should've seen the red flags of someone who whole heartily sang the praises of Ernest Hemmingway, but she didn't. He understood the other side of her. The side of her that her family never understood. They were always supportive of her; they just didn't understand someone who found as much joy reading books as they did playing hockey.

When she was growing up, she almost felt like two

different people. She was a beast on the ice with her broth-ers, but when she wasn't doing that, she was holed up in her room reading Jane Austen and Stephen King. It was easy to disappear into that second persona after hockey, and Jason made it easy to do.

She found herself thinking about him a lot today. He had also been a big part of why she stopped playing hockey. Jason hated hockey and hockey had just broken her heart. He always talked about how low brow it was. They lived together for four years before she finally found it in herself to leave and moved back home to Mystic Falls. By that time, she'd been in that terrible relationship so long, she was a shell of a person. She had been putting back together the pieces of herself since then, but there was one big piece miss-ing. One piece that was still painful, and that piece was hockey. But she had done it. She had gotten back in front of the net, for her dad.

Now she was just about to walk out her front door to pick up a hockey player that she was NOT going on a date with. She popped some more ibuprofen--because damn her shoulders and legs were sore after this morning--and grabbed her purse to head out the door. Hopefully he would be ready, she didn't want to deal with Conner. She would be meeting him later tonight anyway, along with her brothers at the Elbow Room.

As she pulled up, he was waiting for her. She was glad for that at least, less explaining to do.

"Hey," he said as he got in the car.

"I'm surprised you were waiting outside. It's getting cold out."

"It was loud in there, plus it's not that cold. This has nothing on Minnesota winters," he said as he buckled himself in.

"I thought you were from Detroit?" she asked.

"I was born in Detroit. My family is still there, but I went to Minnesota to play AAA hockey when I was thirteen."

They got to the restaurant and parked. He opened the door for her as they walked into the restaurant, and it did make her smile. What was it about him? She couldn't put her finger on it. She had always been attracted to more serious guys, and he was a goofball off the ice and a cocky little shit on the ice. What was even happening with her right now?

"So, you said you played AAA in Minnesota. Did your family come with you?"

"No, they're all still in Detroit. My coach from Detroit got a job and asked my mom if she would let him take me to Minnesota and play for him," he said as he took a sip from his water.

"Wow, I can't believe you left home that young to play hockey."

He just shrugged. "It was for the best. Hockey was my saving grace. I'm not sure what would have happened if I'd stayed in Detroit."

Kate had grown up in a loud, busy house. Her brother's and their friends were always around getting up to something. Her only escape was when she would sneak away to her room and get lost in her books. It must have been so different for him.

The waitress stopped by for their orders.

"Hey there, Kate," she said. Glancing over at Wes who gave her a friendly smile. "Are you Wes Darling? You play for the Magic with Conner, right?"

"Yeah, I'm visiting Mystic Falls with him," he said.

"Could we maybe talk you into signing a picture? We would love to hang it up on the wall.

"Of course," he answered back.

"Now what can I get for you two?"

"I'll have a cheeseburger and fries," Kate said.

"I'll take a chicken Caesar salad," Wes said.

"Coming right up!"

Kate was surprised at how easily the conversation flowed between them. She was also irritated at how her heart fluttered when he touched her hand to ask her about her Claddagh ring.

"I've seen these before," he said as he held her hand and grazed his thumb over her ring. "If you wear them a certain way it shows if you're single or whatever, right?"

She nodded.

"What does this way mean?" he asked, holding her fingers in his hand.

"This way definitely means single. It's been that way for over a year now," she said as she attempted to quiet her traitorous heart that was still thumping away in her chest. She should take her hand back, but she just couldn't seem to manage it.

"So, tell me about you. I know you're secretly an amazing goalie. You work in a bookstore, and you're my teammate's sister, but what else?"

"There's not much else to tell," she said with a small shrug of her shoulder.

"That can't be true. So, you played hockey in college?" trying to get her to open up to him.

"I did, and that was the last time I really played. I only played this morning for my dad. Conner guilted me into it with the dad card," she said as she took a sip from her beer. "I'm glad I did. It was good to get back on the ice with my brothers. I may have been a little rusty, but I can still shut down Conner," she said with a small grin. "That felt good at least. He always said it wasn't fair and I used the twin connection against him. He just doesn't like to lose. But you could probably tell, none of the McPhee's like to lose."

Wes laughed. "Yeah, I did notice that," he said with a smile as his thumb continued to graze over her fingers.

What was she doing? She should take her hand back. She did not date hockey players, not now, not ever. That had been a hard fast rule for her since she was young. She especially didn't date hockey players who were considerably younger than she was.

"I have to say, I was distracted by you today. Then when you skated out and shoved Conner down, I was a goner. I knew you were someone I needed to get to know. It was fucking sexy."

That did it. She was on fire. The heartbeat she had felt pounding away in her chest, was now also pounding away between her thighs.

Luckily, right then the waitress came with their food. She set it down in front of them and pulled out a photo and sharpie for him to sign.

"Thank you," she said as she grinned at him taking the photo back.

"When you hang that up, hang it above Conner's," he said with a wicked grin.

"We'll see," said the waitress with a smile that made Kate feel a type of way. That feeling was not jealousy.

Nope.

Because that would be silly. Luckily, with the distraction she was able to pull her hand back and also some modicum of self-control that seemed to go away when he touched her. Noted. No more touching. She didn't want to touch him anyway, because hello, she did not date hockey players.

Wes took a sip of water, and she watched his throat bob. This was getting out of hand.

"How old are you?" she asked bluntly. He was a baby. That would help to nip the heart flutters in the bud.

"I'm twenty-four."

"Twenty-four," she said, her eyes getting bigger. That should do it.

"Is that a problem?" he asked, one eyebrow slightly cocked.

"I mean, it doesn't matter to me how old you are. We're simply getting dinner because you somehow tricked me into making a bet with you," she said now keeping his eye contact.

"How old are you?" he asked.

"Older than you," she said.

"Turning twenty-nine this year, September first if I remember correctly," he grinned back at her.

"Did you internet stalk me?" she asked, sounding offended.

"No. Your twin brother is my teammate," he said. "Not only my teammate, but we play on the same line. I like to know these things about people."

"Oh...yeah. That makes sense I guess," she said feeling a little embarrassed.

"So, tell me about you. What have you been up to after college?"

That was the dreaded question, wasn't it? She had been lost when her hockey career ended. Lost and found by a pompous, arrogant boyfriend who she pretzeled herself out of shape for to try and be a good fit. She tried for four years, moved with him to his first teaching gig in Glendale, only to find him fucking his TA when she stopped by to surprise him one day. And sadly, it tracked. When he was a TA, he slept with his students. As a professor, he slept with his TAs. Not anything she ever wanted talked about with Wes or anyone.

"I dated someone for a while, but eventually moved home and started working at the bookstore."

"How do you like working there?" he asked.

Now this was something she could talk about.

"I really love it. Luis and Sofia own the bookstore, but

they are getting older, and they pretty much let me do what I want. I love looking for the new books to order, making sure I have a wide span of authors and stories available. When I started it was just a dusty, small-town bookstore, but I like to think I have made it into a community spot," she said.

"Oh yeah? I'll have to stop in and see it before we head out of town."

"I mean, don't go out of your way. I know books stores probably aren't your thing." He just cocked his head and looked at her with an expression she couldn't read. "I just mean, you're such a kid at heart. It's cute...you seemed to do well with the kids today."

"Yeah, I guess. Tell me more about the bookstore."

"I'm just glad Mystic Falls is so open to the things I've been implementing, like our BIPOC book club, drag story hour, and LGBTQ+ club the high schoolers run. It has become a haven of sorts for some people. I think that's what bookstores should be, and with all the book banning and stuff, it is important to support local indie bookstores," she said.

"Yeah, I totally agree," he said.

"Really?" she asked, taken aback.

"You act like I've never read a book," he said, joking with her.

"I just can't imagine you reading, it doesn't really seem like anything your speed."

He looked down at his lap and wiped his hands on his napkin. For a moment, the lightness behind his eyes went away. Kate was kicking herself for saying that.

"I'm sorry if I offended you. I get it, reading is not for everyone. I don't think Conner's read a book since college."

"Yeah, us hockey players don't read much," he said quietly.

The waitress once again interrupted this awkward moment and brought the check.

"Can I get anything else for you guys?" she asked, smiling right at Wes.

Wes looked at Kate to see if she needed anything, since the waitress wasn't seeming to.

"Nope, we're good."

"Alright, I'll take this when you are ready," she said, her hand lingering on Wes's as she set the bill on the table. Kate tried to fool herself that she was only angry because the waitress was being so forward, not because a small part of her already felt connected to him. That would be silly.

Kate went to reach for her purse. Wes took the bill off the table. "You better not be doing what I think you're doing," he said to her with an arched brow.

"You don't have to pay for me," she said quietly.

"Of course, I do. I always pay for my dates," he gave her a cocky grin and she was mad at herself for swooning a little bit. "Plus, I'm paid way too much. I'm guessing the same doesn't go for you."

That stopped her. He was right about that. Finances were tough for her. Luckily college had been a full ride, so she wasn't drowning in student debt like many of her peers. And even though the bookstore paid her as much as they could, it wasn't much.

"Thank you for dinner," she said quietly, sneaking a look at him. Damn it, if that flutter in her heart didn't start right back up. What the hell was happening? He was a hockey player, not only that but he was a baby. What would they possibly have in common?

"How come you never come to see us play? I've seen your parents and brothers at games before, but never you," he asked thoughtfully.

That was the million-dollar question. The question her family had finally stopped asking. The question that had turned her life into two distinct acts. She had her hockey life, and her post hockey life. How does someone say 'I let an asshole of a man change who I was. And when I watch hockey, it reminds me of who I used to be, and I can't stand it.' Because that was the truth of it. That unique mixture of shame and regret was hard to move past. She was on the mend from that wrong turn her life took, but hockey was still too painful.

"I've just been busy," she lied. "And like you said, I don't make much money."

Of course, Conner had offered to buy her tickets. She knew she was hurting his feelings by staying away for so long, but she couldn't bring herself to go see a game. But if she made it through today, maybe she should try to go to see him.

"Come to our next home game. It's Tuesday, and don't say you're busy. Glendale is only an hour away."

She looked at him. She wanted to say yes, but she just couldn't bring herself to do it. He seemed to be able to sense that in her. She followed his eyes to the dart board in the corner.

"If I can beat you at darts, you have to come to our game," he said with a smirk.

Kate downed her beer. "You're on."

After they finished settling up, they made their way over to the dart board. As much as she hated it, she found herself being pulled to him. As they played, she propped herself up on the bar a bit too close to his stool. His hand found the small of her back a few times, and each time it sent chills through her whole body. The pull she felt to him was intense. It was just physical, it had to be. What could they possibly have in common? Even so, if this was such a bad idea, why did she find herself keeping the score even?

She was about to throw her last dart. She could easily hit the points she needed to win the bet, but as she looked over at him, she couldn't help it. She threw the dart, hitting a ten on purpose. She could have destroyed him, but as competitive as she was, she let him win.

She looked back at him when the dart landed. And he fucking winked at her. She didn't have to feign anger, the anger she felt was real, but it was at herself, not him. What was she doing? She rested herself against the bar, her thigh lightly touching his knee. That small touch still sent waves of desire through her body.

He leaned in next to her and gently tugged on one of her red curls and smiled as it bounced back in place. "You let me win, didn't you?"

She looked down at her feet. She shouldn't be feeling this way. This was a bad idea. A really bad idea. He gently lifted her chin. He was so close now she could smell him. Somewhere intermixed with his cologne she could smell something minty, he smelled cold. He smelled like ice. And that ice was setting her on fire. "Don't worry. It'll be our little secret," he said.

She thought he was going to kiss her. She WANTED him to kiss her. She shook her head and moved away from him. "Nope, you won fair and square." The words didn't even come out naturally. She needed to get some space between them right now. "Excuse me, I need to use the restroom."

Kate made her way to the restroom and looked in the mirror. 'Pull yourself together,' she thought. 'You don't date hockey players. You don't date your brothers' teammates, and you don't date kids who you have nothing in common with.' She splashed a little bit of water on her face.

Well, maybe they didn't have to date, maybe they could just put the chemistry that existed between them to a carnal use. She'd read her fair share of romance novels. Maybe there was some validity to 'banging one out.'

She took a deep breath. He was leaving tomorrow, and

really, she had let him win. It had been too long since she watched Conner play. And this weekend did make her realize one thing, she missed hockey.

She knew she missed it, but she had been afraid it would be too painful to face after so much time. It was painful. There was so much regret, but if she was ever going to move past the breakup that had nearly broken her in more ways than one, maybe reconnecting with this part of herself was good. It was time. What it was not time for was some cocky hockey boy. She knew better than to get real feelings for a guy like him. She couldn't help it if her body had other ideas in mind.

As she was leaving the bathroom, her phone dinged.

Conner – At Elbow now with Patrick, Padma, and Dylan. Come on down when you guys are done.

Good, this was just the distraction they needed.

"Hey, my brother just texted. Everyone is at a bar a few blocks down. Should we head down there?"

He gave her a knowing glance. It was like he knew she was trying to create space between them. Fuck, she was in trouble.

CHAPTER 6

WES

*W*es helped Kate into her coat before pulling on his own. She bit back the grin that wanted to stretch across her face at the gesture. It was only there briefly, but he saw it. It was a three-block walk to the Elbow Room, but on this cold January night, it seemed longer. He watched as she pulled her coat tightly around her.

"Are you sure you don't want to drive?" he asked, concern pinching his brow. "You look cold."

"No, it's only a couple blocks. Let's just walk fast," she said as she picked up the pace.

He hoped this walk didn't give her a chance to cool off. He had a feeling he was starting to make headway. There was still so much about her he was dying to know. What made her leave hockey? Why didn't she date hockey players? Something had happened, and he wanted to know what it was. He also just liked hanging out with her. She was a cool chick, despite her constantly throwing blocks up. It was a good thing Wes had always prized himself for being a player who knew how to find his window. He would get to know Kate McPhee, and he would love every minute of it.

Being around the McPhee family had been bittersweet for Wes. He didn't come from a family like this one. It was just him and his mom before he left for Minnesota with his coach. Living with him and his family had given him a taste of what it would be like, but there was so much guilt for leaving his mom. He knew now it had been the right choice but telling that to a thirteen-year-old boy who felt like he needed to be the man of the house wasn't easy. But living with his coach and his family, and being taken in by his teammate's family, had been life changing for him.

That teammate was a big reason he was where he was now. He played with Ethan Yellowtail all through AAA and was happy to be back on the ice with him now. Ethan's sister had been a big influence on him. Although he never had a serious girlfriend, she took it upon herself to make sure Ethan and Wes turned into decent guys in that aspect. So while he would have loved to have grown up in a family like the McPhee's, he had his own hockey family.

He shoved those thoughts aside. Right now, he was more than happy to focus on the girl next to him as they made their way past the town square still filled with a skating rink and fairy lights. He'd been intrigued by her the moment he saw her but watching her on the ice was a revelation. He loved the competitive spark in her eyes. There was something between them, he just wished he knew why she was so skittish.

"Here we are," she said as she opened the door to the retro karaoke bar. Someone was already up on the stage singing an off-key rendition of Burning Love.

"Wow, this is quite the bar," Wes said, taking it all in.

It really was quite a bar. Wes had never been in one quite like it. It looked stuck in time, from the sticky books filled with song choices, to the hodge podge of decor. The walls were teal and there were surfboards on the wall along with a picture of Jimmy Buffet. There was also a giant taxidermy bear in the corner. None of it should work, but something about it did.

"Are you going to sing?" he asked her with a cheeky smile.

"No."

"No? Then why did you bring me to a karaoke bar?"

"Conner."

"Conner's going to sing?"

"Oh yeah, he is."

She spotted her brothers across the bar, not that three tall red-haired men were hard to spot in a small-town bar.

"Up next, we have Mystic Falls' own Conner McPhee."

Conner grinned at them as he made his way up to the stage. Was Conner really going to sing?

"A little Tina Turner?" Kate asked as Conner passed them on his way to the microphone.

"You know it," he said, grinning at her.

"Your brother is going to sing Tina Turner?" Wes asked, his eyes wide, and a smile stretched across his face.

The music to The Best started as Conner took the microphone.

"Would it be wrong to record this?" Wes asked, almost gleeful.

Kate just laughed and made her way over to the table that now had her other two brothers and Patrick's wife, Padma. Wes stopped at the bar to get them each a beer, but he couldn't stop watching Conner sing. This was a song he sang at the top of his lungs after a good win, but this was a whole other level. A small chuckle escaped his mouth as he thought what the rest of the team would say watching their fearless leader sing and dance on stage.

He pulled out his wallet to get some cash. "No need, it's on the house," said the bartender with a wink. That was one thing the poor kid growing up in Detroit never quite got over; now that he had the money to buy almost anything he could ever want, people gave him things for free.

"Thank you," he said, leaving her a tip equal to the price of the drinks.

Wes joined Kate at the table and slid a beer across the table to her with a cocky smile. He could tell she loved it but was trying not to, and that made him want to do it so much more.

"Thanks," she said. By then Conner had finished to a big round of applause.

"You better watch out, Conner. With Liam James moving into Mystic Falls, your favorite singer status might slip," Kate said once he got back to the table, trying to get a rise out of him.

"I heard that Liam James moved here. How on earth did that happen?" asked Padma.

"It was super weird. His bus broke down here for some reason. Then he started dating Lexi Turner and then he just never left. He seems nice though."

"Lexi…is she the one who works with your mom?" Padma asked Patrick.

"Yeah, she manages the inn."

"Used to…I think they just hired another manager full time," Kate chimed in.

"Speaking of the Turners," said Dylan. "I'm surprised Poppy and Josh aren't here."

"You guys have been gone too long. Poppy's pregnant, I think she is due at the end of March."

As they all talked about old times and caught up, Kate snuck a glance at Wes. He should have been bored out of his mind, but everything she said was helping to fill in the beautiful picture of who Kate McPhee was. He could feel eyes on him, and he was aware people were watching him and Conner, but he didn't care. He was here with these people.

"Where did you grow up?" Padma asked, trying to bring him into the conversation.

"I'm from Detroit, but I moved to Minneapolis when I was thirteen."

"I'm from Minneapolis," Padma said with a smile.

"Oh wow, that's awesome."

Wes snuck a glance over at Kate, she was picking at the label on her beer. He ached to take her hand. Nervous energy was radiating off her, and he just wanted to make her feel comfortable. But he also knew taking her hand wouldn't help him in that goal.

"Are you going to sing?" Dylan asked Kate.

"Are you new?" she asked him.

"I just thought maybe you'd become a karaoke star in all your free time," he said needling her. "I mean you don't hang out with us anymore."

"Your guilt is worse than mom's," she said with a glare at her little brother.

"Conner?" They turned and two women were there. "It's so good to see you," one of them said brazenly.

"Thanks, it's good to be back," he said with his easy charm.

"I'm Michelle," said one of the women as she put her hand on Wes's forearm. He could feel Kate's eyes on them, so he politely moved his arm.

"I'm Wes, nice to meet you," he said. But that was it, he didn't engage after that.

"I know who you are, I've seen you play. You're really good." She found his arm again and her fingers started to trace his forearm.

"Excuse me, I'll be right back." Kate made her way to the bathroom.

He watched as she went. When it was just the two of them, she was much more relaxed. He could see the love that existed between her and her brothers, but he also saw the tension written all over her face. Kate McPhee was a mystery to him, and she was one he was determined to figure out.

He picked up her beer as she left and noticed it was empty. He made his way to the bar.

"Can I get another?" he said, holding up the bottle. "And two bottles of water?"

The bartender nodded and turned to get them. He was done drinking for the night, and he didn't know if Kate would want another beer or water, but he had her no matter what she wanted.

"Wes?"

He turned and saw the girl who had been hitting on him earlier.

"How can I help you?" he said with a curt edge of politeness.

She looked at him with a cocked eyebrow and her lip between her teeth. Wes was tempted to just turn around and go find Kate, but he didn't want to be rude.

"I just wanted to give you this," she said, sliding him her number. "You should come home with me."

He had to give it to her for getting to the point, at least now they could stop doing this dance. "I appreciate that," he said, sliding the napkin with her number back into her hand. "But I'm here with someone."

She just shrugged, "If you change your mind," she said, putting it back in his hand. He turned and grabbed the bottles, leaving the number on the bar, and made his way back to the table. As he turned, he noticed Kate leaving.

"Where's she going?" he asked Conner as he set the bottles down on the table.

"She said she was sore from this morning and needed to head home. She hasn't played in a long–"

He didn't even wait to hear the rest of what Conner said.

He needed to get to her. He weaved his way to the door and pushed it open. The cold January wind bit into him, but he could see Kate about a block away.

"Are you leaving?" he called.

"Yeah, I'm tired and a little sore from the game."

"Let me grab my coat. I'll go with you," he said as he turned to head back into the bar.

"No, Conner can take you home. It's silly to go back just because I want to go home," she said. He studied her with a critical eye. "Plus, it looks like you might get lucky."

"What?" he said, shaking his head. Did she really think he was interested in that woman at the bar?

"Have a good night, I need to go," she said as she turned and started to walk.

"Kate," he called out again and jogged after her. "Are we good?" he asked once he was in front of her. He really didn't want to end the night this way. He wasn't sure exactly how he wanted to end the night, but he knew this wasn't it.

"Yeah, why?"

"Just making sure," he said, a little unsure of himself. "Are you sure you don't want me to go with you?"

"Nope, you stay. I'm good."

"At least let me walk you to your car," he said.

"This is Mystic Falls. What do you think is going to happen?"

"I don't know... I..."

"Wes, it's cold. I'm tired and going home. Go back inside. You seemed to be having a good time."

That time her face gave her away a bit. She wasn't quite ready for the night to be over either, but he wouldn't push her. All the things Anna Yellowtail had told him about moments like this played through his head. Pushing someone like Kate McPhee was a good way to fuck everything up.

"That's what you want? You want me to go back inside?"

"Yes."

He evaluated her. He could see it in her eyes. "You're such a liar, but I'm going to go. I'll see you around, Kate."

And at that he turned and walked back. His mind wandered to Mystic Falls Books, and hoped she would be working tomorrow, because he would definitely be stopping by.

CHAPTER 7

KATE

The next morning Kate was happy to be at the bookstore. Yesterday had not gone like she had expected, from getting out in front of the net again to whatever happened between her and Wes at dinner. She got up early that morning and had breakfast with her loud crazy family, tried not to ogle Wes as he played video games with her nephews, and said goodbye. Patrick and Dylan were already on the road and Conner and Wes were leading one more practice with the high school team before going.

She was in her happy place, putting together a display on banned books. She was doing a social media series on the banned books she was putting up. It had already shown some pretty big sales in their online store. Mystic Falls Book's online business was getting bigger than the storefront. It felt good to see something that had been solely her idea doing so well. She was hoping at some point they might be able to hire another person so she could focus more of her time on the online store and social media. That's what was bringing in all the new business.

The bell sounded and Kate turned to see who was coming in. First, she saw Bridget coming around the corner.

"Here for your morning cup of tea and chat?" Kate asked. She had grown quite fond of her morning chats with Bridget.

"Aye, and it looks like I found a handsome fellow for ye as well," she said with a mischievous grin as she walked over to the drink station and made herself a cup of tea.

As she stood, she saw Wes standing by the door with his blond hair tousled around his blue eyes with a big smile. Her fucking heart did the flutter thing. He was too attractive for his own good.

Bridget looked between them and smiled. "I think I'll be taking my tea to go this morning," she said as she slipped out of the store, leaving Wes and Kate alone.

"Hey," he said. The air was heavy between them. "I just wanted to stop by and get your phone number so I can get you tickets for the game," he said. His swagger from yesterday was gone, he seemed calmer. Kate almost missed it, she kind of liked his cocky swagger, even if she pretended it drove her insane.

"Just leave them at will call, I'll be there. You won fair and square," she said, turning back to her display.

"What are you working on?" he asked.

"This is a banned book display. All of these books have recently been banned by school boards," she said.

He picked up a copy of *Gender Queer* she had just shelved and flipped through it. "What would you suggest I buy?"

"From this selection?" she asked.

"Sure," he said.

"Well, that one you're holding is the most banned book in the country right now," she said.

"Okay, well I should pick it up and see what all the fuss is about. What else would you recommend?"

"What do you like to read?" she asked, studying him.

"Oh, you know me, I don't read much." he said, echoing her sentiment from the night before. "Give me your top ten favorite books," he said.

Kate wasn't sure why, but that made her heart sing. "You want to know my top ten favorite books?"

"Yeah, maybe I can start a book collection of my own," he said with a small smile.

"You don't have to do that. It's not necessary," she said, feeling suddenly unsure of herself.

"It looks like this bookstore is doing wonderful things for this community. Let me use some of my 'hockey bro' money as you put it and support the cause."

"Are you serious?"

"Absolutely. Hit me with your best."

"Okay," a big dopey grin spread across her face. It felt unnatural, but she couldn't stop it if she tried. "Follow me, first stop sci-fi, Octavia Butler. She's a must." She took the copy of *The Kindred* she pulled off the shelf. "Next stop, classics."

He followed behind her and Kate could feel the weight of his gaze and she wished it didn't feel so good.

"Okay, Jane Austen because, of course. But also, Mary Shelly and Tolkien." *Pride and Prejudice, Frankenstein,* and *The Hobbit* adding to the pile of books he carried. Moving to another shelf she searched. "This one is one of my favorite reads from last year," she said and added it to his growing pile.

"I'm headed to romance now, are you ready for that?" she asked looking behind her with a grin on her face.

"Lead the way," he said, motioning for her to proceed. He seemed to be having just as much fun as she was.

"Bridgerton. It's popular for a reason," she said, handing him a copy of *The Duke and I* by Julia Quinn. Before they left that section, she had added two more contemporary romances to the growing pile in his arms.

"Brief stop in horror," she said scanning the shelf for "*The Stand,* I mean Stephen King is a must."

The grin on her face got even bigger when she looked back at him and the growing stack of books he was holding. Now this was even more fun than beating him in foosball.

"Now you want my actual favorites or the pretend ones I tell people?" she asked, feeling almost giddy.

"Of course, the real ones," he said.

"Okay, follow me," she said as they headed into the children's section.

She turned around holding a copy of *Where the Wild Things Are,* "I mean...It's so good."

He took it from her with a smile on his face. "Last one, what do ya got for me?"

"Okay, this is a deep dive, but you wanted my favorites, and this one I read over and over again growing up," she said as she headed over to the wall of chapter books. "*Wait Till Helen Comes,* my first ghost story, which led to a high school Stephen King obsession."

"Alright, it looks like I have some reading material for the flight I have coming up this week," he said.

"You don't have to buy all of these," she said.

"Oh, this hockey bro is buying these books. Gotta support the indie bookstores, right?"

"Okay, maybe you're not a hockey bro," she said as they made their way up to the cash register.

"So, can I have your number? Just to get you the tickets of course," he said with the cocky grin she was actually starting to like. What was wrong with her?

She rang up his last book and wrote her number on the back of the bookmark with the store's information. She glanced up at him and caught a hint of a real smile. "There. For the tickets."

As she handed him two bags full of books, she felt like the grinch must have on the day his heart grew two sizes, because hers was about to explode out of her chest.

"Well, I think we're about to get out of town. But I have to say, Mystic Falls may be one of my new favorite places. I might have to visit again," he said with a wink and turned around and left.

Kate collapsed on the office chair behind the counter. What the hell just happened?

Later that afternoon, Bridget popped back over.

"Who was that handsome lad in the store this morning? He seemed smitten with ye?"

"He's no one," Kate lied through her teeth. "He's just my brother's teammate. He came with him to help lead the hockey training camp for the high schoolers."

"AND he's smitten with ye," Bridget said with a smirk.

"Even if he liked me a little, I don't date hockey players," Kate protested.

"Well, it doesn't seem fair to rule out a whole group of men simply because they play a sport. Yere father is a good man and he played hockey, yes?"

"Yes..."

"And yere brother, he seems like a stand-up fellow."

"I see where you are going with this. But I've known guys like him my whole life. I'm not interested."

"I saw that man leave this store with bags full of books and a grin bigger than a cat who just found the cream. That tells me this one might be different," she said with a gaze that held Kate in place. She was right, he did seem different than the other guys, but it would never work.

"All I'm saying is keep an open mind with this one, he might surprise ye," she said as she patted Kate's hand. "Well,

I'm on my way to visit Poppy and Josh. I think their wee one will be coming soon. Care to put a wager on the pool the town has going?"

"I already claimed April Fool's Day. It seems like something Poppy would do," she said with a smile. She knew Sam better than she knew Poppy because she had played hockey with him, but she knew Poppy enough to know a baby on a day like that fit her brand.

"I got my money on that day too, I think it's a pretty safe bet," she said as she turned to leave.

Just then her phone dinged with an unknown number.

Unknown - Which one should I read first?

It was a picture of *Bridgerton* and *Wait till Helen Comes*. There her heart went again...she was done. She needed to figure out what to do about this situation.

Kate - I'll let you make the call. Spooky kid ghost story or horny regency novel.

She saved his name in her phone with that uncharacteristic goofy grin on her face.

Wes - Now that's a tough choice. I'll let you know what I pick later.

Kate - Are you really going to read them?

Wes - There's a first time for everything.

Kate - Don't strain yourself, you have some important games coming up.

Wes - How do you know how important the games are? Unless you were looking me up.

Kate - Don't make me regret giving you my number.

Wes - Never.

Kate - Text me when you've finished a book.

Wes - You'll be hearing from me soon.

Kate - Good, I call that a win for literacy.

Wes - Ouch! If I didn't have such a playful nature, you might hurt my feelings.

Kate - Hockey Bros don't have feelings.

Wes - I'll talk to you after my nightly reading.

Nightly reading....what was happening?

Later that night when she was getting ready for bed, she got another text. It was a picture of his lap in a comfy bed holding a cup of tea and his newly purchased copy of *Wait till Helen Comes* sitting on his lap.

Wes - Family buying a creepy farmhouse next to a cemetery...What could go wrong? I'm calling you if I have nightmares.

Kate - It is a book for middle schoolers. You can be brave.

Wes - You've been warned.

Wes - Good night, Kate.

Kate - Good night

Kate got into bed and tried to ignore the smile on her face. She would go to his game, and he would move on to something else, someone else. That though made her sad, yet she wasn't sure why. She would just ignore it. Best course of action, right?

But when Kate woke up and looked at her phone, she had a new message.

> Wes - Good morning, Red. I hope you have a good day. Nightmare free over here in case you were worried.

And her heart fluttered.

CHAPTER 8

KATE

It was Tuesday. Kate was at the bookstore getting things ready for the Queer Spaces that would be meeting in their backroom today, but she would be lying if she said she wasn't distracted. Much to her surprise, Wes had been consistently texting her throughout the week. He was sending her book updates and other random texts throughout the day. She wanted to hate it, she wanted to be annoyed by it, but her traitorous heart fluttered every goddamn time. And she was beginning to think maybe she had misjudged him. He had finished the first book and was halfway through *The Duke and I*. He was putting the effort in, she had to give him that.

She heard her phone ding and went to check it. Maybe Wes had gotten to the wedding night, she chuckled to herself.

Wes - Care for one final bet, Red?

Kate - I'm a little scared to ask.

Wes - If I get a hat trick, you have to come home with me tonight.

Kate was stunned, she just kept reading it over and over. Was he kidding?

"Hey Kate!" said Ashton Murray, one of the leaders of the Queer Spaces club.

Kate gave a little squeak and her phone nearly jumped out of her hand.

"Hi Ashton, the room is ready for you. You can head on back," she said quickly as she bent over to pick up her phone. Only to find, much to her horror, when her phone slipped out of her hands, she had FaceTimed Wes. They had never even talked on the phone before, and she was FaceTiming him. Crap! She tried to hit the end button, but there he was smiling at her.

"Oh umm hi," she said breathlessly. "I didn't mean to call you. My phone slipped out of my hand."

He just raised an eyebrow and said, "Likely story." And fuck it all if it didn't shoot straight between her legs. "What do you say, Red? Are you game for another bet?"

She looked down at him. Damn he was hot. And she needed to do something to get him out of her head. Maybe it was time to 'bang one out.'

"You're on," she tried to say in her most sultry tone.

"Are you serious?"

She couldn't help but smile as the glee that danced behind his eyes before he recovered.

"Okay, after my hat trick--which I will get--meet me by the gate."

"IF you get a hat trick, I'll see you then," she said with a smirk.

"When I get a hat trick, I'll see you tonight. I gotta run,

Kate, but thanks for the call. It was nice to see your face again."

"It was an accident. I already told you."

"I choose not to believe that. I choose to believe you couldn't wait to see my handsome face."

"You're a cocky little shit, you know that."

"I've been told. I'll see you tonight."

"Bye," she said as she hung up. Now she just had to decide whether she actually wanted him to get a hat trick.

After work, Kate had just enough time to go home and get ready for the game. She still didn't know how she felt, but she did shave her legs and put on cute underwear just in case. Better safe than sorry. She was on her way to her seat that was down by the ice, next to the penalty box. She had assumed she would be in a family section somewhere or maybe in a box. Somehow, Wes had managed to get her tickets down close to the ice. This could complicate things. She watched as the players warmed up. The smell of the ice and the sound of the pucks being hit settled in her soul. Hockey had been such a big part of her life. Before Jason she would never have missed one of Conner's home games. It was good to be here.

Wes caught sight of her and skated over, tapping on the glass right in front of her, waving. She smiled and waved back. At that moment, she caught Conner's eye as well and he did a double take as his mouth fell open. Then he waved at her.

"Excuse me, do you know Conner McPhee and Wes Darling?" asked the woman sitting right behind her.

"Yeah, Conner's my brother," she said. She was trying to find her center in all of this. It was overwhelming.

"Oh, you look alike," she said. "Could you introduce me?"

"Ummmm..." Right at that moment a puck hit the glass right in front of her and Wes winked. That's when it all came crashing down on her. She was here at the arena, watching them play. Conner had to be wondering why she was here. She had seen a couple of his games, but she always sat in the boxes with her family. It wasn't the same as being down on the ice. She needed to get out of here. She stood up and bee lined to the bathroom. Why did she come? What was she thinking?

She made it to the bathroom and splashed some water on her face. She checked her phone and read over the texts that Wes had been sending her over the last few days. She was here because she needed to get him out of her system. She needed things to go back to normal.

She would also have to explain to her brother why she was here. How had she not thought of that? Well...she had assumed he would never know. She would be lost in a sea of fans in a giant arena, but she was on the ice, and she should not have been surprised. Well, it was too late to back out now, she was already here. She might as well make the most of it. Before going back, she picked up a giant pretzel and a beer to calm her nerves.

By the time she made it back, the game had already started. As she sat down in her seat, the goal siren went off and the chorus of 'Do You Believe in Magic' started to play. Someone had just scored a goal, and of course that someone was Wes. He skated right by her holding up one finger. This was going to be an interesting night.

The game continued and Kate settled into it. She was really impressed with Wes. She knew he was good, but he was *really* good. Conner's game seemed to be off though. He had some sloppy passes and a shot he could easily have made but went wide. Guilt bubbled in the back of her mind. Was her surprise presence throwing off his game?

It was mid-way through the second period when Wes got a breakaway and scored another goal. Once again skating by her with a smile holding up two fingers. He just might get a hat trick. And Kate had decided she really hoped he did. She might even still go home with him if he didn't.

At the top of the third period Wes got a penalty for hooking. He came to the penalty box right next to her and grinned at her and mouthed the words one more. All she could do was smile.

The third period finished, and Wes didn't score. She was feeling a little disappointed. It was tied 3-3 and they were getting ready for overtime. Conner and Wes were on the ice with another teammate for the three-on-three sudden death. There had been a close call down by the other team's net. Kate was on her feet cheering. This was an exciting game. Conner got control of the puck and started bringing it back down the ice. Wes was waiting for him closer to the net. Conner passed it to him, and Wes shot it. It went five hole, and the goal sirens went off. The crowd went wild, it almost drowned out 'Do You Believe in Magic' blaring on the speaker. Kate found herself jumping up and down right along with them.

People were making their way down to the ice tossing hats over because Wes had done it. He got his hat trick. After he was out of the teammate's huddles of congratulations, he skated over and stopped right in front of her and held up three fingers and pointed to her and back at himself. She couldn't help but smile at him as the hats flew over her head and onto the ice.

After the game, Kate waited by the back gate for Wes to come and get her. She could hardly keep her heart from pounding out of her chest. The excitement of the game and going home with Wes was turning her into a jumble of nerves and emotions. One of the security guards came up to her. "Are you Kate McPhee?"

"Yes," she responded tentatively.

"Come on back." He led her further down a hallway towards the locker room. Wes walked out of the locker room grinning at her.

"I got a hat trick," he said with his cocky swagger.

"Yes, you did," she said, trying to keep the smile from her face. "You won fair and square."

"That I did."

"Seriously though, congratulations, you played great tonight. What was that? Your third hat trick of the season?"

"The hat trick of hat tricks," he said. He had yet to reach out and touch her like he had in the bar, and she found herself being pulled towards him.

"So, do you want to go out with the team for drinks? I must warn you, there are going to be hockey players there and I know how you feel about hockey players," he said.

She elbowed him, "Yeah, that sounds good."

"Come this way. We can take my car," he said, slipping his arm around her shoulder. He pulled her close to him and her core flashed molten when she felt the press of his hard body against her. He smelled of that cologne and a hint of minty freshness. Whatever that was, she wanted to devour it. Let that ice chill the heat setting her on fire right now.

He slid his hand to the small of her back and guided her out the back.

They got to the bar, and she left her coat in the car. Luckily, it was more of a pub than a night club because her sweater and leggings would not be appropriate for that, but she could do a pub. He slid his arm around her as they walked the block to the pub. Walking in, it was already loud and most of the team wasn't even there yet.

It was only then that she looked around at the crowd. The college crowd. She had almost forgotten how close to campus they were. That thought made her heart race and not in a good way. He wouldn't be here. He was a professor. He didn't hang out with undergrads at a pub.

"Ya okay?" Wes whispered in her ear. She just nodded, feeling a little out of sorts. "What do you want to drink?"

"Just get me whatever IPAs on tap," she said.

"The team usually sits up there," he said, gesturing up the stairs. "If you want to head up and get a seat, I'll be right up."

She made her way up the stairs to find a place to sit. Looking down at the sea of college students she was feeling out of sorts. It was giving her a moment to stop and think after the excitement of the game. Time to cool after talking to Wes. She was strongly questioning her decision to come to a pub with Wes. But he did get a hat trick, he should celebrate with his team. This was a big game and put them in a good spot for the playoffs. He deserved to celebrate. She heard a big booming laugh coming up the stairs and turned to see Ethan Yellowtail, the goalie for the Magic, laughing and walking with her brother...another thing she stupidly didn't put together.

"Hey, you're McPhee's little sister, right?" asked Ethan.

"Twin sister," she corrected as she looked at Conner. "You played amazing out there, Conner."

"Thanks. I have to say, I was surprised to see you out in the crowd tonight," he said with a cocked eyebrow.

"Well, I lost a bet, so here I am," she said.

"You lost a bet?" Ethan said. "What kind of bet?"

"If Wes beat me at darts, I told him I would come to his game," she said.

"And he beat you?" Conner asked. "Wes beat YOU at darts?" His voice was thick with disbelief but luckily, at that moment, Wes came up the stairs and set the beer down in front of her and opened himself a bottle of water.

"So, all it took to get you to the game was a good bet? I should have done that a long time ago," Conner said.

"Yes, but you would have to win the bet," Kate said flatly, but Conner's grin settled in her.

"OOOOOH! That's harsh!" Ethan called. Kate had to bite back a grin of her own.

As the night went on, she had a good time hanging out with all the players and some of the girlfriends. It felt familiar. Guys like this had always been around growing up. It brought up feelings, good nostalgic ones. But that nostalgia was laced with regret of what could have been if things had played out differently. She had tried to bend herself to be the person for Jason. Giving up hockey had been something she had done out of self-preservation, but she probably wouldn't have stayed away from it so long if she didn't lose herself in him. She could see that now, but her feelings around all of it were still so complicated.

"You okay?" Wes whispered in her ear as he rested his hand on her thigh under the table.

"Yep, I'm good."

"Do you need another drink?" he asked.

"No, I think I'm just going to run to the restroom really quick," she said.

She got up and made her way down the stairs to the restrooms. It was undergrad central. There was something wonderful about women's bathrooms. No one was in your corner quite like a room full of drunk women. She could hear the pep talks and gossip and it made her think of her own college experience that felt so long ago.

As she was washing her hands, she caught a bit of a conversation next to her. "Did you hear the professor is sleeping with our TA?"

"Are you serious?"

"Yes! And I saw him out there with her. He's hot for a professor!"

"Isn't it against the rules to sleep with your TA?"

"Maybe, but he doesn't seem to care."

Her heart was in her throat. What were the odds? Surely there were other professors who slept with their TAs. That did not mean that Jason was out there right now. But that thought was not enough to stop her heart from pounding in her chest. Not the nice flutters she got around Wes, but big panic filled thuds that she could hear pounding in her head. She took a deep breath and left the room. No Jason. She just had to make it up to Wes, then it would be fine. But oh my god, what if Conner saw him? Conner didn't know everything that went down between them, but he had figured enough out to know that a guy he hated to begin with had hurt her, and that's really all he needed to start a fight.

She was almost to the stairs when she saw him. Her heart dropped out of her chest; she wasn't even sure how she was still standing. It had been over a year since she'd seen him. He still looked exactly the same, a thin frame, short brown wavy hair, a well-kept beard, and an air of superiority. The need to run overtook her, but she was frozen in place.

She didn't know how she had missed him before, but there, at two tables away from the stairs was Jason, sipping on whiskey. His eyes locked on her, and she froze. She couldn't move. She didn't know what to do.

"Kate? Is that you?"

"Yep, it's me," she said. Her eyes frantically searching for Wes or anyone other than Conner. Fuck! This was not happening!

He got up and walked over to her and hugged her. She felt like she was going to crawl out of her skin. Her clammy hand pushed him away slightly trying to find enough space to breathe, but when they were in the same building, that space didn't exist.

"How have you been?" he asked her like she was some

pathetic child. "Are you still working at that bookstore back home?"

Her eyes searched again, but this time they caught Wes's.

"Yep, I'm still there. I'm really enjoying myself working there," she said.

His hand found her upper arm and gave a little squeeze, then started to slowly rub.

"I'm glad you are enjoying yourself. I'll have to stop by and see it." He stopped talking and his eyes perused her body. She wanted to disappear. "We should get a drink. We have so much to catch up on. I have to say—"

And thankfully before he could finish that thought, Wes slid in next to her and put his hand on the small of her back. "I was wondering what was taking you so long, Red. Hi, I'm Wes," he said with the same cocky look on his face and stuck out his hand to Jason.

Jason looked at him with an unsure expression and took his hand. "Jason," was all he said.

"Are you ready to go?" she asked Wes.

"Yep, let's get out of here."

"You're leaving with him?" Jason asked, shock in his voice.

"Yeah, and you might want to think about heading out. Conner is upstairs and he won't be happy if he sees you."

Wes wasn't sure what was going on, but his cocky grin had turned into a glare after she said that.

"Why is he worried about Conner?" Wes asked, still giving Jason a hard look.

"It's nothing. Please let's just get out of here."

Without another word, Wes began to guide her away. He parted the crowd, getting her out of there safely and out into the car.

She slipped her coat on, but it was cold from being in the car and didn't do much to warm her up. Wes turned on the seat warmers and the soft leather seats beneath her started to warm. Finally, she took a deep breath.

"Thanks, sorry about that," she said, not looking him in the eye.

He put his hand on her knee and she almost jumped at the zing that shot through her. "You have nothing to apologize for. Who was that guy?"

"Just an ex. Now are you going to take me home or what?" she asked.

And at that Wes put the car into drive and was on his way.

CHAPTER 9

WES

es kept stealing little glances over at Kate on their way home. He wanted to ask more about that guy. The look on her face when she made eye contact told him something was wrong. Pride swelled deep down in his soul knowing she looked for him when she felt uncomfortable. He wanted to be that for her.

He had never been serious about anyone like this, but Wes was someone who trusted his gut and went all in. That was part of the reason he was good at hockey. He knew what he wanted, and he went for it. When he played timid hockey, not only did he suck, but it was also dangerous. When a player was in their head too much, mistakes happen. So, the fact that Wes saw what he wanted and went after it served him well in his career, but he was hoping it would serve him well here too.

But there was the other side of him that wanted to punch that guy for making Kate uncomfortable. If she was that uncomfortable just running into him, he knew he was no good. And the way Kate was trying to keep Conner from seeing him told him all he needed to know. He would not be getting anywhere near her again.

He pulled into the underground parking for his condo and glanced over at her. She smiled at him, and his heart skipped a beat. He had never felt that way except on the ice. He had gotten a hat trick, and he was making major inroads with Kate in one night. He knew he still had a way to go until she trusted him completely. There was something about her relationship to hockey and hockey players that was strained. It wasn't something he understood yet, but he would. He would be patient, because that is what she seemed to need him to be. He would show her that he wasn't going anywhere, and that he was an intelligent and compassionate person. She could trust him.

He pulled into his parking spot and looked over at her. "You ready for this," he said with a glint in his eye.

She looked at him and bit her bottom lip, nodding. They got out of the car and walked up to his place. As he opened the door, he took a breath, trying to settle his nerves. His condo wasn't big, but it was nice. His living room looked like what one might think a twenty-four-year-old NHL players condo would look like. Everything was sleek and modern. Lots of white, clean lines, a big leather sectional with a large tv, video games, and a VR headset and all sorts of stuff he bought when he got drafted. Going from being a kid with next to nothing to a nineteen-year-old making millions had caused some extreme spending for a couple years, but that wasn't what he did anymore.

"So, this is your place, huh?" she asked, looking around.

"This is it. Can I get you something to drink?"

"Sure," she said quietly. She looked different here in his space. Her confidence seemed to be faltering a bit, and that just wouldn't do. He loved how tough she was and how much shit she gave him. When they had met there was so much fight in her spirit, he adored that about her.

He went into the kitchen and got her a beer from the fridge. It was the same kind she had ordered when they were out at dinner in Mystic Falls. "Is this okay? I have wine or water if you would rather have that."

"This is good." She walked over to him and took the beer from his hand, leaning back against the counter. She took a sip. He watched as she swallowed, not making eye contact. He hadn't been this attracted to anyone in a long time. It was everything, from her attitude to her wild red curls, to the decadent curves of her body. He wanted to get lost in Kate McPhee.

He leaned his hip against the counter facing her. He reached out and wrapped her silky red curls around one of his fingers.

"I'm really glad you came tonight," he said, leaning in a little bit.

She set her beer down on the counter and turned to look at him more fully. "I am too." The air felt heavy between them. The tension of their nearness was palpable. He wanted to touch her and feel that warmth that took him over every time he touched her. That magic spark that seemed to dance between them was intoxicating. He was barely holding on. His eyes were drawn to her bottom lip as she nervously chewed it.

"Can I kiss you?" he asked as he let the finger that had just been wrapped around one of her curls lightly trace her jaw. The electricity hung in the air as he waited for her answer.

She looked up at him through her lashes. A hint of a smile danced across her face, and she gave a small nod. He slid his hand to the back of her head, cradling it. Slowly he lowered his lips to hers. The moment their lips met he felt a jolt of electricity shoot straight through him. A low moan escaped him at the surprise of the feeling. He moved closer and deepened the kiss. She opened to him, and he swept his tongue into her mouth. He pulled her closer, one hand still cradling her head and the other sliding around her back. All of her delicious curves pressed into him, filling all the spaces of his hard body with her softness. He wanted to sink all the way into her.

He started to kiss down her jaw and she fisted one hand in his hair, pulling him closer to her neck. She smelled warm, like vanilla and maybe a hint of cinnamon. He wanted to curl up and just hold her. And he hadn't told her yet, but that is exactly what he was planning on doing tonight.

"Where's your bedroom?" she asked in a sultry voice that had him questioning his original intent on bringing her here. But he knew it was what he wanted to do.

"I have to tell you something first," he said, pulling away and looking at her. His willpower was being tested with how good she felt. "I don't want to have sex tonight," he said.

She tensed beneath him, and a wrinkle formed between her eyes. "I don't understand."

"Kate, I know you think I'm just some hockey bro. You're probably confused about why you like me, and you might even be thinking about...What do they call it in romance novels? 'Banging one out of your system'."

She looked down and gave a little chuckle. "Am I that transparent?" she asked.

"I just want you to know, I think this could be something special. I'm not going to sleep with you for the first time on a bet."

She looked up at him with an eyebrow cocked. "Then what was the point of said bet?"

"Just to get you to give me a chance. So please, can we start with a blank slate? I'm not a hockey bro. I'm just a guy who desperately wants to get to know you." He held his breath while she just looked at him, evaluated him.

"You're serious?"

He nodded while his hands rested on either side of her hips pinning her against the counter.

"Cause…" She looked down between them at the growing erection tenting his suit pants. "I'm not sure someone got the memo."

"Don't pay any attention to him. He'll do anything for the attention of a pretty girl," he said slowly lowering his face to hers.

"What if I want to pay attention to him?" she said, looking at him through her lashes.

"Then you are just going to have to be patient," he said as he kissed her slowly, exploring her mouth, pinning her to the counter.

"Can we still make out? Because I'm not sure if anyone ever told you this Wes, but you're pretty hot," she said, tracing her hand up his back.

"Oh, there will be so much making out."

"Okay, then can you show me your room?"

He pushed off the counter. "Follow me."

He led her into his room. He was excited for this, not only to have her in his bed, which was something he had been fantasizing about, but also because he had a feeling she was in for a pretty big surprise.

"Are you ready?" he asked her with a grin.

"Are you about to show me where the magic happens?" she asked.

"All kinds of magic," he said as he pushed the door open and stepped aside allowing her to walk into his bedroom.

She walked in and gasped.

CHAPTER 10

KATE

"Oh my god, Wes! Look at this!" She walked over to the wall opposite the door. In the middle was a fireplace with a big screen tv above it, and on either side of it were giant, custom-made floor to ceiling bookshelves. He even had a rolling ladder for the books closer to the vaulted ceilings. She was not expecting this.

"Why do you have so many books?"

"Believe it or not, it is because I like to read. I spend a lot of time on the road, and I have since I was thirteen. I read when we travel."

She walked over to the shelves and traced her hands along the books. "You have even more books than I do," she said. "Why did you let me go on like that in the bookstore?"

She came to one shelf that was all Tolkien. Some beautiful old collector editions and some that look like they have been read time and time again. "You have three copies of *The Hobbit* now. Why didn't you tell me that?"

She turned and saw him grinning from ear to ear. "You assumed I didn't read," he said.

"And you assumed I couldn't skate," she said with a

sheepish smile. "I think we both made some incorrect snap judgments of each other."

"That we did. Although, I'm just gonna say, I assumed a cute little bookworm wouldn't know how to ice skate, and you assumed that simply because I play hockey I wasn't as smart as you," he said.

"I never said you weren't smart!" she protested.

"No, you just questioned my ability to read," he said.

"I'm sorry. I was wrong, you clearly know how to read."

There was a big comfy chair that sat next to the bookshelves. On the table next to it were the stack of books he had bought from the bookstore. "But seriously you now have three copies of *The Hobbit*."

"Yes, but you see, I needed another one," he said in all seriousness.

"And why is that?"

"Well," he said as he walked over to his shelves. "I have this copy, which is a first edition. I can't read that. It's no good on a road trip. Then I have this copy," and he gently pulled a very used copy from the shelf. The cover was barely hanging on and the spine was cracked. It looked like it had been read over and over. "And I'm not sure this one would take another reading without just falling apart in my hands. So, I clearly needed another one. My mom actually gave me this one before I moved to Minnesota. Growing up, there was a library next to where she waited tables. I spent days in that library."

"I was wrong about you. You're never what I expect you to be," she said before trapping her plump bottom lip between her teeth.

"So why don't you stop expecting things of me and just get to know me."

She looked down at the carpet. She hadn't been fair to him. He was proving to be a good guy time and time again.

Looking back at him, his gaze still holding hers, the intimacy of this moment had her buzzing. It was teetering between anxiety and just plain excitement. "I think I can do that," she said quietly.

And with that he turned on the fireplace and lamp, and turned off the overhead light. His room was filled with warmth and soft light and all she wanted to do was jump him, but he had taken that off the table. Although he was standing there by his bed, giving her eyes that told a different story.

"Come here," he said.

She walked over to him and slipped her arms around his waist, laying her head against his chest. His heart was pounding like hers. She sighed and melted into him. Seeing him in this new light had thrown her. She was hoping they would be having some hot sex right now, but instead she was in his space, learning that she might actually like him. He would've been the first person she slept with since Jason. She had thought he was just some cocky hockey player who would show her a good time, and then they could both move on. It would be easier than feeling vulnerable again because she wasn't entirely sure she knew how to do that.

"This is different now," she said. Her voice was muffled by his chest.

"Not for me. I've known this is something special the moment I saw you take off your helmet and push Conner down on the ice," he said as he kissed the top of her head.

She looked up at him, her arms still wrapped tightly around him. "Really? That's what did it for you?"

"Oh yeah. A bookworm who's lethal on the ice? Red, you've gotta know that's my type."

She chuckled, burying her face in his chest. This was not at all what she thought it would be. It wasn't as safe as she thought it would be. She was terrified at the thought of being in love with someone else. And while she wasn't in love with him, she knew that's the kind of relationship he wanted. That was NOT the kind of relationship she felt ready for. Her body started to tremble at the thought of letting someone in again. She didn't know if she could do it.

"Hey, are you okay?" He tried to pull back to look at her, but she knew if he did that she would cry. And she would not cry tonight.

So, she buried her face in his chest. "That guy we ran into at the bar," she said. Her face was still buried in his chest, comforted by the Wes smell of ice. "I told you he was my ex, but he really did a number on me. I'm not sure if I'm ready for what you want. I like you, but I'm just not ready yet." Tears burned in her sinuses, but she would not let them out. She had cried too much over Jason. She would not let him ruin this too, but she didn't know how to do this anymore. "Please be patient with me."

He held her tight and rubbed her back. The warmth of his embrace was easy to get lost in. Then, he did pull away and tip her chin up to him, forcing her to look him in the eyes. All she wanted to do was run and hide.

"I'm here." He said it so plainly before dropping a sweet kiss on her forehead. "I'm not going anywhere. I'll be as patient as you need me to be. I'm not going to rush this because I trust my gut, and my gut is telling me this is something special."

She closed her eyes because this moment was too much. This was not what she expected. Then she felt his lips find hers in the sweetest barely-there kiss. Something inside of her broke, and a tear rolled down her cheek. He simply wiped it away and held her. This felt painfully vulnerable, but she couldn't bring herself to put an end to it. She wanted this, but she just didn't know if she could do it again.

Then he kissed her a little harder. His mouth parted and

she opened, letting him sweep into her mouth. This one small gesture burned the paper-thin vulnerability she felt and set it on fire. She was ablaze for him. Before, it had just been about having sex with someone who is undeniably attractive and who seemed to want her too, but this was more. And while she still felt so fucking scared, in this moment, desire started to win the emotional battle taking place inside of her.

"So, I know I said I don't want to have sex tonight, but that doesn't mean I can't make you come," he rasped in her ear.

She pulled back and looked at him. "Yeah?"

He nodded and walked her back until her knees hit the bed and she fell with a gentle huff. She looked up at him and all the fear was burned away by the heat of his gaze. He kneeled before her and kissed her. This kiss was not like any of their previous kisses. This kiss was pure fire. His hands found the hem of her sweater and started to tug it up. She helped him and his hands ran over her breast, trying to pinch her nipples through her entirely too supportive bra. She reached behind herself and undid the clasp, pulling it off her shoulders. Then his hands were all over her. He pushed her back on the bed, crawling over her. He was still in his suit pants and shirt, and she started to pull at his buttons. She watched with anticipation as each new bit of skin appeared. She wanted to feel him holding her and get lost in those strong arms.

"You are so beautiful," he said, as he took her in and ran his hands over her breasts. He stood and took off his pants, then laid down next to her. He kissed her and kissed her until she was dizzy with desire. She had never felt this taken care of her entire life. After an eternity of kissing, he pulled back and gazed at her, gently brushing her hair out of her eyes. "I just love these curls," he said, wrapping another around his finger. He kissed her again and then started peppering light kisses down her neck.

"What do you want, Red. Do you want to come?"

"Yes," she said, pulling at his body.

"Okay, just you though. Don't forget. I couldn't stand it even a second if you thought I was just trying to get you in bed. I also don't want you to think we're just doing this because of the bet."

"Okay, but maybe tomorrow..." she said looking up at him.

"Yeah," he said, then licked his lips. "Maybe tomorrow."

Then he was kissing her again, his hand sliding down her belly. His mouth kissed her jaw and down her chest until he gently flicked his tongue over her nipple. Her body cried out with need.

"Is this okay?" he asked as he started to pull down her leggings.

"Oh my god, yes!" she said, helping him slide them off her hips. His mouth stayed at her breasts, slowly sucking and flicking as his hand trailed up her leg until he was at the apex between her thighs. He slid a finger between her folds, and she was shamelessly wet and needy. He let out a low guttural sound as he slid a finger inside of her. He sucked her nipple more fully into his mouth. She could feel herself falling fast. His wet finger slid out of her and swirled around her clit. He stayed there, working slow circles.

"Do you like that?" he asked between kisses.

"Yes, just like that," and he listened. He didn't speed up or use more pressure, he stayed just like that. The build was intensifying, and she started to grab at the sheets. Her body arched and pleasure jolted through her. He pulled back, her nipple leaving his mouth with a pop. Hlooked at her. The look on his face was one of reverence, and it broke her. They locked eyes as her orgasm came in wave after wave of perfect pleasure. He stayed steady, circling her clit just like she had said she liked until she collapsed on the bed, all the pleasure wrung from her body.

"Oh my god," she panted as he collapsed next to her.

"That was fun," he whispered in her ear and pulled her close and cradled her naked body.

"It was. I know you said you don't want the favor returned tonight, but I just need you to know, the offer is most definitely on the table for your taking," she said.

He kissed her forehead. "I appreciate that, but I can wait."

Just then, something on the bedside table caught her eye. Right there with a bookmark about half the way through was the copy of *The Duke and I*.

"You're really reading the books you bought?"

"Of course!" he said as he wound a curl around his finger.

'You're perfect' is what she wanted to say, but she didn't say anything. She just laid there with him, enjoying the feel of his body against hers.

"I liked watching you play hockey," she said quietly.

He kissed the top of her head. He had no idea what that statement meant. He didn't know that the absence of hockey was like a giant gaping hole in her heart she didn't know how to fill. So she had just built up walls around it and was careful not to fall in. Losing hockey after college had left her questioning who she was, and Jason had been there to build her into who he wanted her to be. That was until it was time for an upgrade, and she was tossed aside like an old model.

Maybe it was time she started putting the pieces of her old self back together. It had started when Conner got her back on the ice. As scared as she was, she thought maybe learning to love hockey again, and letting Wes into the spaces she kept everyone out of might help. She knew she had a lot of work to do on herself, but if he was willing, maybe he could be there to hold her hand when she faced it all.

Her eyes started to get heavier, and her breathing slowed.

"Are you falling asleep?" he whispered in her ear.

"No," she said in a weak protest.

He kissed her and got out of bed, turning off the fire and the lamps before crawling back into bed. He settled behind her holding her back tightly to his chest as they both fell asleep.

CHAPTER 11

KATE

Kate woke up with the sun starting to peek through the curtains of Wes's room. He was sleeping next to her peacefully, but she was in a panic. She had been woken up by severe cramps and a damp feeling on the sheets. She did not just get her period all over his sheets. No, that simply wasn't possible. The universe was not cruel enough to do that.

She slowly lifted the sheet and Wes's white sheets looked like a massacre had been committed. Fuck! Her heart was pounding, and her head couldn't figure out the next step. She quietly got out of bed and made it to the bathroom off Wes's bedroom. She would shower and figure out what to do about the bleeding, and sneak home. She didn't want to even think about what would happen when he woke up to see blood all over his sheets.

She turned on the hot water and started to cry. And this was not just a few tears slipping down her face. This was an ugly cry from all those emotions swirling around inside of her, from hockey entering her life again to whatever was starting here with Wes.

And that was over. She would never be able to look him in the eyes again. She'd never known a guy who wasn't weird about periods. Her first memory of learning about periods was when Patrick chased Conner around the house trying to stick a pad on him. It was clean of course, and he got in trouble, but nine-year-old Kate had gotten the message. Boys think periods are gross. And every guy she had dated had enforced that assumption. She once asked Jason to pick her up some tampons at the store and he freaked out and refused. He refused to even touch her when she was on her period. He acted like they were living in the past, and she needed to go live in the red tent. That was after they'd been together for over a year.

Now she had just bled all over Wes's sheets. This twenty-four-year-old kid who had just invited her back to his house on a bet. Though she learned last night that all the assumptions she had made about him were wrong and possibly even a little unkind, this...this was something else entirely. This was something that would give grown men pause.

The tears stopped and she let the hot water run over her until it turned cold. The thought of trying to sneak out of his window did cross her mind, but she didn't have her clothes in here. They were still all over Wes's floor. And she wouldn't be climbing anywhere...they were in a high rise, but also, she had terrible cramps. That's the thing about PCOS, irregular periods, heavy periods, and debilitating cramps, that's where she was. She didn't want to be dealing with this. She was humiliated and in pain. This may be one of the lowest points of her life.

Okay, now the water was going from tepid to cold, she needed to get out. Stepping out of the glasswork shower she saw a towel sitting next to a pair of old comfy looking sweats and on top of that was a little woven basket with a lid on it.

She lifted the lid and found a variety of pads and

tampons. Wes must have snuck in when she was in the shower. Now she was crying again. How on earth did he have these on hand? And there was no way she would fit in his sweats, because she had gained weight after she quit playing hockey, and he was slender. But when she picked them up, she let out another sob because these were over-sized, comfy looking sweats. She got herself all taken care of and went out to face Wes. Maybe he wouldn't be terrible about this. She hoped so, because she was now all taken care of and in some comfy sweats. She was growing entirely too fond of him.

She left the bathroom, and the bed was all made up, but no Wes. When she found him in the kitchen making pancakes, she started to cry all over again. She was a mess.

He looked up and just gave her a small smile as he plated up the pancakes and handed her the plate and set the syrup next to it. He had made her chocolate chip pancakes.

"How are you feeling? Do you need anything?" he asked.

"No, I'm good. You took care of everything," she said, tugging on the sweatshirt. "I'm so sorry. I'm so embarrassed."

"Why?"

"Ummmm...because I bled all over your sheets."

"Kate, half of the population has had or will have a period. I assure you, it's fine. The sheets are in the wash, and every-thing is taken care of. Please don't worry about it. Besides, I'm a hockey player, I've dealt with my fair share of blood, mine and other people's," he said as he walked over and gave her a kiss.

"Thank you...for everything. Are these chocolate chip pancakes? They're my favorite. How did you know?"

"It may have come up at breakfast with your family," he said as he took a drink from his smoothie.

"No pancakes for you?" she asked.

"No. I try to stick to a pretty strict diet during the season. Do you need to get back today?" he asked.

"No, I'm off today," she said as she got a forkful of pancakes.

"Me too," he said sitting down next to her at the breakfast bar in his kitchen.

A particularly bad wave of cramps hit her. She stilled, bending over slightly as she took a careful breath.

"You okay?" he asked with concern clouding his face.

"Do you have any pain killers?" she asked.

"Yeah, let me go grab you some."

He left to go to the bathroom as Kate took another bite of pancakes. They were delicious. Once again, Wes had been better than she could have even imagined. This would have caused an awkward morning for most guys, but he was being so great.

He returned with a bottle of ibuprofen and a clay heating pad he tossed in the microwave.

"Since we are both off today, and you're feeling kinda crummy, what would you say to a good cuddle and a Lord of the Rings marathon?"

She smiled as another tear ran down her face. She was going to blame the hormones, and not the feelings she was fighting for this thoughtful man.

"I think that sounds amazing," she said with a small smile.

He just smiled back at her and wiped the tear away. With a sigh, he kissed her head.

"You are just a surprise at every turn," she said as she leaned into him. He took her plate and put it in the dishwasher and got the heated pad from the microwave.

"To Middle Earth?" he asked, taking her hand.

"I never would have guessed you were such a nerd," she said playfully.

"Yeah, I keep it on the D.L." he said as he led them back into bed.

Once they got back in his room, Wes lit the fire then headed back to the bed and jumped on it with a big flop. He scooted himself up and got the pillows and blankets all situated in a cute little nest and patted the space right next to him. Kate watched him and smiled. Even her painful cramps weren't enough to drown out her heart flutters. Maybe it was time she gave Wes a proper chance.

She was still afraid, but at every turn he had shown he was someone she could trust. She crawled in bed next to him as the opening scene of The Fellowship of the Ring started to play. She curled right into him. Her head on his chest. He helped her situate the heating pad and put his arm around her. They fit together perfectly. As she rested her head on his chest, she melted into the soothing sound of his heartbeat, and realized that it was keeping time with her own.

"The extended edition?" she asked.

"Of course," he said in feigned offense. "Is there any other way to watch it?"

"Nope," she said as she settled back in next to him.

The sound of the hobbits celebrating soothed her. The medicine was kicking in, the heating pad was warming her, and Wes was holding her hand. This moment felt pretty close to perfect. She could say it now, she had misjudged Wes. She had gravely misjudged him. She needed to work through her shit, because if she could make this work, it had potential to be life changing.

Kate looked and watched him for a moment while he watched the movie. His soft blond hair pulled away from his face like he had just ran his hand through it, his ice blue eyes watching the movie, he really did look young. Yes, twenty-four was young, but he had a baby face. He was not the serious academic her two previous boyfriends had been, but that was a good thing. He was different, a surprise at every turn. She gave a contented sigh, and he looked down at her.

When he looked down at her, a small smile crept across his face before he dropped a small kiss on top of her head.

"Thank you, Wes," she said, trying to push away the emotion that had clouded her voice.

"For what?" he asked as he traced her jaw, one corner of his mouth slightly upturned.

"For being a constant surprise, and for being you," she said quietly.

He slid his hand to cradle the back of her head and lowered himself and pressed a small, sweet kiss to her mouth. It broke something inside of her. She had never in her life been treated like this, like she was something to be cherished. She didn't really know how to handle it.

"What is it exactly that you are looking for here?" she asked. She figured being blunt was the way to go. She needed to figure out right now if she was going to be able to give him what he wanted. She was still such a mess, but part of her did want to try with him.

"I just want you."

"How can you know that? I wasn't even particularly nice to you in Mystic Falls," she said, feeling a little ashamed of what she had thought of him before she got to know him.

He chuckled. "I know, but I like a challenge," he said grinning from ear to ear.

"Well, that's not particularly healthy," she shot back at him with a half-smile.

"I get it, but here's the thing. I live my life and make decisions based on my gut. That is part of being a good hockey player, you know that. If I am wishy washy or play it too safe, I could get injured or injure those around me. I need to be confident in the choices I make. The worst mistake of my life was made when I went against what my gut was telling me to do. After I got out of that mess, I vowed to always trust my gut. And now my gut is telling me there is something special here," he said with such certainty.

"What decision was it you made when you didn't trust your gut? I mean, if you feel comfortable telling me," she added on quickly.

"My life is an open book for you, Red. It was when I got drafted to Florida. Hockey teams have always been like a second family to me and that was not the culture of the team down there. When they drafted me, I knew it wasn't going to be a good fit, but I didn't think I could say no. I didn't want to be seen as some cocky nineteen-year-old thinking he was too good for an NHL team, so I went down there knowing it was a mistake...I was right. It was awful. The team culture was brutal, the coaches were rough. I mean I get it; coaches push you and don't have to coddle you. I wouldn't want that anyway, but there was name calling on and off the ice. And the way many of the players and staff talked about and treated women was fucked up. After some stuff went down with one player in particular, I got out of there as fast as I could."

He paused and looked down at her, winding one of her curls around his finger.

"I was supposed to be there another two years, but I worked on getting traded early. Ethan Yellowtail and I played together in Minnesota growing up. The Magic always had a good reputation as a team, and Ethan said he loved it. It was the year that David Anders' knee went out. I knew they would be looking for a shooter with speed to play with your brother and I thought I might be a good fit. It's worked out pretty well for the past two years and I'm really hoping to stay here and be a franchise player like Conner. This is a great team. Plus, I'm closer to my mom, I mean not super close, but closer than Florida."

"I'm glad you ended up here," she said.

"Me too. Playing with your brother is great and of course being with Ethan is amazing. He's like a brother to me. And Coach Wagner is amazing. I mean he's tough, but I know he has all our backs. So, all that being said, I trust my gut. And I'm not trying to scare you, but as soon as you whipped off that helmet and this mess of red curls popped out, I knew I had to find a way to make you mine."

Is it possible for your heart to race and flutter at the same time? Because that's how Kate felt right now. There was something about Wes that was already so comforting. He had been different than she thought he would be, he was perfect, but she still didn't know if she could trust him. While her heart was telling her she could trust Wes, she just couldn't get her brain on board. Her traitorous brain was still waiting for the shoe to drop.

He was lying next to her holding her, looking at her with patience. He deserved more than what she could give him.

"I want to try," she said timidly. "But I'm just not sure if I'm ready for something serious."

"Okay," he said as he brushed her hair away from her face.

"But you just said you wanted more."

"I do, but if you are not ready, then you're not ready. I'm not going anywhere. If you need time to trust me, then I'll give you that time. I mean, we have only been on one date," he said.

"But that wasn't a date," she said with a small smile.

"Right, of course it wasn't. So then, why don't we go on a date?"

"Yeah?"

"Yeah. I'm heading out for a road trip tomorrow, but I'll be back next Friday. Do you have plans for Friday night?"

She shook her head.

"Okay, I'll pick you up at seven and you can show me a good time in Mystic Falls."

"Seriously?"

"Of course! Does that sound okay to you? You can plan something, or I can, whatever you want."

"I'll plan something. And can we not tell anyone yet?"

He looked at her with a look she had yet to see, and she didn't like it. His cockiness was gone, and it looked like she might have hurt his feelings.

"It's not that I want to hide or anything, it's just complicated. You're my brother's teammate. My family just started leaving me alone about why I have distanced myself from hockey. I just need some time to wrap my head around everything."

"Of course. We'll take things slow."

She snuggled back into him, and he held her close. How on earth did he feel so good? AND smell so good, always. He smelled like ice every time, and it was everything. They settled back into the movie and watched the fight for Middle Earth curled up on Wes's big bed. Kate wasn't sure if she had ever felt this safe and happy. She could do this. She trusted Wes, now she just needed to trust herself.

CHAPTER 12

*L*ater that week, Kate opened the bookstore and got the coffee brewing. She was trying to get back to normal, but the events of the past week were playing in her mind on an endless loop. She had been living back in Mystic Falls for almost a year. When she moved back, she had stayed with her parents for a few months which had been terrible.

Her parents were amazing, supportive people, but at the time, she was just so broken. She had a little bit of money saved up, but was starting over. At first, her dad kept trying to relate to her about hockey because hockey had always been something the entire family bonded over. But it was hard to leave hockey and not see a place for herself in the profession like her brothers all did. Grieving the loss of hockey in a toxic relationship with someone who thought hockey was pointless had messed with her head. But she was glad Conner got her back on the ice.

It seemed to be a perfect storm of events. Bridget talking to her about hockey, then Conner came in and played the dad card. It had been great getting back out there, but she was still trying to play it down, because she wasn't sure she could trust it.

As she poured herself a cup of coffee, Bridget walked in.

"Hello lass, I noticed ye weren't in yesterday," Bridget said with a knowing smile.

"Yeah, I scheduled myself for the weekend instead," Kate said.

"Oh yeah, anything new and exciting happen?"

"I just went to see my brother's hockey game," she said, trying to seem as nonchalant as possible.

"Just yere brother's game? Not the handsome blonde lad he had with him?" she said with a raised eyebrow.

"Well, I mean it was his game too, of course," she added.

"He seems like a nice young man."

Kate couldn't help the smile that spread across her face at that comment. He was a nice young man, and not at all what she had expected.

"Yeah, he's a good guy."

"And handsome too!" added Bridget, wagging her eyebrows.

"Yes...he is," Kate said, trying to play it off.

Bridget nodded and Kate couldn't help but feel like she already knew what had happened.

"Can I tell you something?" Kate asked.

"Of course, Lass."

"I always said I wouldn't date hockey players. I think it all came from a bad experience when I was young but was only solidified by being around too many locker room conversations I would never want to be on the other side of, but I think I might want to date Wes," she said.

"Well, I think it isn't wise to have rules that cut ye off from so many people, especially when yere family seems so fond of the sport," she said.

Kate let the words sink in. She was right, and Wes wasn't

like so many of the guys she grew up around. He was one of the good ones. But the real problem was Jason, and she knew it.

"I think I'm just scared. I don't talk about it much, but the last guy I dated really messed me up. I'm just not sure I'm ready to do it again. I'm not even sure I can do it again."

"My dear," Bridget said with kindness as she reached out and took Kate's hand. "I've known ye for a while now, and I consider ye a dear friend, but I have noticed ye seem apprehensive to let people in. Most of us do, but being hurt is not a reason to cut yereself off from others. It is hard to find happiness again, trusting others and finding yere own worth is hard when ye've had someone take those things from ye, but I do think it is a worthwhile venture. Do ye think young Wes would hurt ye?"

"I don't know...I don't think he would on purpose, but something could happen."

"Yer're right, something could happen. Something wonderful could also happen. Do you really want to cut yereself off from those things as well in an effort to protect yereself from hurt?"

Kate took a moment. She knew Bridget was right, but she wasn't sure if she was strong enough. The moment was broken by the sound of the bell tinkling above to alert them to a customer.

"Hannah, my dear, if it isn't another one of my favorite women of Mystic Falls. How are you and your fine fellow doing?"

"Hi Bridget! Good. Graham is working with Sam. I have some news about the book I'm writing, and I'm hoping that Kate here might want to help me with a release party," said Hannah smiling over at Kate.

"Well, isn't that great news. I'll let ye chat. Think about

what I said though, Kate," she said before making her way to the door.

"So do you have a release day for your book?" asked Kate.

"Yep! I'm hoping to do a signing here."

"That sounds amazing! We can totally work something out."

"Perfect! I'll find out more from the publicist and get back to you with more details."

A release party would be fun, it was just another reminder of how far her little bookstore had come since taking it over. Maybe it was time she started pouring as much into her recovery as she did into Mystic Falls Books.

On Friday, Kate was finishing up a new window display before heading out to get ready for her date. She was nervous. Things with Wes had been surprising and wonderful, but still so far outside of her comfort zone. But she had to at least try.

She had talked to her dad earlier to get some things set up. Luckily, he hadn't asked too many questions. She didn't want to take him anywhere, because she didn't want anyone to know she was seeing him. Sure, Bridget knew, but she wasn't ready to have anyone else know quite yet. But she did have something planned for tonight. This was their first official date, no matter what Wes said. Even just thinking that made her smile. She was in so much trouble.

After everything was set up, she went home to get ready.

Wes - I'm leaving Glendale, is there anything you need me to bring or pick up?

Kate - Just your handsome face.

She pulled on a sweater. It was a casual type of a date. Her phone dinging again. When she got it, there was a picture of Wes's smiling face.

Wes- This handsome face?

Kate - That's the one.

Wes - See you soon.

Now she just had to wait. Well, wait and try to calm the hundreds of butterflies in her belly. This was a completely new feeling, and she wasn't mad at it.

She checked her clock at 6:56. He should be here soon. At 6:58 there was a knock on her door. He was punctual, another plus for him.

She opened the door and there he was, in jeans and a gray pea coat. His cheeks were red from the cold and his light blonde hair fell around his face. He had his big, cocky smile and a giant bouquet of roses in his hand.

"Hi," she said breathlessly.

"Hi," he said back with a grin.

She just stood there until he tilted his head and gave a small chuckle. "Are you going to invite me in?"

"Oh, right, sorry! Yes, come in! Are those for me?"

"Nah, I just thought you might want to look at them," he said as he handed her the flowers.

"Sorry, I'm a little thrown off. Thank you very much. They're beautiful." she said, taking them from him. "I'm just going to go find a vase."

"Hold on," he said and grabbed her hand and pulled her to him. "Let me do this first. You look beautiful," he said then he leaned in and gave her a kiss that almost made her knees buckle.

"So, this is your place?" he asked, looking around.

"This is it," she said as she walked into the kitchen to get a vase. "I've been here a little over a year."

It was a small little house right on the edge of town with

two bedrooms, a tiny kitchen, and a fenced yard with a cherry tree. It wasn't much, but it was perfect for her. It was her sanctuary after leaving Glendale.

"Now, why don't we get going? I have something special planned," she said, trying to fight the nerves in her stomach. She could do this.

"Oh yeah? Well, lead the way. I'm excited for whatever you have planned."

She went to the hall closet to get her coat. Wes took it from her and helped her into it. He may be the first guy to have ever done that for her. This twenty-four-year-old kid was completely showing up all the older men she had dated, and she just smiled. She could do this.

"Let's do this," she said as they headed out the door.

CHAPTER 13

WES

es didn't like that Kate was driving, but she had planned the date, so he was just along for the ride. He was hoping he would be able to plan the next date though. He got the feeling that Kate could use a little forethought and pampering, but he was just happy to finally be with her again.

Mystic Falls was something out of a storybook. The skating rink in the town square was gone, but there was still a picturesque Main Street and gazebo in the middle of the square. All the little shops were locally owned, and it looked like a perfect place to raise a family. And that is not the kind of thought he was used to having. Not one he felt like acting on any time soon, but being with Kate did make him think about those things.

The car pulled up to the high school and Kate pulled into a spot back by the arena. He looked at her with a questioning look on his face. "Why are we here?" he asked.

"You'll see. Just follow me."

She dug some keys out of her bag and unlocked the big

metal doors. "I happen to know the coach," she said with a smirk.

He had to admit, this piqued his interest. The doors shut with a bang behind them. It was dark, but there was the unmistakable smell of ice. He had no idea what they were doing, but if he got to see her on the ice again, he was here for it. The lights clicked on with a hum. They were dimmed, and over next to the bleachers was a table all set with some candles and fairy lights hanging from the Plexiglass around the ice.

"What is this?" he asked. "You didn't have to go to all this trouble."

"It was kinda fun. Plus, if we went anywhere in Mystic Falls it would be everywhere in this town. You know how small towns are. I'm just not ready for all that. But I did want to say thank you for being so great when I stayed at your house."

"I mean to be fair, all I did was act like a decent person and show my nerdy side, you went to a lot more trouble." He took her by the hand and pulled her into a hug. Her body was so soft in his arms. He had been good when she was in his bed, but he wouldn't hold himself to such high standards this time. This time, he was ready and willing to see where she wanted to take this. He was ready for whatever she had planned here. And really, he had been on plenty of dates with plenty of women, but he was not what you would consider a playboy by any stretch of the imagination. None of those women had ever planned anything or done anything like this. Just another reason he knew that Kate McPhee was going to be his. He knew it, but he would wait until she was ready.

"Go have a seat. I have dinner for us staying warm in the concessions stand. I tried to stay on your eating plan as much as possible. I remember those days."

She disappeared behind a door and Wes sat down at the table waiting for her to join him. He took note of two pairs of skates sitting next to the table. He picked them up and sure enough one of them was his size. He was excited to get on the ice with her. Being in a rink like this was something he had never experienced but was something out of every hockey kid's dream.

She came out carrying two plates filled with chicken, rice and roasted veggies. "If I had my way, we would be eating hot dogs and nachos straight from the snack hut, but this will do."

"Next time," he said as she joined him at the table.

She smiled and looked down at the table. "Next time," she agreed quietly, and his heart soared.

They sat down to eat as Kate lit two candles. Wes stopped for a moment to take a mental snapshot of this moment. Sitting across the table from Kate, her red curls framing her face, her round cheeks slightly rosy from the chill in the air, and the smattering of freckles that danced across her nose and cheeks, the smell of the ice and peace it always brought him. And thinking that someone went to all this trouble for him. He couldn't remember the last time anyone had done something like this for him, but he was pretty sure no one ever had.

"What are you thinking about?" she asked timidly.

"I'm just taking a mental snapshot of this. This is perfect," he said, taking her hand.

"A mental snapshot?"

"Yeah, it is something my mom taught me to do when I was younger. A way of remembering the good times."

"I like that." She tucked her hair behind her ear. She looked so beautiful. "Are you close with your mom?"

"Yeah, I don't get to see them as much as I would like, but we talk often."

"Do you have any siblings?"

"I have a little sister, but we weren't raised together. She's ten. After I went to Minnesota, my mom ended up marrying a great guy."

"But it was just the two of you growing up?"

He nodded, finishing the bite he had in his mouth. "Yeah, she was a single mom and did the best she could. We didn't have much growing up, and she was always working. I was pretty much raised on sitcoms and spaghetti o's while she worked, but she was a good mom."

"Wow, that sounds rough."

He just shrugged. "It wasn't so bad. I grew up quickly because I had to look after myself so much, but when she was around, she was great."

"Was it hard leaving at such a young age?"

He took a long pause. This wasn't his favorite subject to talk about. "It was. I had a lot of guilt leaving her behind, but it was clearly for the best. My life would be completely different if I hadn't left Detroit."

He glanced up into her eyes. She was looking at him with such kindness, though he tried to ignore the pity he thought he saw there.

"What about you? Tell me a little more about Kate McPhee."

"I mean, there's not a whole lot to tell."

"Now that can't be true. Tell me anything. First kiss. Favorite meal. Favorite song. I wanna know it all."

She bit her lip slightly and smiled at him. "Dereck Fipp, my mom's lasagna, and how could I possibly pick."

"Derek Fipp, huh? That's a punchable name."

"It is…that's why I punched him."

He grinned at her and couldn't stop the laughter that came out of him. "Oh, now this I gotta hear."

"I was fourteen. He was sixteen. He was on the team with

Patrick and was talking about it in the locker room the next day. My brother almost punched him, but my dad stopped him. So, I took care of it myself after their next game. That was the beginning of my vow to never date hockey players. It's something else now, but there ya go."

He just sat across the table, smiling at her. With every wall that came down he fell a little harder for her.

After they finished eating Kate turned to him, "Care to skate?"

"Let's do this," he said with a small smile.

They laced up the skates and Wes opened the gate to the ice. "How did you know my size?"

"You are a popular NHL player. I could find out everything I needed to know with very little online sleuthing," she said with a grin as she slid onto the ice.

"I see. You've been reading up on me," he said as he closed the door. She easily maneuvered to be skating backwards and grinned at him.

"Of course, I have. If we're going to do this, I need as much information as possible," she said.

"All you have to do is ask. I'm an open book," he said as he skated closer to her. She easily pivoted back to forward skating as he slipped his hand into hers. There was this magic that danced between them every time they touched, and it felt entirely too hot to be safe on the ice.

"How do I know you aren't just trying to play the game and tell me what I want to hear?" she said to him, still grinning like she had said something playful. He didn't like it. Did she still really think so poorly of him? Dropping her hand, he stopped and she skated on and turned to look at him. "What is it?"

"So, you still think I'm a player? What do I have to do to convince you I'm not like that? Because I swear, I'm not. Ask your brother. Ask Ethan, he's known me since I was fourteen." He looked down at his skates, his thoughts racing through his head.

Kate skated over to him. "You're right. I'm sorry. I don't even think that. I'm not sure why I said it. You've been great. I'm just not sure I know how to do this. I want to try. I mean clearly..." she said gesturing around to the romantic ice side table and the fairy lights romantically lighting their private skate. "I'm just not sure how to do all of this anymore."

"Do what? All I'm asking is to get to know you."

The look on her face changed and she seemed to disappear behind her eyes. He could tell she was scared, and he wanted to be patient, but he wouldn't put himself in a position to be hurt either. She looked down at their skates. Wes cupped her face with his hands and pulled her face up to look at him.

"What's going on?" he asked.

"I don't know..." she said looking up at him, emotion clear on her face. "I'm trying. I am. I'm just not sure I can do this."

"What is this exactly?" he said as he took her hand, and they slowly began to glide across the ice.

"This," she said again gliding with him hand in hand. "Being on the ice again and being in a relationship again."

If there was anything true about Wes, it was that he trusted his gut. His gut was telling him this was his girl. She was endgame for him. His gut was also telling him to shut up and skate. His gut told him that a lot, but this time, he was rewarded with a little more.

"I guess it's probably because they are the two things that have caused me the most pain in my life," she said. She held tightly to his hand as they skated. They made a couple laps around the rink in silence with nothing but the sounds of their skates cutting through the ice in unison.

"The pain of an awful relationship I just got out of," she said with a sigh. "Well, I didn't just get out of it. It's been over a year, but I'm not sure who I am right now. I'm not even sure if that makes sense. Clearly, I know who I am, but I spent years of my life trying to be someone different. I guess I'm just trying to figure out who I am now, what pieces of that person were actually me, and what pieces were who he wanted me to be."

"I don't want you to be anything other than yourself, Kate. I hope you know that."

"I do," she said without a second thought. That made him feel a little better at least. "I'm just still trying to figure that out."

"I'm here. I'll give you space, I just hope that you don't push me away."

"I'll try..." she said.

Once again, the only sound was their skates on the ice. He wanted to fill the silence and make jokes, but he could tell she was still working through stuff. So, he would be patient.

After a few more laps he was rewarded with a little more.

"And really, ever since I played Saturday my emotions have been all over the place. I told myself I left hockey behind me. But being back on the ice, seeing you and my brother play, being immersed back in it has been hard," she said, and her voice caught on the last word.

He stopped them and skated in front of her until he was facing her. Her eyes were glistening, and she wouldn't meet his eyes. "Can I ask why?"

She looked up at him with her bottom lip caught between her teeth. "I don't really know how to explain it." She said taking his hand again and skating.

Okay, if she would talk and skate, he would skate laps around this rink all night to learn more.

"Growing up, hockey was everything. We all played, and we all loved it. We all played in high school. It was my whole life, if I wasn't on the ice I was with the team, and if I wasn't with the team, I was in a quiet corner reading my books. It was just how life was. We all played in college. My brothers all went on and had careers in hockey. There aren't many opportunities for women after college. I mean, I could have gone out for the national team, I maybe even had a shot, but it just wasn't as straightforward for me."

Once again, they were skating. He wanted to say 'there are more opportunities for women in hockey than there used to be', and while that was true, he also knew it wasn't the same. He wanted to say 'but you're so good of course you would have made it', and while he believed that to be true, his gut told him to shut up and listen.

"After my last game senior year, I decided to leave hockey behind me. Cold turkey. If I couldn't play anymore, it was too painful. I might have gotten over that in time, but then I was with Jason. He got a side of me my family didn't get. He was my TA for my American Lit class. He could talk to me about books and appreciated that part of me that my family never really understood."

The pieces were slotting together, but he just skated beside her holding her hand waiting for more.

"Jason didn't like sports. He understood I played hockey because I was on a full ride. But when the season was over my senior year, he didn't understand why I was so upset. We made it to the final four and that was it for me."

There was another pause in the conversation. Wes could see the wheels turning in her head.

"Conner was at Notre Dame with me at the same time. He was captain of the men's team, and they went on to win first place that year. I was there, cheering him on. I sat with my family, and I heard all of them gushing about it. The scouts were all over him after that. He was signed right away, and it was all encompassing. I tried to be happy for him. I really fucking did," she said her voice catching again, but this time he didn't stop her, he just held her hand a little tighter. "But I had just lost my final game and I knew my hockey time was over. This thing that had been my whole life, had been my whole family's life, was just over. I didn't know how to do that. And everyone was so happy for Conner. Everyone was so focused on his next move and everything that was lining up for him. No one even stopped to realize how hard that was for me. Even MY teammates were obsessed with Conner and what team he would play for. It was just really hard for me."

They continued to skate, but he was putting together the pieces. How had no one seen how hard that must have been for her?

"The only person in my life who wasn't obsessed with Conner's career was Jason," she said with a small sniffle as she started to collect herself. "He hated hockey. It was a safe haven. He made me feel smart and he fed my other interests that were safe at the time. I think that is why I wrote off hockey entirely and stayed long after he showed his true colors."

"That makes sense," Wes said quietly as he rubbed his thumb over hers.

"I vowed to never get back on the ice. I saw a handful of my brother's games out of family obligation, but I shut the door on hockey. I didn't put my pads back on until Conner talked me into it for my dad's birthday. And then you came, and I guess I'm just feeling a little swept away right now. And because of that, I keep saying things and making assumptions about you that I shouldn't."

He got it, he really did. He couldn't imagine what that must have been like to watch her brother go on and do all of these amazing things in a sport they both loved while knowing her career was over.

"This guy Jason, he was the one at the bar?" he asked.

"Yeah. I stayed in Indiana with him for a couple years while he finished. Then he got a job teaching in Glendale. I had mixed feelings about it because it would be nice to be close to home, but also being in the same town as Conner and the Magic opened me up to even more hockey questions from my family. I had to draw some hard boundaries around hockey. None of them understood, but they respected it. I know Conner didn't understand. It wasn't his fault and I always felt bad that I was hurting him."

"He was really happy you were at the game this week," Wes said, trying to encourage her.

"I know, that is another reason why I want to take this slow. My family finally started to leave me alone about hockey, and it all feels like a lot. There were some pretty big fights, especially with my mom. She didn't understand why I stopped coming home and going to Conner's games. My dad tried to tell her I just needed time, but things were rough for a while. That's why I don't want anyone to know about this yet."

While he did understand that more now, he still didn't like it. Partly because he wanted to be with her out in the open. He wanted to take her on dates and show her off. He wanted her in the stands with his jersey on, cheering for him. He wanted her hanging out with him and the team. He just wanted her without having to worry about that stuff. He didn't want to be something she was ashamed of. While he didn't think she was meaning to make him feel that way, being so secretive about things made him feel like that. But that was a problem for another day.

"I get it," he said as they skated.

She came around in front of him skating backwards with ease. He surged forward snaking his arms around her waist and kissed her. His whole body lit up as she opened and slid her tongue into his mouth. His cock was instantly rock hard, and all he could think about was getting her back to her house and doing some very dirty things to her, but he wasn't sure that was the right move.

That didn't matter right now though. Right now, here on the ice, he could kiss her. He could give her some better memories on the ice.

She pulled away and looked up at him with a playful quirk. "Race ya!" she said as she spun out of his arms and took off on the ice. He watched with amusement for a split second before he took off after her. He caught up to her easily and pinned her against the rail and kissed her. They stayed there for a while, kissing on the ice. The ice that was his safe space and a space she was trying to reclaim, but a place they had both felt at home for a large part of their lives.

"I have never known anyone like you, Kate," he said as he rested his forehead against hers.

"I can safely say the same about you, Wes. I mean it. I know I've been fucking this up, but I'm trying."

"Hey, I get it. You don't owe me anything, not even an explanation. I'm glad you shared everything you did because I feel like I know you better. I'm grateful for every piece you give." He tucked a stray curl behind her ear, and she leaned her face into his hand. The simple gesture pulled at him. They both had a complicated past, but whatever it was that existed between them was simple. When they focused on that, everything else fell away.

"Well, I need to get all this cleaned up before we leave since there's practice tomorrow. Wanna help?"

"Of course," he said. "But first," he said as he bent his head down and kissed her again. And she melted into him. She kept putting up walls, but he was there finding his way in, and she was letting him. That felt good.

After they got everything cleaned up, they were back at Kate's house. "Do you want to come in?" she asked.

"I don't think I should," he said. He wanted to, he really fucking wanted to, but he had morning skate, and he could tell she still wasn't quite in it yet. He was already gone for her, and he knew that if they took things to the next level and things didn't work out, it would crush him. He wanted her to be sure.

"Are you serious?" she pulled back and asked.

"Yeah...I have an early morning, and I want you to be sure. I don't want to be an experiment to see if you have this guy out of your system or anything like that. I'm here. I'm not going anywhere. And I can wait."

"You can wait, but I'm not sure I can. Damn Wes, what does a girl have to do to get a little action?"

He laughed and cupped her face. "Oh Red, I want to. I just want it to mean something. Call me old fashioned, but that's just how I am. I want us both on the same page."

"Okay, when can I see you again?" she asked.

That question settled in him, maybe she was as eager as he was.

"I leave Sunday for a week-long road trip. But when I get back, I'll have a few days off. Do you want to come to Glendale next Saturday? I can plan a date."

"Yeah, I would like that," she said as she leaned forward and kissed him. He kissed her right back and they may have sat in her car making out like a couple of teenagers until they were both cold, and finally ready to part from one another. He hadn't felt like this in a long time, it was nice.

CHAPTER 14

KATE

Things were going well for Kate and Wes. She was still surprised that he hadn't wanted to come in on their last date, but she really did need to stop being surprised by him, because he was never going to be what she suspected. She was starting to feel safe with him. Being with someone who understood both sides of her was something she had never experienced before. She had her book friends, and she had her hockey friends, she had never found someone who was both before. Wes had been reading the books she had given him. He had already read Tolkien and Frankenstein and Octavia Butler, to her surprise, but the rest were new to him.

He had called her one night from the road to talk about *The Duke and I*. They had made plans for a *Bridgerton* marathon once he had some time.

Tonight, however, she was curled up on her couch with a bowl of popcorn and the Magics game on. They were playing Minnesota tonight. Watching hockey again felt good. At the moment, it was still something she was doing in secret. She just couldn't bring herself to let anyone else in on this yet.

Her mom and dad would be in their basement in front of their big screen watching the game, and she knew they would love her company. Smokey's would have a crowd of people cheering for Conner. Both of those are places she had once felt at home, but that felt like a lifetime ago.

So here she was, by herself, watching her brother and her...Wes...play. They hadn't really talked about what was going on between them. He was so damn respectful; she told him she needed to take it slow, and he was respecting her wish. Part of her wanted him to push a little. It might make it seem less vulnerable to put herself out there, but that wasn't his style. He wanted to make sure she was with him every step of the way, and while that was commendable...It was also slightly infuriating.

But still she cheered for him by herself. She hadn't told Wes, but they shared a number. And something about looking for him on the ice by trying to find the number 98 felt right.

Watching Conner on the ice was bittersweet. She saw the leader her brother had grown into. He always commanded the ice, but not like he did now. The players and fans respected him. He'd had this amazing career and she'd missed it. Wes was something else entirely on the ice. He scored tonight and made his victory lap amping up the crowd, which isn't easy to do on another team's ice, but people couldn't help but love him.

He was interviewed during the second intermission, and after his interview he winked at the camera. She knew it was for her, and it just made her heart soar. She needed to just rip off the band aid. Tell her family she was with Wes, and get back into the McPhee madness, but something was still stopping her.

After their win, she started getting ready for bed. It was late considering the time difference, but she knew Wes would be boarding the plane soon to head to California for a game tomorrow. Then, after one more game, he would be home. Hopefully she could keep herself from putting her foot in her mouth this time. She didn't know why she kept saying insulting things to him. It was probably because she had been trying for so long to distance herself from the game, but she was ready for that to be over. While she may be a closeted hockey fan for now, she needed to change that.

She was just getting into bed when her phone went off.

Wes - I have a bone to pick with you.

Kate - ???

Wes - I am sitting next to you brother right now, very uncomfortably trying to hide a boner.

Kate - I'm sorry what? And how on earth is that my fault?

Wes - Warn a man before you give him porn to read while sitting next to his girl's brother on a plane.

Kate - hahahaha oh my god!

She couldn't help it. She was laughing out loud at the thought of that.

Wes - I'm glad this amuses you, if he wasn't busy bickering with Sasha, this could be awkward.

Kate - I hate to tell you this, but the romances I gave you were tame compared to some...

Wes - Seriously? I should have started reading romance a long time ago.

Kate - I'm telling you, there is a reason romance is the most popular genre. It single-handedly sells e-readers.

Wes - Why? No one should be ashamed of reading these. This is a good book, story, sex, and all.

Kate – No one is ashamed... we just need a free hand for the really good books.

Kate watched in amusement as the three dots appeared and then went away. Then appeared again and disappeared one more time.

Wes – You are killing me over here, Red.

Kate – I might just have to get lost in a particularly smutty hockey romance tonight. I got a good one loaded up on my e-reader, ready for some one-handed reading.

Again, she watched as the dots flashed to life several different times. She smiled thinking about what she must be doing to him. Served him right for playing hard to get over their last couple dates.

Wes - I don't even know how to respond to that. You've broken me. I'm going to say good night because you are not making the situation any better. I can't wait to see you in a few days.

Kate - I can't wait either. I miss you.

Wes - I miss you too. Sweet dreams.

Kate - Goodnight, enjoy the rest of the book
<winky face>

Kate went to bed with one thought. Tomorrow, when she closed the bookstore, she would go down to Smokey's and order some onion rings and a beer and watch the game. It seemed like nothing. Something many people could do without thinking about, but it was a major step for her. A step she finally felt able to make. Wes was helping her reclaim a large part of herself she had shut off a long time ago, and she was ready. Hopefully he would be ready the next time she saw him, because it had only been a couple weeks, but she was growing so fond of this hockey kid from Detroit.

The next day, after closing the store, she did it. At first, she felt herself making excuses and just wanting to go home, but she could do this. She walked down the few blocks to Smokey's and walked in. Up on the big screen was the pre-game. She sat down at one of the high tops, ordered some food, and texted Wes good luck. She knew he wouldn't see it until after the game, but it was what they did.

After a while, Sam Smith and Lucas Fipp walked in and sat at the bar. They didn't notice her at first. Sam was quite a bit older than her and Conner were. They were freshmen his senior year, but they had played with Lucas a couple years. They ordered a couple of beers and settled in for the game. Conner scored the first goal of the night, and the bar erupted in cheers.

It was then they saw her and came over.

"Hey Kate, I haven't seen you around for a while," Lucas said.

"Yeah, I just thought I would stop in and watch the game for a bit," she said, trying to act as nonchalant as possible.

"Would you like some company?" he asked.

"Sure."

He and Sam joined her at the table, and they watched the game. She felt pretty good about this decision. They all talked about hockey and there was no pressure. They hadn't been close in years, but she and Lucas had been good friends in high school, and everyone in Mystic Falls knew Sam. It was nice to sit there with people who knew and cared about the game but didn't know the complicated relationship with hockey she had. They had all played together and grown up together, but hockey wasn't their life like it was for the McPhee's. It was just a fun way to pass the time. She had never experienced it like this before, and it was wonderful.

Sadly, the Magic didn't win, so they all went home a little bummed.

"It was nice watching with you, Kate," Sam said as they walked to their cars.

"We should do this again," said Lucas, giving her a genuine smile.

"Yeah, we should," she said. She walked to her car feeling pretty good about things, even with a loss.

It was Saturday. This whole week had been a journey for her. Slowly but surely, she was letting hockey back in. But tonight was going to be better than that. Kate was excited to go see Wes. She didn't know what he had planned, but man she was ready to see him. Hopefully this time she would be able to see a little more of him. This would be their third date and she was finally hoping to get lucky. He had told her to go ahead and park in the deck for his building and that the door man would let her up. The giddiness at seeing him again was new, and she was living for it. Something inside of her was healing, and she had Wes Darling to thank for that.

She parked, grabbed her bag from the back, and headed in. She walked into a gorgeous lobby. They hadn't come through here the last time, so she was taking it all in.

"May I help you?" asked a man in a suit behind the front desk.

"Umm, yes. I am here to see Wes Darling."

"And you are?"

"Oh right! I'm Kate McPhee."

He typed her name into a computer. "You're on the list. Head on up."

She went over to the elevator. As she was waiting, the door to the building opened.

"Hello Mr. Yellowtail. How are you this evening?"

"I'm good, just getting back from taking Oscar for a walk. Talk to you later, Ernie."

Then around the corner to the elevator came Ethan Yellowtail. She hadn't seen him since the bar when she went briefly with Wes.

"Hey! You're Kate, right?" he said with a smile.

"Yeah! I wasn't sure if you would remember me," she said pleasantly surprised.

"Yeah, Conner's sister who left the bar with Wes. Who has been oddly quiet about the whole thing," he said with a raised eyebrow.

"And who is this?" she said, smiling down at his golden retriever.

"This is Oscar. He's a good boy." he said, giving him a scratch behind the ears.

"Can I pet him?"

"Of course," he said warmly.

Kate bent down and gave him a good two-handed scratch as the dog wagged his tail and his tongue hung out of his mouth, panting happily. "You're a good boy," she said as his tongue lapped her face.

"He likes you," Ethan said with his big booming laugh she had heard at the bar.

The elevator dinged and the doors slid open. Kate picked up her bag and stepped inside the elevator with Ethan.

"What floor?" he asked.

"Tenth."

He pushed the ten for her and the eighth for himself.

"Tenth?" he said, looking over at her with raised eyebrows. "Wes's floor."

"Yeah, I'm here to see Wes."

"Interesting. He's been holding out on me. My best friend is dating our teammate's sister?"

The panic made her heart race. She still wasn't sure what was happening here. She didn't want to hide anything, but she didn't want Conner to know yet. Every time she talked about keeping it a secret, Wes got a funny look on his face she absolutely hated, and she was really hoping to finally get laid tonight.

"It's new."

She was hoping he would drop it there and not tell Conner. Fuck. She would have to talk to Wes about this.

"No problem, I got it. It's complicated. But he's a great guy," he said with an easy smile.

"Yeah, I'm starting to figure that out," she said, her panic subsiding.

The elevator stopped and the doors opened. "See ya around, Kate."

"Yeah, see ya," she said as the door slid shut. Two more floors till Wes, and she couldn't wait.

She got to his door and knocked. It had only been a little over a week since she had seen him last. They'd been in constant contact almost the entire time. They texted on their breaks. They talked on nights he didn't have late games. He was this incredible hockey player that fans drooled over, but he was also a book nerd who had taken care of her and watched movies with her while she felt like crap. She had opened up to him on the ice. Talking while they skated helped her to come to terms with some things. She liked him, but more importantly, she trusted him. He had been so sure that this was the start of something special, and he was right. There was no denying it now. She still wasn't ready to tell her brother, but she was getting closer.

He opened the door, and her heart skipped a beat. There he was in jeans and a sweater, with his blonde hair framing his face. She had to resist the urge to just fall into his arms.

"Hey there, Red," he said, opening the door wider and taking her bag.

"Hi," she said, feeling slightly unsure of herself.

As he shut the door behind them, he sat her bag on the table and pulled her into his arms.

"I've been thinking about this for way too long," he said as he pulled her into a hug and kissed her.

She snaked her arms around his waist and kissed him back with a satisfied hum. And they just stood like that for a long while, holding each other and kissing. She could stay like this forever, but she could also move this to the bedroom. Hopefully tonight things would progress like she kept thinking they would. Like she so desperately wanted them too.

He pulled back and smiled down at her.

"I have something for you," he said with a grin.

"You do?"

"Yep," he said, as he let go of her and turned for the living room and handed her a purple gift bag with teal tissue paper, the colors for the Magic.

She took it from him and bit her lip to try and keep the grin from creeping across her face. "You didn't have to do this," she said.

"You don't even know what I did yet," he said.

She reached in and pulled out a jersey. It was a Magic jersey, and she had a feeling what was on the back. She flipped it around and held it up. Sure enough, it read Darling 98. He had given her a jersey with his number. Something about that warmed her heart. She knew if she wore this, she would have to finally answer the question about what was going on between them. She wished she was as confident as he seemed to be, but she wanted to try being more open. She could do that; he has proven himself time after time, from the way he was attentive even when he was on the road, to the way he handled the situation last time she was here. He was right, she wasn't scared of him, she was scared of getting hurt again. Hurt by him, hurt by hockey, hurt by truly caring for someone again, only to have it end painfully.

She held up the jersey to her, "You got me a jersey?" she asked, eyeing him.

"I got you my jersey to wear to my games you're going to start coming to," he said with his cocky smile as he crossed the room. His hands found her waist and pulled her to him. The butterflies were fluttering as he leaned closer and kissed her. This was a good kiss. A kiss with promise. All she had to do was not fuck it up this time. This was all new to her. Usually, when she wanted to have sex with a guy, all she had to do was allow it. Wes seemed to be making her work for it. So, if she could just get out of her own head and allow herself to be here with him, hopefully, she would finally get a little more action.

"Thank you, I can't wait to wear it," she said, smiling up at him. And to her own surprise, there was honesty in those words.

"Are you hungry?" he asked.

"I could eat. Are we going out to dinner?"

"Kind of," he said.

"Kind of?"

"I know you don't want many people to know yet, and I hate to tell you this, Red, but I'm kind of a big deal," he said with the infuriatingly cute look on his face. She slapped his chest, and he caught her hand and kissed it. "But seriously, one private romantic dinner deserves another."

She looked up at him and cocked her head.

"Come with me," he said as he took her hand and led her out of his apartment and to the elevator. She was confused when he pressed the button to go up.

They stood hand in hand, waiting. Anticipation buzzed in her chest right along with those busy butterflies. "Where are we going? I didn't even grab my purse," she protested.

"You don't need it. We aren't leaving."

The elevator doors slid open before them. They stepped in, and he pushed the button that said roof.

"We are going to the roof? It's like thirty-three degrees out!"

"Just trust me, Red."

And she did. She did trust him, that much she knew.

The door slid open into a glass enclosure. On the roof was a pool that was shut down for winter and a few seating areas, but over in the corner was a tent with clear walls, inside was a little romantic dinner for two and an outdoor heater.

She looked up at him with a smile. "This is incredible," she said.

The tent was nice and warm as they stepped in. He held out her seat and lifted the lid in front of her. She was expecting something fancy and gourmet, but to her surprise, in front of her were concession stand nachos and a hot dog.

"What is all of this?"

She asked as he handed her a beer he had sitting in the wine cooler.

"Cheat day," he said, lifting the lid to show his own concession stand food and joining her in a beer.

"This is perfect," she said, grinning at him. He raised his beer, and they clinked bottles.

After they were finished with their dinner, he cleared the plates and sat back at the table across from her holding her hand. He traced over a tattoo she had there.

"I've never noticed this before," he said as his fingers lightly tracing the inside of her forearm, sending shivers to her core. "Is that white ink? What does it say?"

Her heart stuttered in her chest for a moment. If he noticed the scar this tattoo was covering, he didn't say anything. Even if he had, many hockey players had scars. Maybe he assumed it was from that. Either way, that scar was not something she could talk about.

"Out of the Ash. It's a Sylvia Plath quote. I got it to remind myself to be strong."

"I like it," he said, bringing it to his mouth and pressing a quick kiss to it, and damn it she didn't feel that kiss in other places. "Do you have any other tattoos?"

She did. She did and she was almost dreading him finding it as well, but for entirely different reasons.

"You do, don't you?"

She nodded. "One more."

"Where? How have I never seen it? Is it somewhere hidden?"

Kate just closed her eyes and shook her head.

"It is! Where is it?"

"It's nowhere weird. I got it in college my senior year. All the seniors on the team got them after training camp."

"Is it on your butt?"

She just glared at him.

"Come on, Red. Give me a hint," he said. She would be irritated at this if he wasn't so fucking cute.

"It's on my back," she said.

"Show me!"

"I'm not taking off my shirt out here to show you."

"Well then, let's go inside and you can take your shirt off there," he said with a molten look on his face that shot straight to her core.

A flush began to creep up her chest and she could feel the heat spreading across her cheeks. Being a natural redhead meant she blushed, and with the heat she felt right now, she had to be turning beet red. "I'd like that," she said breathlessly.

Wes leaned over and blew out the candles between them and held his hand out to her.

When they were safe in his warm apartment, he turned on her. "Okay, show me," he said, looking like a kid in a candy store.

She turned so her back was to him. "Alright, are you ready?" she asked unsure if she was ready for what she knew would happen when she showed him. She reached down to the hem of her sweater and pulled it off over her head, her back now bare to him, and she waited. Because there, between her shoulder blades, was the number 98.

He was still for too long. She turned to look at him. His hands flew to her shoulders keeping her facing away from him. After what felt like an eternity he finally said, "You have my number on your back."

She spun in his arms. "No, I have MY number on my back," she protested.

He firmly grasped her shoulders, spinning her back around, and she couldn't help but laugh. His hand lightly traces the numbers, and she was on fire. Turning to face him again, this time she registered the heat in his eyes. He appeared to have gone hockey caveman at the sight of the number on her back. His mouth came crashing down onto her and he claimed her. Fuck. She needed him. Right now.

He seemed to share the sentiment, because his hands traced down to her ass and then lifted her up. She wrapped her legs around his waist. He carried her into his bedroom and dropped her down on the bed before climbing over her. Somehow, they both managed to shake off their shoes as they climbed into the bed together.

"Is this finally happening?" she gasped as his hands roamed her body. His mouth was kissing down her neck.

"Oh, this is fucking happening," he said as he pulled the cup of her bra down and sucked her nipple into his mouth.

"Thank fucking god," she said. Then they were a mess of mouths and hands, ripping at each other's clothes. Before she knew it, her bra was off, and he was pulling at her pants. She shifted her weight, and he pulled them down over the swells of her hips. He kissed his way back up her leg. Reaching down for the button of his jeans, he aided her in taking off his own pants. He was kneeling between her legs, wearing only his boxer briefs. She was splayed out before him in her lacy cheeky underwear. Reaching up, she let her finger trail down between his pecs, slowly down the line between his well-defined abs, to the waistband of his underwear. She was ready to see all of him. She hadn't seen past here before, and she was ready.

She stroked him through his boxers. He groaned and threw his head back, biting down on his lip. She liked that. She reached inside of his boxers, wrapped her hand around his length, and gave him a good stroke.

"Fuck, Red," he said pushing into her hand. Pulling at the waistband, he somehow managed to pull them down and kick them aside. He was still kneeling between her legs. She sat up and looked at him. He was like a chiseled Adonis, all blond and hard and beautiful right before her. She sat up and wrapped her hand around his cock, giving one more stroke before lowering her head and flicking her tongue across the head. He groaned and she sucked more of him into her mouth. Looking up at him with her mouth wrapped around his cock set her on fire. He was gazing down at her with an expression that was half adoring, half sex god, and fully Wes. His hand fisted into her hair as she began to work him.

"Fuck," he groaned out holding perfectly still. "You are going to finish this before it even begins if you keep that up much longer." She pulled off with a pop and looked up at him. He growled and pushed her back down to the bed. Then, he began to pull at her underwear. Pulling them off her, he pushed her legs apart and positioned himself between them. He pushed his fingers in, swirling her wetness all around. She was already wet and ready for him. Then she felt his tongue lick her from opening to her clit, and her whole body jolted with desire. He slid in a finger and lightly flicked his tongue over her clit again.

"Fuck, Wes. That feels good."

He added another finger and stayed there, his tongue flicking over her clit. She had been wound so tight with want for this man she thought she was going to explode. He stayed there steady between her legs.

"More," she gasped.

His tongue flicked with a bit more pressure, and she cried out. Her hips started to grind against his face and her hand fisted into his silky blond hair. Then, he sucked her clit into her mouth, and she broke. She cried out as waves of pleasure swept over her, grinding against him as she held his face to her core. He stayed there, intensifying each wave until she pushed his head away panting.

"Fuck, you've been holding out on me," she said panting as he crawled over her.

"That's just the beginning, baby," he said as he reached over her and got a condom out of his drawer. "Is this okay?"

"Yes, please," she said.

He rolled it over his cock and positioned himself between her legs as he kissed her deeply, the taste of herself still clinging to his mouth. He pushed himself up and their eyes connected as he pushed into her. He was a bit bigger than she was used to, and although he was going slowly, the stretch was intense.

"Okay?" he asked as he slowed. She didn't have any words, so she just reached and grabbed his ass pulling him into her. They both moaned as he bottomed out inside of her.

"Just give me a second," she hissed out.

He bent his head down and tenderly kissed her. She didn't know what she wanted more, his tenderness or his heat, but she wouldn't choose. She wanted it all. She slowly started to rock her hips, feeling him slip in and out ever so slightly, and it was delicious. He kissed her deeply while he stayed still above her allowing her to get used to his size. As her rocks got more intense, he started to move with her.

"You feel so good, Wes," she panted as his thrusts began to increase.

"Fuck, Red. You feel even better than I imagined. And I imagined you feeling like heaven so...." she cut him off with a kiss and sucked his bottom lip into her mouth. He took the hint and began to fuck her in earnest. And while Kate was not the most experienced person, she was no stranger to sex, and it had never felt this good before. She felt like her insides were glowing, and the pleasure was once again pooling low in her belly. She had never come from penetration before, but she was about to. She bit his shoulder and began to meet him thrust for thrust.

"Oh my god, Red," he groaned in her ear as his thrust became more urgent and stronger. Her nails dug into his back as her second orgasm came, powerfully pulsing through her. She cried out and Wes dug his fingertips into her soft hips and gave a few last powerful thrusts before both were coming at the same time. He stayed buried deep inside of her until they were both done.

He pulled out, and the ache of his absence made her almost ready to go again. She wanted him back inside of her soon.

He fell onto his back and disposed of the condom in the trash next to his bed.

"Kate," he said, rolling back over to her and kissing her shoulder. "That was amazing."

"It really was. We need to do that again," she panted up to the ceiling. She turned to him smiling. "And again and again and again," she said. Then she kissed him.

And that's just what they did. Again in the bed, and then again in the shower, and then again before they both passed out for the night.

She woke up the next morning to him tracing the numbers on her back. Looking over expecting to find him in bed, she was surprised when she found him kneeling beside the bed, fully dressed.

"Good morning, I have morning skate, but I'll be back when it is over, and we can get something to eat. Okay?"

She nodded and stretched. He kissed the top of her head and headed out the door. She looked over at her phone. It was 7:30. So she rolled over and buried her face in his pillow and the scent of Wes and ice and drifted back off to sleep.

CHAPTER 15

WES

Wes grabbed his bag and headed out the door. He liked the idea that Kate was still asleep in his bed. Last night was incredible. He had never felt like this about anyone before. The sex was, of course, incredible, but it was more than that. He had been right to trust his instincts about Kate. There was something special here. He was even more sure of that now.

As he stepped out of the elevator, Ethan was waiting for him in the lobby.

"Hey Wes, ya ready?"

"Yeah. let's go."

When Wes moved to Glendale, he got a condo in the same building as Ethan, so they usually shared a ride to the practice center. It was the little things like this that made the Magic feel like a family. Ethan had always been the closest thing Wes ever had to a brother, so having him this close was amazing. When he moved here from his time in Florida, he needed family around him.

Even though the people Wes considered close friends were a small group, he had never been on his own until his time in Florida, and it had been such a shit show. Not that his childhood had been all sunshine and roses, but he never felt alone until he was in Florida. Being close to Ethan and joining a family like the Magic had been healing. The organization also offered a team therapist that had been immensely helpful when he moved. She helped him work through what went down in Florida, and some of the crap from his childhood. He actually had a meeting with her because he would be playing Florida again soon, and it would be the first time he was on the ice against Blake Kelly.

"So...I ran into McPhee's sister in the elevator yesterday," Ethan said to him with a knowing look.

"Yeah, we started talking when I went home with Conner a few weeks ago," he said, trying to appear as nonchalant as possible.

"What's going on with you two?"

"I'm not sure yet. It's still new, but I know it's going to be something incredible."

Ethan didn't say anything, he just looked at Wes with a look on his face.

"What?"

He still didn't say anything, just raised his eyebrows. Those eyebrows said all that needed to be said.

"I know...but it will be okay."

"If you say so, man. The playoffs are almost a month away..." Ethan said as they made their way to Wes's car.

"Don't tell anyone," Wes said quietly.

Ethan stopped and looked at him again. "What the fuck man?"

Wes raked his hand through his hair. He knew. He knew keeping this a secret was a bad idea, but it was Kate's decision. As much as he fucking hated it, he had to respect it.

"I know, it's not my idea. She doesn't want people to

know yet. So please man, just keep it between us for a little bit."

"You're serious?"

"Yeah, I am. I really like her, Ethan. I think she's it for me," he said plainly and simply, because that's how he felt. He knew she was it for him. He knew that beyond a doubt. If she needed some time to come to that conclusion as well, he would give it to her.

"Dating your teammate's and your team captain's sister...what could go wrong?"

"Conner wouldn't be all possessive like that. He's a good guy."

"He is and so are you. Which is why you should tell him. You can't risk making things weird with him this close to playoffs, especially since he's your line mate. You guys dominate the ice, something like this could throw that off and you know it."

"I know," he said, raking his hand through his hair again. He fucking hated this. "But man...I have to tell you, she's something else. I made a fool out of myself when I first met her. I hit on her not knowing she was Conner's sister and tried to get her to skate with me, but then Conner came, and she started flying around the ice with him. And then during the scrimmage when she came flying away from the net, pushed Conner down, and ripped off her helmet, that was it, man. I was done."

"She's a goalie?" Ethan said with an approving nod.

"A really fucking good one. She played in college."

"At least she plays a good position," Ethan said as they got into Wes's car.

"And while Conner doesn't know we've been seeing each other, I did ask him if he would be okay with me asking her out before I made a move," he said. "So, yeah, me continuing to date her while he doesn't know isn't great, it's not like he'll be completely blindsided. It has more to do with her complicated relationship with hockey and her family than anything else, I think."

"Is she worth all the shit this could cause?" Ethan asked him plainly.

"Without a fucking doubt."

"Okay then, tell him soon. Shit just got back on track for you after the Florida debacle. I don't want to see you stuck in it again."

"I know," he said with a deep sigh. "I'll let him know as soon as she's okay with it...but I just have to tell you this..." He paused and Ethan looked at him, gesturing for him to continue. "She has my number tattooed on her back. Even if I wasn't certain of it before that after I saw that it was over. She's mine."

"What?"

"Okay, she says she has her number tattooed on her back, but all I know is last night when I saw that 98 on her back my brain short circuited for a minute. You'll have to be my best man."

"Let's just get to the ice and hope her brother doesn't kill you before you marry her, lover boy."

Wes knew Ethan was right. He knew he was playing with fire dating Conner's sister. But Conner had told him he could ask her out, and he had no intention of ever hurting her. So, if that's what he feared he knew it would be okay.

What was really bothering him about this situation was he couldn't figure out why she was so set on keeping it private. He knew she had only dated intellectual types before, and her attitude towards hockey players on their first date--whether she admitted it was a date or not--had gotten to him. He worried she was ashamed of being with him. He didn't have a fancy degree, or any college degree for that matter. He made it through high school, but then he went straight into playing hockey. No matter how many times he told himself her choice for privacy had nothing to do with him and more to do with her ex and her relationship with hockey, there was a voice in the back of his head that kept telling him she was ashamed to be with him. Still, he would give her time if that was what she needed.

After practice, Wes made his way home. He was excited to see her again. Ethan had stayed at the ice to hang out with some of the guys and get another workout with the trainers. Wes normally would have too, but he had a cute girl at home in his bed. So, he decided he would much rather be there instead.

He opened the door and set his bag down under the side table and dropped his keys in the bowl. Toeing out of his shoes, he was looking forward to crawling back into bed with Kate. When he opened the door, he saw her curled up in one of his chairs in his sweats, her red curls in a messy bun on top of her head. If he could drop to his knees and worship at her feet, he just might.

"Hey Red, you look good," he said.

She jumped a little bit and then looked up at him with a big smile on her face and his heart was fit to burst. "Hey yourself," she said as she put the book down next to her. "How was it?"

"Good, but I'm glad to be home," he said, crossing the room to her. "What are you reading?"

"A true classic," she said, holding up his well-loved copy of *The Stand*. There was something intimate about her reading one of his favorite books. He wasn't sure why, but the sight of it just made his heart sing.

"Excellent choice," he said as he reached out for her hand pulling her up.

"It's the only choice where Stephen King is concerned," she said, smiling up at him.

He wrapped one of her red curls that had slipped out of her bun around his finger and bent his head low to kiss her. "What do you say we actually leave the house for some food this time?"

"Yeah, I think that sounds good. Just let me get ready really quick."

Well, that was a good sign. Being willing to be seen in public with him was one step closer to not hiding it. He wouldn't push her, but he was eager for that dynamic to change.

Whatever the reason for privacy, he could tell she was walking around carrying some extra baggage. He could see that because he was himself. After he left Florida, he had been a mess. Even though he had moved on from that mess, it was starting to weigh on him more and more with their upcoming game. It reminded him all he had gone through down there.

The worst of it happened right before he got traded. One of the players, Blake Kelly, had assaulted a woman, and Wes was set to testify against him, until it got settled out of court. That was also why he had been traded, but he was grateful. He was also pissed that the guy was still playing and got off with a slap on the wrist. Because of fucking course he did. He had a meeting this week with the organization because the team had petitioned to keep them from meeting on the ice in a few weeks. Okay, he needed to stop going down that memory lane. Nothing could put him in a foul mood like thinking about his time in Florida and Blake Kelly. He was not looking forward to playing them, but right now, he had a lovely redheaded distraction in his bathroom.

After another moment the bathroom door opened, and Kate walked out. Her red hair pulled up with some curls framing her face, a green low-cut sweater, and some tight jeans.

"I mean...We don't have to leave...We could just stay here," he said as he walked over and kissed her. Then he splayed his hands wide on her ass and pulled her to him.

"Nope, you promised me breakfast." she said with a smile. "And I want a mimosa."

"Well, let's hit the road, Red. There's a great brunch place a couple minutes away." he said with one last kiss. "You go first so I can watch your ass while you walk," he said, giving it an appreciative spank.

She grinned up at him and they made their way to breakfast.

CHAPTER 16

KATE

*K*ate was at work setting up the back room for a book club that would be meeting in the store tonight. She heard the front door open and stepped out to find Hannah had come in. They were going to touch base about her release party for her debut novel. It was the first time she had planned something like that, and she was excited to work with Hannah.

Working here had been something to do at a time in her life when she was at her lowest. After she finally left Jason, she was in a really bad place. She had lost hockey years ago, and with that on some level she had lost her family. Not saying that they weren't still trying, because they were always trying. She still remembered the look on her dad's face the day she had yelled at him that there was more to life than hockey and basically told them all to leave her alone. The sad look in her dad's eyes and the disbelief in Conner's still haunted her.

When she was with Jason, things had been good...until they weren't. Then they went south and fast. After moving to Glendale, things seemed to be getting better. She was helping him get settled in his new job, but then she found a job and worked briefly at the university library. She liked that, but there, her life was all about Jason. After their first year there, something was off, but she couldn't figure it out. He became more temperamental. Though that was normal for him, this was different. He had always made her feel like she wasn't as smart as he was, that she wasn't as capable as she always was. After a while, she started to believe it. She put her life on pause and seemed to exist only as an extension of him. By that time, she had pushed her family away completely. He seemed to prefer it that way.

But then one day, she was stopping in to bring him dinner and she walked into his office and found him fucking his TA. She shouldn't have been surprised, he had done stuff like that back in Indiana, only she had been the student and he was the TA. Now he was the professor, and he was fucking a TA. That had been the wakeup call she needed to finally leave.

When he came home that night her bags were already packed. He was so angry.

"You're leaving? Where are you going?"

"I'm going to go stay with my parents until I figure that out."

"Don't do that, stay here. I'll stop seeing her. But maybe you can try and fix some of the problems here."

"Me? What on earth do I need to fix? You're the one fucking your TA."

"It's just physical. I don't love her. I love you."

"And that's supposed to make me feel better?"

"Kate, I'm just not attracted to you anymore, but I think we can work on that?"

"What?"

"You just don't take care of yourself like you used to..."

She just glared at him. Had her body changed since they

got together...of fucking course it had. When they got together, she was twenty-one and working out every day. She was playing hockey and her body showed it. She was athletic and had the body of an athletic twenty-one-year-old. She was no longer twenty-one and she no longer worked out every day, her body had changed. She was a little self-conscious about it, but that was just what happens. She was someone who just held onto a little more weight than other people did. Eventually, she stopped gaining weight, and her body found where it comfortably sat when she was no longer on the ice for hours every week. She was happy with that. She wouldn't kill herself to have some ideal body because the one she had was great. It did everything she needed it to do, but it apparently wasn't enough for him.

She wished she could say she left right then and there. She had been ready. Her bags were packed, but somehow Jason had talked her into staying. And even worse, she started working out more, she started counting her calories, and judging herself in the mirror. She had lost hockey, next she lost herself in him. She was becoming someone who existed for him. She was gone entirely.

Two months later, when the excuses for being late started up again, this time she blamed herself.

It wasn't until one day when Conner had finally talked her into going out for dinner when they ran into him at a restaurant entirely too cozy with the same TA. She froze and panicked. Conner was pissed. Conner was ready to walk right up to him and punch him in the face.

"Conner, don't. Let's just leave."

Conner did, but then he was there all the time. He had been giving her space, but after that, it was over. He was checking in every day. He was dropping by on his days off. He didn't tell anyone, but he also wasn't going to let her be alone in this, and she loved him for that. So, when she walked in on him with a different TA. That time she was ready to leave.

She went home and started packing. He came home drunk and pissed. She really wished Conner wasn't on the road, but he was. She packed a bag and was heading to Conner's house to stay there until she figured out something else. Then Jason came in and wasn't going to let her leave. He was standing in front of the door. She tried to push him out of the way when he backhanded her.

The shame of what her life had become set in. If she stayed, it would always be like this. So, she got up and tried to leave again, that time he grabbed her by the hair and pulled her back from the door. She fell into the glass table they had by the door, and it shattered. Blood was dripping from her arm, but she didn't stop to see. She grabbed her bag and her phone and ran to her car. She tied an old t-shirt around her arm to stop the bleeding and drove to Conner's house.

After she examined her cut and figured out she didn't need stitches, she broke. Jason was already calling her and apologizing and swearing things would be different. She blocked his number and stayed at Conner's house until he came home from his road trip eight days later.

After Conner was back, he went with her to their apartment while she packed up her stuff and did the encouraging brother slash intimidating hockey player role perfectly. Then she stayed with him for a few months before she figured out what she was going to do.

She moved back to Mystic Falls and stayed with her parents, saving money, and working at the bookstore. The bookstore was not thriving, and she wasn't thriving herself. She still had a long way to go, but she was getting there. As she built up the bookstore, she slowly built her confidence back up too. Her family was just glad she had finally come out of the funk and thankfully left her alone about hockey. She went to a couple of Conner's games, but that was it. That was it until she let Conner talk her into getting onto the ice one last time for her dad, and as hard as it had been she was glad she had done it.

And now there was Wes, he was fixing her in ways he wasn't even aware of, probably even in ways she wasn't even aware of. She didn't trust it yet, but that was because she didn't trust herself yet. All she knew was every time her phone buzzed, she hoped it was him. He was the first thing she thought about in the morning and the last thing she thought about before she went to bed. He texted her and reassured her and didn't push her. This hockey player, who was five years younger than her, was helping to heal part of herself she didn't even know was still there. She didn't know what the future looked like for them, but she was ready for it. And that wasn't a thought she had had in a very long time.

Between Wes healing her heart, and the bookstore helping to restore her confidence in herself and her decisions, she knew she was on the right path.

"Hey Hannah, we've already seen quite a few preorders for your release party."

"That's amazing. The dust jackets should be in soon. Do you want to see the art?" she asked

"Yes, I would love to," said Kate.

She pulled out her phone and showed her an old-style clinch cover.

"I love it! It reminds me of the romance novels my grannie used to read. I love that old clinch covers are coming back into style, this is wonderful. Send me that when you are ready to announce, and I'll put it out on social media."

"Awesome! I'll be sure to get it to you. A bunch of us are going over to Poppy's tonight to hang out. Did you want to come? It's a good time."

Kate thought about it. This was the first time she had been invited. She knew they were nice, and if she was a bit more of a joiner, she knew they would gladly invite her more often. But she just hadn't really felt ready to venture out of the comfort of her store or house yet, but she was beginning to think it was time that she emerged from the cocoon she had been living in for the past year and a half, but tonight she had plans.

"Can I have a raincheck? I actually have plans tonight," said Kate.

"Of course! What are you up to tonight?" asked Hannah.

"I'm headed over to Glendale to see my brother's game."

"Oh right, your brother plays for the Magic. I always forget about that. He's good. I used to watch hockey with my dad growing up. We should all go to a game sometime. I haven't been to one in forever."

"Yeah! I think it would be fun to get a group of us going. Let's look at the schedule and pick a date. I'm sure Conner can get us tickets," said Kate.

"That sounds good, I'll take that rain check though. Poppy and Josh have weekly game nights, so you should totally come next time."

"I will. That sounds fun."

Hannah left, and she was busy thinking about what they had discussed. It was time to get back out there. She really liked Hannah, and she had grown up with Poppy, but they had traveled in different circles. Kate, of course, was all hockey all the time, and when she wasn't on ice or with the team, she was somewhere quietly escaping into a book. Poppy had been busy with the drama stuff, but she always seemed nice. She knew Sam a little better because he did play hockey, but he was older than her and Conner were. She knew Sam was still a part of the league that played here. The thought of joining the league wasn't even something she had considered, but after the scrimmage, the thought had crossed her mind. She moved back to Mystic Falls because it really was a special little town, but she hadn't been participating in the events much. She needed to change that.

After she got done tonight, she would be heading over to Glendale to watch Wes play, and she hoped that after that she could play a little game of her own with Wes. She hadn't seen him since the last time she was there, and they had finally had sex for the first time. It was by far the best sex she'd ever had. Yes, he was skilled and attentive, and she was insanely attracted to him, but there was something else about it. There was this spark that danced between them she had never experienced before. It was like every touch lit her up on the inside.

When it was time to close for the day, she headed home to get ready for the game. She pulled out the jersey Wes had given her. Looking at it made her smile. She did love that his number was her old number and having a 98 on her back again was a nice feeling, but she couldn't bring herself to put it on. She still just wasn't ready for everyone to know yet. He was this wonderful little secret.

Her life was complicated. Her relationship with hockey was complicated. Her relationship with her brother was complicated. Her past relationships with men had been complicated. And while things should be complicated with Wes, they weren't. It was delightfully simple. She liked him and he liked her. Once people knew about them, things would get complicated again, and she wasn't ready for that. Two things in her life were simple and made her feel sane, Wes and the bookstore.

Part of her wanted to wear it, but the part that wasn't quite ready won. So, she hung it back up in her closet and finished getting ready. There would be other games to wear it too, and she did plan on going to more.

She made it to the arena close to puck drop, but by the time she got to her seat, the players' warm up was already over. Her parents were here tonight too, but they were probably in the family box. Kate was sitting down close to the ice again. She liked this more than being in the box anyway. Here, she got to experience the game again, and that felt good. She was reclaiming herself, bit by bit.

Unfortunately, this game didn't go as well as the last one she had been at. It had been close, but the Magic were behind going into the third period, and they just couldn't pull it out. Wes has lost some games on the road, but she had never been around him after he lost a game before. On the road when they had lost, they would text back and forth but that wasn't the same as being in person. They had made plans to hang out after the game, so she headed back to the hallway to wait for him.

He was one of the first ones out and he looked for her and smiled at her the second he saw her. Something settled inside, he didn't seem like he was going to be in a foul mood like her brother often was when he lost.

"Hey Red, ya wanna get out of here?" he asked, holding his hand out to her.

She had been relieved when he decided not to go out with some of the team and just head back to his place for the night. Once they were there, he went to the fridge and got them both out a beer. He popped the top and handed it to her.

Taking it from his hand, she took a sip. He had been quieter than usual tonight, but that was to be expected after a loss, right? Being a little withdrawn was better than being angry. They went and sat on the couch, and he pulled her close to him putting his arm around her and he took a long slow breath.

"You were really good tonight. It was a tough loss, but you played well," she said, trying to comfort him.

He just nodded and took a long sip from his beer. Glancing up at him, she smiled, and he looked away. If this was Wes in a bad mood, she could handle it. It was way better than Jason in a bad mood. Jason in a bad mood usually involved lots of yelling and blaming. This was something she could handle. Kate laid her head on his shoulder and his hand ran over her arm.

"Can I ask you something?" Wes asked.

"Of course," she said, turning to face him.

"Why didn't you wear the jersey I got you?"

He wouldn't meet her eye. She didn't like it. Wes should never be upset. If he was upset because of something she had done, and not just bummed because of the loss, that was something she needed to make right.

"Is that why you're upset?"

"It's part of it," he said, finally looking over at her.

"I... I don't know...I just...it felt like a big statement or something," she said and once it was out of her mouth, she wanted to take it back in. Wes just nodded and they sat there.

"What are we doing here, Kate? I like you a lot. You know that. And you seem to like me, but I don't want to be a secret. I don't want to lie to your brother. I understand things are complicated for you, but it doesn't feel good."

Those words cut her to the quick. He was right. She had been so wrapped up in how all of this affected her, and how hard all of this was for her. She hadn't really stopped to think about what it might feel like for Wes. Most guys would be fine with a little booty in private, not needing a label or anything like that, but Wes had proven time and time again he was not like other guys.

"I'm sorry. You're right. I guess I didn't think about it like that," she said quietly.

He looked at her and wrapped his finger around one of her curls. "I get it, Kate. I do. I just want to be able to be with my girl in public. I want her in the stands cheering for me. But also, the longer we keep this from Conner, the more it is going to mess things up when we tell him. He's your brother, you can tell him when you're ready, but he's my teammate and my captain, it puts me in an awkward situation. I am trying to be patient, but damn...."

"Hey," she said as she cupped his face. "I'm sorry. I've only really been considering how all of this affected me, and that wasn't fair. Yes, this is complicated for me, but I don't want to hurt you. I'll talk to Conner."

"I don't want to push you, but I just need to be honest with my feelings. I was expecting to see you in the stands tonight in my jersey, maybe that was presumptuous. You totally don't have to wear it; I just didn't know what to think. I know you don't date hockey players and I thought that you were ashamed to be with me. It didn't feel good. I want to tell everyone we are together. I can barely keep it in, and it just sucks that it's not the same for you."

"Wes. I am not ashamed to be with you. It's not about that at all. You are wonderful. I mean that. You have been surprising at every fucking turn." She was now turned completely on the couch facing him because he needed to know this. "It's not about you. It's about me. It's about me, but that isn't fair to you. I'll talk to Conner tomorrow. We can tell people. I need to work through my shit, but I don't want you for one second thinking that I am ashamed to be with you."

He smiled at her. Finally, a good smile that went up to his eyes. The relief that smile gave her was overwhelming. She climbed onto his lap straddling him, and he put his hands on her ass and pulled her close. "I'm serious, Wes. You have to know how incredible I think you are. You're smart and talented and strong and so fucking sexy I can't stand it." She dropped her face to his and kissed him. And there it was, that glow that filled her every time they connected like this. "I'll proudly wear your name and number on my back."

"Are you sure?" he asked. "I don't want to push you. I just wanted to be honest with my feelings," he said with his hands still cupping her ass.

"Yes, I need to be brave. Me not facing my fears made you feel like this, and I need to fix that. You're helping me, not pushing me. You're giving me a reason to finally deal with everything I've been pushing away. I'm not going to promise it will be easy. I'll make mistakes, but you are worth it. You are worth everything, and you need to feel that. I really like you Wes, and I want people to know about us."

"You wanna tell everyone you're my girlfriend?"

"Girlfriend?" she asked, testing the word out. That word was a bit of a jump, but here with him, it felt like one she might be able to take.

He raised his eyebrows and nodded to her waiting for her to answer.

"Let's do it. I'll call Conner tomorrow and tell him. And then everyone can know I'm Wes Darling's girlfriend." She waited for the pit in her stomach to form, but it didn't. She just felt happy.

He cradled her head in his hands and brought her down to kiss him. And this time he didn't stop. She opened her mouth and his tongue swept in. She ground against him feeling the heat stir inside of her.

"Take me to bed," she said to him in a breathy plea.

CHAPTER 17

WES

He stood up with her legs still wrapped around him. His legs were a little weak from the game, but he had enough strength for this. He was relieved that Conner would finally know so he could stop dreading the fall out, but mostly he was just glad that Kate was willing to claim him publicly. He loved her. He'd known that for a while. He knew she needed time to get there, and he could give that to her, but this felt good. Kate McPhee, this gorgeous strong woman he was carrying to his bed, had chosen him. That felt better than being the number one draft pick. This was important. She was important.

When they got into his room, he dropped her down on the bed.

"I'm going to need you naked. Right now," he said as he began to unbutton his shirt.

She stood pulled her sweater over her head and the sight of her breasts and pale shoulders covered with a smattering of freckles lit him on fire. She turned to take her pants off. And the sight of his number on her back did something to him, something he couldn't explain. While he had been disappointed when he saw her in the crowd without his jersey on, knowing his number was still on her did make him feel a bit better. After he had his own pants off, he walked over to her and traced the numbers on her back as he undid the clasp of her bra.

She turned and the look in her eye was pure fire. His mouth came crashing down onto hers and he once again pulled her up and she wrapped her legs around him and they dropped to the bed. He was kissing her and grinding his already painful erect cock into her soft core. The only thing keeping them from connecting was two thin pieces of fabric.

He moved them further up the bed until her head was resting on his pillow, then he began to kiss down her body, stopping to pay some attention to her breasts. He sucked one into his mouth and his tongue flicked over the nipple while his other kneaded her other breast and slightly pinched the nipple. She squirmed and moaned, and he loved it. He craved her. He craved her moans and her kisses and her taste. He kissed down over the mound of her soft belly and pulled at the elastic band of her underwear. She shifted and he pulled them off quickly, throwing them somewhere and then he was there kneeling before her legs.

He pushed them wide and just looked at her. He looked at her perfectly plump, pink pussy and he couldn't wait to sink into it, but right now he needed to taste it. He slid his finger down over the seam and pushed in.

"You are already so wet," he said as he pushed in a finger. She felt like heaven. He slid his fingers higher to the sensitive little bundle of nerves and she moaned and squirmed. He loved every second of this. He lowered his head and pushed in two fingers as he kissed her clit.

"You taste so fucking good, Red," he said. Then he licked his lips. The look of sheer lust on her face set him back into motion and he worked the fingers inside of her and flicked his tongue over her clit. She cried out and fisted her hand into his hair.

"Oh my god, Wes. Don't stop," she cried out.

And he didn't intend to. He was here, and he intended to be here until her pussy squeezed his fingers tight with her pleasure. He increased the pressure with his tongue over her clit. His fingers found the bit of thicker tissue inside of her and he massaged it as she began to grind against his face. Her hands fisted so hard in his hair it began to sting, but it was amazing. He could spend days between this woman's dimpled thighs, and it would never be enough. He sucked her clit into his mouth and her moans got louder. He matched her intensity. Then she screamed out his name and broke. He could feel her pussy throbbing around his fingers as he sucked on her clit flicking his tongue over it.

When she was finished, he kissed his way back up her body and she lay there panting. He kissed her lips again. The way she clung to him and moaned when he was on top of her made him forget about the game he had lost. All that mattered was here. She was everything.

She stopped kissing him and pushed him away slightly. Pulling back and seeing the look in her eyes was enough to make him come right here, but when she pushed him to the side and rolled on top of him, he was a goner. The feel of her warm soft body pressing into him was incredible. The energy that danced between them was like nothing he had ever experienced. It was better than anything he could have ever imagined.

She leaned over and pulled out a condom from his bedside table and gave him a sinful sexy look. She sat kneeling over him and ripped the foil packet and rolled the condom down his length. He willed his hips not to buck into her hands. Then she began to lower herself slowly down his length. It took a while as she adjusted, but once he was sheathed fully inside of her she began rocking her hips. He grabbed her ass and pulled her down hard to him, feeling that delicious softness enveloping him.

"Damn, Kate. You're so fucking sexy," he rasped out.

Putting her hands on his chest, he rocked her hips and moaned. And with one more rock, he was thanking his lucky stars that she was his girl. The thought of their conversation moments ago, when Kate McPhee had just agreed to be his girlfriend, made him wild with need. He slammed her down against him, and she cried out in surprise. As she ground against him and he got close to coming. He needed her to come again first. Letting her set the speed, he brought his hand up and rubbed his thumb over her clit as she rode him.

"Oh my god, Wes," she cried out as she began to rock against him with more speed.

When he could tell she was getting close, he started to buck beneath her.

She cried out and pulsed around him. He slammed her down on his dick one final time before following her over the edge.

She fell to his side panting. "Oh my god, Wes. We are so good at that," she said with a smile.

Disposing of the condom, he turned on his side and lightly traced her soft jaw. "You can say that again."

His heart was fit to burst at the sight of her. She was laying there looking so satisfied, her curls slightly stuck to her sweaty forehead. He bent his head and kissed her slow and long, relishing in the fact that she was his. He wanted to shout it from the rooftops, and he was going to be able to soon.

"Do you have to work tomorrow?"

"Nope," she answered.

"Are you going to come to my game tomorrow?"

"I was planning on it," she said with a smile as she pushed his blond hair out of his eyes.

"After the game, if you want, we can tell Conner together."

She bit her bottom lip, and a little crease found her brow. "I appreciate that, but I think I should tell him on my own."

"Whatever you think is best," he said snuggling into her. "Just know I'm here if you want me to be with you."

"I've never been with anyone like you, Wes. I'm so glad you wouldn't take no for an answer," she said, giving him a cheeky grin.

The playful side of her was something new, and he loved it. He grabbed her sides and tickled her. She squealed and tried to wiggle out of his grasp, giggling the whole time. He had her, and he wasn't letting go.

CHAPTER 18

KATE

The next morning Kate woke up and took a shower. Wes was making some breakfast and Kate decided it was time to tell Conner.

Kate - Hey, do you want to get lunch today?

Conner - Why? Are you still in town?

Kate - Do you want to get lunch or not?

Conner - yeah, meet me at Mary Anne's Diner at 1?

Kate - Sounds good

Heading out into the kitchen, she saw Wes plating them both up an omelet.

"You're going to spoil me if you keep cooking for me like that."

"That's the point," he said. "I like spoiling you." He brought her the plate and gave her a quick kiss.

"I just texted Conner. I'm going out to lunch with him to come clean." It wasn't that she was feeling nervous necessarily. Conner was protective in the way a friend is protective, like a 'hurt her and I'll help her burn your shit' kind of vibe, not in a patriarchal bull shit kind of way. But she was still just nervous about committing to this. If she let other people know, it opened them up to more questions and complications.

"I can go with you if you want," he said.

"No, I think I should do this. I've never really explained to him why I cut hockey out of my life, and maybe him a little bit because of that. I need to do this on my own," she said.

"I'm here if you need me. You know that right?"

She nodded and took a bite of her omelet. She did know that, and it was making her feel guilty. She knew he would be there for her in any way he could, no questions asked and here she was not even ready to say they were together. Why was she like this? He was perfect and she was going to mess it all up, she could tell. She was going to run, because she already felt it. Just the thought of talking to Conner about all of this made her a mess.

"Can you take me to my car later so I can go meet Conner?"

"Of course, we can go get it after breakfast. I have a guest parking pass I can give you to put in your car so you can park here whenever you need to," he said.

"Thanks," she said, fighting her knee jerk reaction to say it wasn't necessary. That was a boyfriend thing to do right? And that's what they were now. It had felt better last night, but now she just wasn't sure. She was going to mess this up and hurt him. He didn't deserve that. He deserved someone less...broken than she was.

Later that day, she was scrolling on her phone waiting for Conner at a diner. She smiled as she scrolled through some of the social media the Magic was starting to put out. It was engaging, whoever did their social media knew what they were doing. Wes and Ethan had some goofy stuff going on. Conner had some hockey tips videos, it was fun. Although there was a video of him in his suit walking in for game night with a look on his face she didn't really want to see her brother making.

"Ya know, it's pretty weird to find your sister looking at a thirst trap of you, right?" Conner said as he sat down across from her.

"I get it...I'm the one who has to try and keep down a meal now," she said, smiling at him. "Whoever is doing your social media is doing a fantastic job."

"They just hired a new person. She's irritating, but it seems to be working...so it is what it is," he said as he picked up the menu. "As much as I love a surprise lunch with you, I am a little curious what this is all about."

"Can't a person just want to hang out with their brother?"

"Yeah, and we used to all the time, but not in the past couple years."

"Stop, it hasn't been that long," she said defensively.

"Yeah, it has Kate, but I'm not going to complain. So, what's up?"

"What do you mean what's up?"

"Are we gonna do this dance, or are you going to tell me what is going on? I've had to drag you to my games once a year and suddenly you have been to two of them."

"Yeah..." she said, fidgeting with her menu.

"Can I take your order?" asked the waitress. Kate was relieved for a moment to collect her thoughts. Why was this so hard for her?

After the waitress left, Conner just looked at her, eyebrows raised.

"It's hard to explain, and I know that I do owe you an

explanation. It's just hard to talk about." She paused and took a breath. Conner was probably the person she trusted most in her life, but she had pushed him away. This was hard. She took a sip of water and continued. It was time she finally did this.

"When I stopped playing hockey, it was really hard to watch you go on to have this amazing career. I was stuck in a toxic relationship, while you and Dylan and Patrick all went on to these wonderful things. It just sucked." She stopped and took a sip of her water. Conner looked like he was about to say something. "Please just let me get this out," she said. His brow furrowed, but he nodded and let her continue.

"I loved hockey as much as you did. But for me it was done when we lost the last game in the semifinals. Then you went on to win, and you were signed, and I was so happy for you, but so messed up myself. I didn't know how to get distance from hockey and not from all of you. I'm not even sure if that makes sense," she said looking out the window trying to fight the emotion clawing at the back of her throat.

"Kate..." His hand reached across the table and squeezed hers. "I didn't realize."

Finding her strength to glance over at him, his eyes were soft with concern.

"I know." Taking back her hand, she took another sip of water and a deep breath. "But that is why I just had to cut it out...it was too hard."

"You could have gone on to play. You were one of the best female goalies out there, you could have been on the national team, or coached like Patrick. You'd be good at that."

"I didn't want to coach...I wanted to play. Options just weren't the same for us. I made a wrong choice. I get that now. And I'm trying to fix it, but it's hard."

"Yeah...I never even thought about it that way. I'm sorry Kate," he said, his voice full of sincerity.

And she knew he meant it. This was what she didn't want. She wanted everyone to be able to go on and live their lives and not have their lights dimmed because she was a dark cloud.

"I'm sorry too, Conner. I should've supported you, or at least told you why I was staying away. But everything with Jason happened, and I didn't even recognize myself anymore," she said as the waitress dropped off their food.

"We're good, Kate. We have been. I still want to kick that fucker's ass," he said with a head shake. "But it's been really nice having you around."

Kate picked up a fry and dipped it in ketchup, trying to work up the courage for the final topic she needed to discuss with him.

"But there is another reason I have been hanging around more…"

"And what reason is that?" he said with a knowing glance.

"Because when Wes was home with you, he asked me out, we kind of hit it off and have been dating since then," she said quickly in one breath. Just ripped the band aid right off.

"I can't believe you actually said yes to him," he said with amusement.

"You knew he asked me out?"

"He asked me if I would have a problem with it when we were home, and I didn't, but I never thought you'd say yes. What happened to 'I don't date hockey players', huh?" he said.

"I know. I tried to turn him down…but he's persistent. And he's a good guy. I really do like him," she said quietly, not meeting his eye.

"He is a good guy, as long as you're both happy, I'm happy for you. But ya know I'll kick his ass if you need me too."

"I'll kick his ass if I need me to," she said to him with a grin.

"That's the old KitKat energy I am talking about." he said,

giving her a five over the table. "Are you coming to the game tonight?"

"I was thinking about it," she said with a small smile.

"Good, I like having you there. We should all go out afterwards."

"Sounds good," she said, relieved that the conversation was over.

"Oh! And guess who's in town tonight and coming to the game?" he asked with a grin.

"Who?"

"Frankie."

"Shut up!"

Frankie was one of her teammates from college. On top of that, they had been roommates in college for years. Frankie went on to play on the national team, but last she heard, she was coaching out in Seattle.

"She emailed me last week and let me know. She's coming out with us after the game."

"That's amazing. I haven't talked to her in so long." Kate was a little worried that Frankie might be mad that they had lost touch after college, but she was pretty sure she would just be glad she finally left Jason. "I'm excited to see her."

The rest of her meal with Conner was enjoyable, but she couldn't shake the apprehension that was setting in. The feeling that somehow, she didn't deserve all of this. Conner was right. She used to be tough. She used to be someone who stood up for herself, who went after what she wanted, but now all of that was gone.

She was hiding. On some level, she had been hiding since her last hockey game. Being a goalie is hard. Being the goalie and having a bad night is brutal. Being a goalie and the reason your team loses its shot at the championship, is devastating. Dealing with that while your twin brother is having all his dreams come true in a sport they both love, the sport that had just chewed her up and spit her out, is what had driven her into Jason's arms, and he was why she was broken. Being back on the ice and being with Wes in his hockey world were making all of that very apparent, and she just wasn't sure how much of it she could safely face.

She made it back to Wes's condo and used the guest pass to park. Walking into the lobby, the security guard recognized her and told her she could 'head on up'. Everything that should make her feel good made her feel like crawling out of her skin. This was not normal, but she didn't know what to do.

She knocked on Wes's door and he immediately opened it, eyebrows raised with a questioning look on his face.

"Well, how did it go?" he asked.

"Good," she said as she came in and set her purse down on the table.

"You gotta give me more than that. Was he pissed?"

"Why didn't you tell me you asked him if it would be okay if you asked me out?"

"It was just a courtesy thing. Is he cool with this? Is he going to punch me when I get into the locker room tonight?"

She looked at him and couldn't help but laugh. All the apprehension she felt seemed to fall away when she was with him.

"No. He was surprised I said yes, but that's about it. He said if you hurt me, he'd kick your ass if I wanted him to. But I said if you hurt me I'd kick your ass myself, so we're all good."

He pulled her into a hug and whatever it was that happened between them when they touched came to life. She looked up at him and sighed.

"That's a very self-satisfied look you have on your face, Red," he said. Then he kissed her.

She wrapped her arms around his neck and opened to

him in a demanding kiss. He groaned and deepened the kiss, splaying his big hands on her ass and pulling her close to him. Lifting her up, he set her on the counter and continued to kiss her. As he sucked her bottom lip into his mouth, she moaned and began to pull at his shirt. He let go of her long enough to remove both their shirts. Then they were back on each other.

Kate didn't remember ever feeling this way before. She had never experienced this absolute hunger for another person before, she needed him. She began to pull at the waistband of his sweatpants, but then his hands found the button of her jeans and undid them. Shifting her weight, he pulled them off along with her underwear and settled back in between her thighs. He kissed a trail down her neck, setting her on fire.

Undoing the clasp of her bra, his mouth found her nipple and she cried out. She felt so alive. Being with Wes like this was like nothing she had ever experienced. She could get lost in him. His mouth continued moving south, and she was in ecstasy. Pushing her legs wide, he pulled back and smiled at the sight before him. Pushing his fingers into her, she was already wet and ready.

"Fuck, Kate. You're perfect," he said as he lowered his head and traced his finger across her clit.

"Stop talking," she said as she pushed his head between her legs. He gave a muffled grunt of approval and got to work, licking and sucking and working her with his fingers. He did something to her. She was almost there, and it had only been moments. She could never get her fill of him. Then he did something to her clit. She wasn't sure what it was, but she knew she never wanted it to stop. "Oh my god, Wes. Don't stop."

And he didn't, he stayed there doing exactly what she needed to send her over the edge.

Pushing his head aside, she sat there on the kitchen counter panting. Wes reached over to the table by the door and grabbed his wallet and pulled out a condom. Then he pulled her down off the counter and moved them a few steps into the living room. He pushed down his sweatpants and bent her over the couch. This was new for her. This primal need she felt for him was nothing she had experienced before, but damn did she love it.

His fingers found her core and she cried out in surprise and pleasure. Then, she felt his fingers trace the 98 on her back and her whole body was on fire.

"You're mine, Red," he growled in her ear. Then plunged deep into her. The delicious stretch made her cry out.

"Say it," he said, driving into her again.

"I'm yours," she cried out. And with that, his restraint was gone. His hands grabbed her hips, his fingertips digging in almost painfully to the soft flesh there, fucking her hard. She cried out as the pleasure overtook her. She was lost in this man, and he was equally lost in her. The search for pleasure drove their every movement.

She felt herself getting close again. "I'm going to come," she cried out. One of his hands let go of her hips and moved up her back, stopping where the tattoo was before moving up further and fisting into her hair. At that she broke and began to throb around his cock, squeezing him.

"Fuck, Kate," he cried out. He gave one last hard thrust and fell on top of her, panting.

They both stayed in the moment, unable to pull away from the passion and the connection. He pulled out of her, and she ached at his absence. She wanted him back inside of her.

Coming back to her, he flopped over the couch pulling her over on top of him.

She let out a little squeal,

"What are you doing?" she asked as he settled her on top of him, their naked bodies stretched out on each other.

"I'm going to crush you," she said, trying to move off him. His arms wrap around her holding her in place.

"I'll let you know if you are crushing me," he said as he wrapped one of her curls around his finger. She loved that he did that. Most guys would just try to run their hands through her hair, making her a mess of red frizz. But the way he did it defined her ringlets. He really was the perfect man.

"I have to tell you, Red. That was probably the hottest moment of my entire life. You drive me crazy," he said, tracing his hands over her back. He widened his legs and she settled in between them, still torso to torso.

"I agree. That was some of your best work," she said, grinning up at him.

Kissing her forehead, he sighed contentedly. She could stay like this forever. When she was with him, all the questions and doubts she had were gone. All that was left was happiness. It had been too long since she had felt simple happiness down to her core, but here it was. She snuggled into him.

"So, things went well with Conner then?"

"Ummm. Wes, if you want to talk about my brother, I'm going to have to put some clothes on," she said with a grin.

"Fair enough," he said as he cupped her face and kissed her. "I'll never bring him up again, and you can just stay naked."

She laughed and snuggled back in, enjoying the way his finger traced her back.

"If you would have told me a few months ago I would be in a relationship with a hockey player and getting back into the sport, I would have laughed at you. But I have to tell you, Wes, I'm really happy. Thank you for giving me multiple chances every time I tried to push you away."

Kissing her forehead, he said, "I told you. I had a gut feeling about you, and I knew this would be life changing. And once again, my gut has not let me down. You're it for me, Red."

She laid there letting those words sink in. While she may not be ready to say them back, when he said them, they didn't scare her.

"Oh! I forgot to mention, Conner told me that one of our old friends from college is in town tonight. I might try and find her during the game, and I told Conner we would go out with them," she said.

"That's awesome. I'm excited to meet them."

"Frankie was one of my teammates and we lived together. I haven't seen her or even talked to her in years. I'm excited to see her…maybe I'm also a little nervous."

"Why are you nervous?"

"Last time I saw her, I was still with Jason and actively avoiding hockey. It's just weird," she sighed as she laid her head back down on his chest and listened to his heartbeat. "Our hearts are beating with the same rhythm." She didn't know why, but the thought of that made her smile.

He took a deep breath and just held her close. "I think it must mean we're soulmates. At least that's what the woman in the store next to the book shop said."

This made her sit all the way up. "Bridget? When did she say that?"

"When I was in Mystic Falls, before I met you. Conner was busy and that woman was offering tarot readings, and I thought why the hell not? Anyway, her reading alluded to me finding my soulmate, and then I found a cute little redhead with her nose in a book."

"That's why you came and talked to me?"

"Partly maybe, but I would have anyway. I'm a sucker for a hot book nerd," he said as he reached up and tickled her sides. Giving a squeal, she squirmed out of his grasp and they both tumbled to the floor, and he pinned her. He held her hands over her head, his face mere inches from her own. And just like that another wave of heat hit her and she reached for him, crashing into his mouth. He was growing hard again between her legs. There were perks to dating a twenty-four-year-old, and they explored all those perks right there on his living room floor.

CHAPTER 19

KATE

Making her way to her seat was a little more nerve wracking than it had been for a while. The past couple games she had really enjoyed herself, and the nerves of the first game she came too had gone away, but she knew who was going to be sitting in the seat next to her. Conner had told her that there was an extra ticket to sit with Frankie, and she took it. She also told Conner not to tell her she was coming. Did she do it as an out in case she chickened out? Maybe. But she was going to do this.

Frankie had been one of her best friends. There was no bad blood, they just lost touch when they graduated. Frankie was an amazing player, and she was a good time. So as nervous as Kate was, she was excited to see her. It had been a long time.

She got to the section. They are behind the team a few rows up. Conner always had amazing seats on reserve. As she made her way, she saw Frankie's long blonde hair pulled into a braid. She was looking down at her phone while the teams warmed up. She found Wes on the ice stretching and her heart smiled. Then she saw Conner, he was looking at her and waved.

Frankie noticed that he was and turned to look. Her mouth fell to the floor. 'Now or never' Kate thought and made her way to her seat.

"KATE! What the hell? Conner didn't tell me you were coming!" she yelled loudly as she pulled her into a hug. Kate had known that Frankie was amazing and wouldn't make it weird, but she was still relieved.

"How the fuck have you been?" Frankie asked.

"Good! How have you been?"

"Good, I'm coaching in Seattle. Living the dream, you know."

"Nice."

"What about you? What the hell have you been up to?"

"Not much. I'm just managing a bookstore in my hometown."

"No shit? That sounds like something you would be doing. Are you still with Jason?" she asked carefully.

"God, no." Kate shook her head.

"Good! That guy was a douche. I always thought so."

"What about you? Are you still with Bear?"

"No, we broke up after graduation. He's playing in Europe." There was a bit of a lull, and they watched the guys warm up. "The Magic is doing pretty good this year. They might have what it takes to go all the way. That's got to make Conner happy."

"You have no idea."

Conner and Wes were talking on the ice and Wes looked over at her with his big grin and a little wave. Frankie didn't miss that, then she realized Kate was wearing a jersey. Then she gently pulled on Kate's shoulder to look at the name on the back of her jersey.

"You are wearing a Wes Darling jersey?"

"Yeah, we've been dating for a while now."

"What!? I didn't think Kate McPhee dated hockey players!" She asked with a big grin.

"I know…" Kate sighed. "It just kind of happened."

"I'm just surprised. You went from not dating hockey players to dating a younger, hotshot player."

"Trust me, no one is as surprised as I am. But Wes isn't what you expect him to be. He's amazing," she said, trying to bite back the stupid grin that wanted to spread across her face.

"Do you still talk to anyone from the team?" Kate asked, looking for a subject change.

"Yeah, I actually just saw a lot of them over the summer at Haley and Kendra's wedding." A look clouded Frankie's face, like she wished she hadn't said anything.

"It's about time they got married. I'm surprised it took them that long," Kate said quickly, trying to let Frankie know it wasn't weird. Even though there was a small part of her that felt a sharp pain of regret. She should have been there. Those women had been her family for years, but she lost touch with all of them quickly after college because of Jason.

"Yeah. It's really good to see you, Kate."

"You too, Frankie. I was excited to see you when Conner told me you'd be here."

"Are you coming out with us afterward?"

"Yeah, Wes and I will be there."

They watched the game together. Kate was pleased at how easy it was. They hadn't seen each other since graduation, but Frankie acted like it was nothing. They talked about the game and old times. Kate was feeling more and more like who she had been all those years ago. It was a good feeling.

She knew she wasn't that person anymore. How could she be? But she was not the person she was when she was with Jason either. Somewhere between those two versions of her was who she was right now, and she was still searching for who that person was. But remembering who she had been when her only care in the world had been winning the next game and keeping up her grades for her scholarship felt good.

Frankie also reminded her of the sisterhood of having a team. She missed that. She was bummed that she hadn't been invited to Haley and Kendra's wedding. She remembered when they got together their junior year, but their life moved on, and Kate's life revolved around Jason. She had a choice, she could spiral in regret of what her shitty life choices had made her miss out on, or she could focus on where she was now. And as the crowd cheered and jumped to their feet, she was reminded of how wonderful her life was right now, and part of the reason had just scored his first goal of the night.

The game was over, and she waited for Wes. Things had gone really well with Frankie, and she was looking forward to spending more time with her tonight. She was looking forward to seeing Wes too. The locker room door opened, and Conner and Cash stepped out.

"Hey Kate, you're going to Westside tonight, right?" Conner asked.

"Yeah, Wes and I'll be there when he's done."

"See you there," he said before he turned and left.

A few minutes later, Ethan and Wes came out of the locker room joking with each other. Her eyes met Wes's and her heart fluttered. How did just being in his presence do that to her? She pushed off the wall and walked over to them. Wes's hand was already out waiting for her to thread her fingers through his.

This was the first time they were out in the open about their relationship like this. Kate had expected for it to feel weird, but it didn't. It just felt right.

"Hey Red," Wes said as she took his hand.

"Kate," Ethan said in a knowing greeting.

"Good game guys."

To her surprise, Wes dropped a quick kiss on her lips. "Thanks."

"That save at the end of the second period was insane," she said to Ethan.

"Ya like that one?" he said with raised eyebrows and a grin cocky enough to rival Wes's.

Kate just sighed and shook her head. What had her life become since January? Here she was, spending all her time with these hockey players reconnecting with her old teammates, and she loved it. That was a plot twist she did not see coming.

Once they made it to the bar, Wes stopped and got them each a beer before they made their way upstairs. Once she was at the top of the stairs, she spotted Frankie sitting with Conner, and two free seats across from them.

Frankie waved and Kate slipped her hand into Wes's as they made their way over to the table.

"Wes, this is Frankie," Kate said. "We played together at Notre Dame." Wes reached out his hand to shake hers. That's when she noticed shots and a drink on the table.

"What's all this?"

"Lemon drops and a cranberry and vodka." She pushed two of the shot glasses over to Kate. "For old times," she said with a grin. Kate looked at the shots apprehensively.

"Come on," Frankie said. "I know you got a ride home and I'm staying at the hotel down the block."

At that, Kate nodded and picked up one of the shots and held it out to Frankie. She clinked her glass to it, and both threw it back.

She settled down in the chair next to Wes and smiled as he slid his arm around her and pulled her close. She didn't realize how tired she was of hiding it until they were here with each other.

"I don't think I've ever seen you drink hard liquor before," he whispered quietly in her ear. Her entire body flushed at the accidental touch of his lips on the shell of her ear.

She turned, his face was mere inches from her own and she gave a small smile. "I don't really anymore," she said as she bit her lip.

"No worries. I got you." Then he gave her a quick kiss. She looked around to the balcony full of players and beautiful women. She might have felt uncomfortable because she didn't fit in with many of them, but between the grasp Wes had on her arm, and the way Conner and Frankie were teasing each other, she felt nothing but belonging. Jason would never have done this. He would never have come, and if he did, he would want to leave and be pissed at her for drinking. But no more thoughts of him tonight.

After the second shot, and halfway through her cranberry and vodka, she felt warm and things were getting swirly and happy. She was laughing with Conner and Frankie about old times.

Kate was on her way back from the bathroom when she heard Frankie call her name. At that moment, she saw a shot glass hurtling through the air at her. On reflex alone, she reached out and snatched it from the air.

"No!" Kate shouted as she put the shot glass on the table. "We are not doing this."

Conner turned to Frankie with a huge grin. "Can Kate Catch It! We haven't played that in years!" he whooped loudly.

"No!" she shouted again in exasperation. But no sooner Conner called out "Kate," and threw his keys at her, which she coolly snatched out of that air. Goalies had quick hands, and her brothers had done this to her for her entire life. She slammed down the keys next to Conner.

"No. We are not doing this." But he just looked up at her with a shit eating grin, and she couldn't help it, she punched her brother in the arm and made her way back to Wes.

"What's that about?" Wes asked with a grin on his face bordering on giddy.

"My brothers used to randomly throw things at me. They said it was to make me a better goalie, but they're actually just fuckers," she said loud enough for Conner to hear. He just raised his eyebrows, the cocky grin never left his face. "When you are at college with your brother, those things follow you."

Later that night Frankie called out her name again and she saw a phone flying through the air, but before she could catch it a large hand snatched it out of the air. She looked up to see Ethan smiling at her. "Goalies stick together," he said. He slipped the phone into his suit pocket and turned to Frankie with a smug look.

"Give me back my phone," she said, evaluating him.

"No."

"No?" she scoffed.

He just shook his head, and Frankie's mouth fell open trying to figure it out.

"Well, as fun as this has been, I think I'm going to head home. Hit me up next time you're in town Frankie," Conner said as he gave Frankie a big hug.

"Of course, it was great to see you, Conner. I'll talk to you later."

"See you later KitKat," Conner said, giving his sister a warm smile.

"See ya," she said with a warm smile.

As he walked down the stairs, she felt warm and smiley inside. That might be the liquor, but she hadn't felt this at ease in a long time. Being here with Frankie and her brother felt familiar, but being here with them with Wes's hand on her thigh felt life changing.

She stood to go to the bathroom with a little wobble.

"You good?" Wes asked.

"Yeah," she answered back with a slight slur. "I gotta go to the bathroom."

"I'll go with you," Frankie said.

They made their way to the bathroom. As Kate was washing her hands, she noticed Frankie preening in the mirror. "Why am I almost wasted, and you seem fine?"

Frankie laughed. "Well, it looks like you can't hold your booze anymore."

"You're probably right. I haven't had hard liquor in years," Kate said.

"Seriously? That would explain it, plus I didn't drink as much as you."

"Rude!" Kate said to her.

"What do you know about Ethan?" Frankie asked.

"Ethan? He's Wes's best friend. They played AAA together. And he's a fucking kick ass goalie. Why?" Kate eyed her suspiciously.

"I don't know...I think he's kinda cute," Frankie said, touching up her hair.

"Seriously? You think a 6'5 tall, tan, monster on the ice is kinda cute?"

"Mmm hmm," she said with a smile.

"Well, go for it. He's a good guy."

"Good to know," she said, zipping her purse and turned and left.

Kate followed her out of the bathroom, but then saw Wes leaning on the wall next to it.

"Hey, Red. Just checking in. You seem a little wobbly on your feet there," he said with a cocked eyebrow.

"Oh, do I?" she said, slipping her arms around him.

"Yeah –" but before he could finish his thought, she kissed him. There was a lot in this kiss. Not just her feelings and desire for him, but there was also something special about tonight. Pieces of her past and what she hoped would be her future had melded together so seamlessly. And they didn't have to hide anymore. She could kiss him whenever and wherever she wanted to, and right now, feeling all warm and glowy from the alcohol and the nearness of Wes, made it all feel magical.

His arms slid around her, and he turned, pinning her on to the wall. She gasped as he kissed down her neck. He pressed her into the wall and now that warm glow had turned to fire. Her hands fisted into his hair, and he grabbed at her hips.

"Take me home," she whispered into his ear.

He pulled back and looked at her. His eyes were hungry. "Let's get out of here."

"I'm going to go say goodbye to Frankie," she said.

They made their way up the stairs where there were still a couple players and a few others. She scanned the space for Frankie. She found her on Ethan's lap, her hands sunk into his black hair, his hands firm on her ass, and their mouths connected.

Kate gave a small chuckle, "She didn't waste any time."

"What's going on?" Wes asked, clearly amused by the whole situation.

"I'll explain later," she said looking back at Frankie and Ethan who didn't seem to be stopping anytime soon. "Why don't you just take me home?"

"Let's go."

They wove through the crowd of people in the bar and made their way to Wes's car. The cold winter air and the walk to the car sobered her up a bit. When he opened her door, she smiled up at him. He wrapped his fingers around one of her curls.

"Tonight was really nice," she said with a half-smile.

"I agree. It was nice to be out with you like that."

"Agreed." She threw her arms around his neck and kissed him.

He groaned and kissed her right back. Finally, he broke the kiss. "It's cold. Let's get home and continue this there."

She got in the car, and he closed the door behind her making his way over to the other side. She gave a contented sigh. Things felt good.

CHAPTER 20

WES

The next day, Wes had been called in early for a meeting. He and Conner had petitioned for him not to meet Blake Kelly on the ice because of the history they had. While Wes wanted to believe that Kelly wouldn't use the ice to get back at him, he wasn't sure.

"Wes, come sit down," Coach Wagner said. He was sitting at the table with the GM. A meeting with the head coach and the GM was a little intimidating.

"We got final word for the league today," said Kyle Durst, the team's general manager.

Wes could already tell it wasn't good news by the look on their face. He raised his eyebrows and waited to hear it.

"The league ruled that since there were no official charges filed, the game will be played as scheduled and the rosters are up to the individual teams," said the GM.

"So, if it hadn't been settled out of court, this might not be happening?"

"It would seem that way," he said with a stern look on his face.

"I'm sorry, Wes," Coach Wagner said, "we tried."

Wes took a deep breath and blew it out of his mouth and raked his hand through his hair. "I know…"

"If you decide to not play the game, we support you. It is your decision," Coach said.

"I appreciate that, but of course I'm playing."

"I figured you would, but just know we support you."

"I appreciate it."

"We'll see you on the plane later this afternoon, son. I wish it would have played out differently."

"Thank you for trying. I appreciate it."

At that, Wes stood and left. He had expected this much. Conner had been the one who had convinced him to bring it up. Even though he wasn't surprised, he still had a gut feeling about this game. The ruling didn't change the pit in his stomach that kept growing every time he thought about playing his old teammate on the ice. When they had previously played Florida, Kelly hadn't been on the ice, but he would this time.

He made his way to the locker room, sat down, and tried to center himself. He could do hard things. He could do this. He didn't have a choice. He dropped his head in his hands.

"How'd it go?" asked a familiar voice. It was a voice he knew in his sleep. A voice that had helped him through so much over the years. Without looking up he felt Ethan sit next to him. "Not good, I take it."

With a deep sigh, Wes picked up his head. "I mean, it was a shot in the dark. Conner had more faith in the system, but we both know how it was going to go. My only hope is that Kelly isn't self-destructive enough to ruin his own career just to end mine."

"You know this whole team has your back and won't hesitate to fuck him up."

Wes just nodded.

"We got this," Ethan said with a reassuring hand on his

shoulder. "I'm gonna hit the shower before we take off. See you on the plane?"

"Yep," Wes said, followed by one more deep breath. He heard his phone vibrating in his bag. Hoping it was Kate, he dug for it. And while it wasn't Kate, it was someone who still managed to make him feel better.

"Hey mom," he said.

"Hey baby, I was just calling to check in. I know you have some pretty tough games coming up. How are you?"

"I'm good. How are you?"

He talked to his mom and tried to feel better. His mom never knew exactly what went down in Florida, she knew it wasn't good. He had his reasons for not telling her, and she respected them. Right now, he just wanted to hear her laugh.

"Did you show Claire the last video the team posted of me and Ethan? That was the dance she was trying to teach me last time I was in Detroit."

"I did," his mother said with a laugh. "She loved it."

The conversation stayed positive and light, and it almost made him forget about the dread setting in.

Almost.

Later that day, he boarded the plane for their road trip. He had some time to come to terms with their meeting. He was trying to focus on the positive, and when he did that, he couldn't help but smile. They had won their last game. He had scored two goals. And he was hopelessly in love with his girlfriend. While she may not be there yet, he knew she was on her way. They had had a wonderful couple of days together full of lots of sex and laughs. And for the first time he found himself enjoying both of those things equally. That's not to say he was a player who used women for sex, but his other short relationships had never felt anything close to this.

The seat he usually sat in was next to Conner. He hadn't

really had a chance to talk to him much after Kate had told him about their relationship. She had said it went well, but every time he went to talk to her about it more, he got a little distracted by his beautiful and sexy girlfriend. Conner wasn't treating him any differently, so that was promising, but he was hoping to talk to him about it on the plane and make sure they were good. With the way the two of them played on the ice, he couldn't risk messing it up.

The team boarded the plane, and everyone was busy getting situated. Conner was upfront talking to coach until it was time to take off. He was feeling pretty good about tonight's game in Texas, but tomorrow night they would be in Florida. He dreaded going back there.

His phone vibrated in his pocket.

Kate - How's it going on the plane? Did Conner say anything to you?

Wes - We haven't taken off yet. He's still up talking to the coach.

Kate - Well in that case...

And then he waited for a moment and a picture popped up and he nearly choked.

It was a picture of Kate in her bathroom wearing nothing but some purple cheeky underwear and his jersey looking over her shoulder with a sultry gaze biting her lip. His brain shorted out and he was instantly hard.

Of course, at that moment her brother sat down next to him. He fumbled his phone in surprise and watched it tumble to the floor. Conner bent down to pick it up. Wes snatched it out of his hand quickly, but not before Conner caught a glance of the photo.

"Oh god, tell me that's not who I think it is," he groaned.

"Uh... It's not who you think it is?"

He quickly shot off a text.

> Wes - your brother just sat down next to me FML

> Wes - but damn Red...more later.

"So, you and my sister, huh?" Conner asked.

"Yeah. We've been dating since the game in Mystic Falls. I wanted to tell you, but I let her make that decision. Are we good?"

"Yeah, we're good...as long as I don't see any more pictures like that," Conner said with a raised eyebrow.

"Noted."

"I still can't believe she went out with you," Conner said.

"Me either, but I'm glad she did. I really like spending time with her. I'm glad we're good."

Conner just nodded.

"Are you good with the Florida game? I know Kelly's gonna be on the ice. I wish we could have gotten him taken off the roster for the game."

Wes nodded. The overhead speaker dinged as the captain let them know it was time for take off. Conner and Wes both clicked their seatbelts.

"You know we all got your back, right?"

"Yeah...I think it's kind of fucked up that I have to play him. I appreciate you guys having my back." He let out a long sigh and ran his hand through his hair. "I would be lying if I said I wasn't worried about it, but it is what it is. I'll show up and do my job, and hopefully, we'll kick their asses."

"Yeah, it's fucked up. You're a good guy...even if you're dating my sister," Conner said.

"Thanks, man. It means a lot."

Conner just nodded and got out his phone.

Wes took this moment to shoot Kate another text.

Wes - Are you going to be up after our game tonight?

Kate - I can be.

Wes - Good, expect a FaceTime when I get back to the hotel.

Kate - Looking forward to it. I think I'm going to go to Smokey's and watch the game there. I'll be cheering you on.

Wes - Thanks.

His fingers itched to type out 'I love you,' but he knew she wasn't there yet, and he didn't want to freak her out, but he knew how he felt. He was head over heels for her. And he couldn't wait until he wasn't next to her brother to take a better look at that picture, because damn he could look at her ass all night long. And the sight of her in his jersey, and her ass was giving him a bit of a problem in his pants. So, he pulled up his reading app and started reading a dense fantasy novel that would make his brain focus on something other than the cute redhead and her ass on his phone.

CHAPTER 21

KATE

It was just about time to close the bookstore with fifteen minutes before closing time when the bell sounded and in walked Ashton.

"Hey Ashton," Kate said. "How's it going?"

"Good," he said, looking a little bit unsure.

"What's up? We're all set for Queer Spaces tomorrow," said Kate.

"Yeah, I know. I just wanted to ask something," he said.

"Okay..." she said, waiting for him to say it.

"You know there aren't many opportunities for work here in Mystic Falls. And I'm looking for a job to help save up for college. If I'm ever able to afford it. I was wondering if you ever thought about hiring someone to help you. I could even just clean and set up for events. I could shelf books. Whatever you need. If it's a silly idea, I get it, but I just thought I would try, because I really enjoy it here, and you've made it a great place and I was just wondering–"

"I think it's a great idea," Kate said, cutting off his rambling.

"You do?" he asked, a grin spreading across his face.

"Yeah. I'll call Luis and Sofie tomorrow and see what they think. It would give me more time to focus on the online store if I had help with the community room and all that stuff. Here," she said, giving him a piece of paper. "Write down your availability and I'll see what they say."

He took the paper from her hand and quickly wrote down his schedule. "Thank you so much! I know it might not work out but thank you so much! It would be so amazing to work here!"

"Hey, I think it would be great too. I'll see what we can do." She took the paper from him.

"Okay, great! I really appreciate it."

"Of course, but I'm getting ready to close up. I'll talk to them and hopefully be able to tell you something tomorrow at Queer Spaces," she said with a warm smile.

"Yeah. See you tomorrow! Thanks, Kate!" he said with a big smile as he left.

As she finished up the last couple things, she started thinking about what having some help would be like. If she had someone here covering the store, she could focus more on the online side, where they were making more money right now. She could do more, and she could do it from anywhere. She could work at the store when Wes was traveling, and work in Glendale when Wes was home. Maybe he could even spend some of his downtime here in Mystic Falls. She was possibly getting ahead of herself, but she did like to think about it. Spending time with him was beginning to become a priority for her, and that hadn't been a priority for her since Jason. But it felt completely different with Wes, because with Jason, there was pressure to be whenever he needed her, but this was different. With Wes, she wanted to be near him all the time, but with his job, it wasn't always an option.

When she had finally gotten away from Jason, her

autonomy was something she protected fiercely. But in the couple of months she and Wes had been seeing each other, he never tried to guilt her into spending time with him. Only convinced her a bit by tapping into her competitive side, but she was glad he did.

Checking her watch, she noticed it was getting close to puck drop. She locked up the store and headed down to Smokey's. She was hoping Sam would be there. She'd had fun watching the past couple away games with him. He reminded her of watching games with Patrick. He knew about the game in and out, but he had a pretty even nature. He also didn't have any expectations of her. They just talked about the game and had easy conversations.

When she walked into Smokey's, she found Sam sitting at a table, but instead of Lucas Fipp, he was with his husband. Kate hadn't really gotten to know Jackson. He moved to Mystic Falls when he and Sam got married a few years ago. He seemed nice, but she didn't really want to intrude on their dinner. So, she walked over to the bar and sat down there. She ordered a beer and started to look over the menu.

"Hey, Kate," Sam called from across the bar. "Do you want to join us?"

"Sure," she said, taking her beer to the table. "I didn't want to intrude."

"No, we just ordered food. I was actually hoping you'd be here. He's not much of a hockey fan," he said, motioning to Jackson.

"Hi, I'm Jackson. I've seen you around, but I don't think we've ever been introduced," he said, reaching out his hand.

"Yeah, I'm Kate. It's nice to meet you," she said, taking his hand.

"Hey Kate, can I take your order?" asked the waitress.

"Yeah, just give me a cheeseburger and onion rings."

"Is the guy you were here with a few months ago playing tonight?" she asked.

"Yeah, he is."

"If you still talk to him, you should tell him we got his picture up. He should come in and see it," she said.

"I'll let him know." She tried to hide the grin that was creeping across her face. It was the same waitress who had hit on him that night. If she only knew what was going on between her and Wes.

"Someone's got the hots for a hockey player?" Jackson laughed.

"I wouldn't say I have the hots for him," Kate said defensively.

"I wasn't talking about you, but I am now," Jackson said with a knowing smile.

"I'm kind of dating him," Kate said softly.

"Dating who?" asked Sam.

"Wes Darling."

"You're dating Wes Darling?" Sam said with an approving nod.

"Is that him?" Jackson said, pointing to the screen where they were doing a pre-game interview with his ridiculously handsome face and cocky self-assured smile.

She looked up at the screen and smiled. "Yeah, that's him."

"Damn, good for you," Jackson said with an agreeable smile.

After their food came and they finished eating, it was the end of the second period. The Magic and Texas were tied. It had been a good game. Conner had scored a goal, but Wes's playing was a bit off. No one who wasn't used to watching him play and knew how he skated would be able to tell, but Kate could tell. She wondered what the problem was.

"Well, I think I'm going to head home. You two stay and finish up the game," Jackson said as he stood up and slipped his coat on. "Kate, you should come to Poppy and Josh's tomorrow. They're having a game night."

"I'll have the game on," Sam said, giving her a knowing look.

"Yeah, Hannah said something about that last time she was in the bookstore. I'll try to make it," Kate said, and to her surprise, she meant it. She had been hanging out with Sam more, and he was great. Hannah had been in the store a lot more recently with her book release party, which was going really well, so yeah, this could be fun. It had been a long time since Kate had a group of friends, probably not since college.

Another piece to rebuilding her life was falling into place.

"Awesome! Well, I'll see you then. I'll see you at home," Jackson said leaning over to give Sam a kiss goodbye.

Sam and Kate finished the game, and the Magic did pull it out for a win. Both of them were pleased about that, Kate especially. Even though Wes was off tonight, and he didn't score, they still won so hopefully he would be in a good mood when they chatted tonight.

Kate made her way home. Hanging her coat in the closet, she was glad to be home. She had been spending so much time with Wes. And while she loved the time she got to spend with him, she did wish they could spend more time at her house. It was a lot cozier than Wes's modern condo. It was a small house, but she made it just how she wanted it. In her living room, she had an overstuffed couch with lots of pillows and blankets. A big screen tv over the fireplace and built-in bookshelves on either side. Her kitchen had retro vibes with lots of pink. It was all just how she wanted it.

While she waited for Wes's call, she decided to dig out a box that had sat buried in her closet since she moved here. Moving all her boots, she pulled it out and opened it. In it were newspaper clippings, pictures, awards, all moments from her time in hockey. She had the puck from her last regular season game from high school where she had played a shutout and stopped thirty-two goals. That was an amazing night that she hadn't thought about in a long time. She took the puck and a few other mementos and made some room on the shelves in her living room. It was time to start putting some of the pieces back together.

Her laptop in her room started dinging and she went in and accepted the call from Wes. She was almost expecting a phone call and not a FaceTime since she thought he might go out for a little bit with the team tonight, but he was already in his hotel room.

"Hey you! Good game tonight," she said with a big smile.

"No, it wasn't," he said matter of factly.

"You guys won, so that's good," she said. She was a little thrown by his demeanor. He seemed upset, and she wasn't sure why. "Are you okay?"

"Yeah... I think I'm just in my head about tomorrow," he said quietly.

Florida. Kate hadn't even thought about that. She knew he had a bad time there, but he never really talked about it.

"Yeah, you'll be back in Florida. You played them last year, right?"

"We did. I hated it then too, but I think I'm worried about playing against Blake Kelly. He was out with an injury last year when we played them."

"If you don't mind talking about it, what happened there?" she asked.

He took a deep breath. She had never seen him look like this before, and she yearned to wrap her arms around him and make that look on his face disappear.

"I told you I never felt right going down there when I got drafted, but what do you do? The team culture wasn't how I liked to play. It wasn't a family feel from either the players or management. I got along with most of the guys well enough, but we just never clicked," he paused, taking another deep breath. "One night, we were at the bar. Blake Kelly was drinking, which was not great because we were midseason, and you know how it is. He'd had too much, and I caught him in the alley trying to force himself on a woman."

He stopped and ran his hand through his hair. "Of course, I pulled him off her and he swung on me. I defended myself until another one of our teammates came out and got him. I'm not sure where they went, but I checked on the woman and asked her if she wanted to go to the cops. She didn't. She was just glad it was over, but it did cause a scene. After that, a few other girls came out saying he had attacked them in the past. The woman from the bar did finally press charges. The organization managed to sweep it all under the rug, but I was called as a witness. Kelly was suspended for the season and had a crazy fine. He should've gone to fucking jail, but now he is back on the ice like nothing happened, and it's the first time I'm playing him since it all went down."

"That's fucked up. You shouldn't have to play him," she said adamantly. She knew some not great stuff had gone down in Florida, but she didn't know it was as bad as it was. "Is there anything they can do?"

"Conner and I went to talk to the coach, and they petitioned the league for us to not have to meet on the ice, but the official ruling was that since it was settled out of court, their hands were tied."

Kate didn't like to see him like this. Wes was usually fun and light. She could sense the heavy weight that was sitting on his shoulders. If she had known it was this bad, she would have figured out how to go to the game to be with him. That thought pulled her up short. She knew she was getting more serious with him, but that was a serious girlfriend thought. The idea of being in that kind of relationship again scared her. Maybe she needed to see someone. That was a thought she wanted to think about even less.

"That sucks. I'm so sorry you have to deal with that. I wish there was something I could do for you," she said.

"It is what it is," he said with a slow breath as he ran his hands through his hair. "What's in the box next to you?" he asked, looking for a subject change.

Sitting on her bed was the box she had dug out of her closet. She didn't realize it was in the frame. Pushing it further down the bed with her foot she said, "What box?"

"The box you just pushed away. Wrong move, Red, now you have to tell me." The quintessential Wes smirk sat on his face. The reappearance of that smirk was the only reason she was going to do it.

"I decided to look through some of my old stuff tonight," she said, pulling the box to her. "I got to talking to Sam tonight at Smokey's about some old hockey memories when we played together, and I just came home and continued the walk down memory lane," she said, taking the lid off the box.

"Is this the Kate McPhee box of hockey memories? Now I really wish I was there. Show me."

"It's nothing really, just some newspaper clippings, pictures, and a few game pucks."

"Like I said, show me," he said, egging her on.

She showed him a few pictures from college of her on the ice and some incredible saves she pulled off.

"Here's this one," she said, holding up a picture of her and her three brothers on the ice.

"How old were you in that one?" he asked.

She turned the picture to check. That smile on her face pulled at something deep inside of her. "Well, if Conner's toothless grin is any indication, I would say we were eight."

"You guys have all been playing together that long?"

She shrugged. "McPhee's play hockey. It's what we do."

"I wanna see you on the ice again."

She just glared at him.

"I said what I said. And I know it's going to happen."

She thought about protesting, but on some level, she hoped he was right. She would love to play again, and that thought was surprising. She had been trying to fight it since she got back on the ice but playing and the walk down memory lane she and Sam had taken had her thinking.

"Don't they have a recreation league there? You should play. I'll come cheer you on," he said.

The thought of him in the crowd for her and of course his normal demeanor returning all settled deep within her. Maybe she could do this.

"I wish there was something I could do to help take your mind off tomorrow," she said.

"Well, there is something you can do for me," he said with a cocked eyebrow.

"Oh, there is? Well, why don't you tell me what you have in mind." She had a pretty good idea of what he had in mind.

"I keep thinking about that picture you sent me of you in my jersey. And I have to tell you Red, I'm hard just thinking about it." The look in his eyes had turned molten and she felt it deep in her core.

"Show me."

"Are we doing this?" he asked, his hand moving down to stroke something that was off camera.

"Just because I'm not there with you doesn't mean I can't distract you with my body from here," she said, trying to be brave. This was out of her comfort zone, but she really wanted to. And if you're dating someone who spends so much time on the road, you have to do what you have to do. And this could be fun.

"I'll be right back," she said, moving off her bed. She went over and put on his jersey...and nothing else. She got back onto her bed and his jaw dropped.

"Damn...you look amazing."

"Take your shirt off," she said.

He immediately obeyed and slipped his t-shirt over his head.

"Now your shorts."

He wiggled his shorts off and laid back against his head-board. His cock was erect, and he began to stroke it lazily.

"Fuck, Wes. You're so hot," she said, neediness creeping into her voice.

"Yeah, you like what you see?" he asked with his cocky smirk.

"You know I do."

"What about you? What are you wearing under that jersey?"

She shifted her weight bringing up her feet, her knees bent showing him that she was not wearing the cheeky underwear she'd had on in the picture. This time she was bare. He took a sharp inhale and began to work himself a little faster.

"Touch yourself for me."

Her hand reached between her legs.

"Damn, you look so fucking good. Are you wet for me?"

She dipped her fingers into her core and brought them back up to circle her clit. "Yes," she moaned.

"I love watching those dirty fingers. You're driving me mad."

She could feel the desire pooling deep inside. She began to work her fingers faster. She plunged them back, deep inside of her.

"That's right, fuck yourself with your fingers," he panted out, his own hand now firmly stroking his cock.

Her breaths turned into pants as she worked her fingers

in and out of her wet center. She was getting close. She brought them up to her clit and began to work circles as she moaned.

"You're so perfect," he growled out as he stroked himself faster.

She felt her release building inside of her. Moans began to escape her lips as she quickly circled her clit.

"That's right, make yourself come for me," he said between his own pants.

And that is just what she did, after a few more circles she gave into the pleasure and pulsed for him.

"Fuck," he groaned out. Her eyes opened just in time to see him pumping his own release all over his taut stomach.

"Damn, that was hot," she said, still laid back against her headboard trying to catch her breath.

"You can say that again. Consider me distracted," he breathed, his cocky smirk returning to his face.

She gave a contented sigh and moved to a more upright position. "I miss you," she said.

"I miss you too. Why don't you get some sleep and I'll go clean up? I'll talk to you tomorrow."

"I'm here if you need anything. I mean that, Wes."

"I appreciate it. I'm just going to get tomorrow over with and come home to you."

"Sounds like a plan. Goodnight."

"Goodnight," he said with a wink.

She closed her laptop and smiled to herself. She had never done anything like that before, but she had a feeling it wouldn't be her last time. Two more nights until she would be in his arms again, and she was ready to be there.

CHAPTER 22

KATE

The next morning Kate had to drag herself out of bed and made it to the store ten minutes late. She wasn't used to being up so late but talking to Wes was worth it. She texted him when she got up wishing him a good day...and she may have sent a picture. That thought made her blush again. It was still hard for her to believe she was in a relationship with a professional hockey player four years younger than she was. And sent him sex pictures. Not nudes, but definitely ones she hoped Conner didn't see this time.

"I was wondering when ye might show up this morning."

Kate looked up only to find Bridget standing right in front of the register. She hadn't even heard her come in.

"I was only a few minutes late," she said.

Bridget only looked at her with a raised eyebrow as she made her tea.

"Have a late night, did ye? I didn't think yere fellow was in town."

"No, he's on the road. We were just up late talking after his game," Kate said.

"Ahh, so at least admitting now that he's yere fellow," said Bridget with a very pleased smile.

"Yes, fine. I'll admit it. Are you happy?"

"I'm very happy, my dear."

"Well, good. Can I ask you something?"

"Of course."

"Did you read Wes's cards at the winter festival?"

"Aye, I did."

"What did you say to him?"

"Well, I can't tell ye that now, can I?" she said with a knowing glance. "Also, I can't say I remember, I read lots of fortunes that day."

"You're right...it was probably a silly thing to ask," she said quickly.

"Not silly at all. I've never read your cards, have I Kate?"

Kate just shook her head. Tarot readings weren't really something she had any vested interest in or any belief in, but there was something about Bridget she could never quite put her finger on. If anyone could tell the future, it was this woman before her. "I haven't had that pleasure."

"Ahh, well lass, we must rectify that as soon as we can," Bridget said with a twinkle in her eye.

"We'll see," Kate said, knowing it would most likely happen.

"Well, I need to get going. Poppy is coming to the store this morning to help me with some reorganizing. Thank you for my cuppa tea," she said as she left.

As she was walking out the door Hannah was walking in.

"Hi Hannah," Kate said. "What can I do for you this morning?"

"Well, I just came to finalize some stuff with you. My book is coming out at the beginning of September."

"That's wonderful! That should give us a good amount of time to plan the launch party and get some good publicity."

"Yeah, that's what I'm hoping for. I would love to have a big event with a Highlands theme. It will be right around Graham's birthday too," she said.

"That sounds perfect. I'll talk to Mr. Fipp and look at the town schedule to see what date works best. Then we can schedule a meeting," Kate said.

"Perfect. And hey, are you busy tonight?"

"Ummm, I was planning on watching the game," she said. She wasn't sure why she didn't say Sam had invited her to game night. It felt weird since it wasn't even his house.

"Poppy and Josh are hosting a game night, and I'm sure Sam will have the game on. It'll be Graham and I, Jackson and Sam, and I believe Liam and Lexi."

"Sam mentioned something about it, I might stop by. I still can't believe Liam James lives here in Mystic Falls. It's weird seeing his face on all the magazines, but then he's next to me in the check-out lane when I'm buying frozen pizza."

"I know, it did take some getting used to and I only moved here a few years before he did. He's really nice though, more down to earth than you would think for a pop super star."

"He does seem that way. What the hell, as long as I can have the game on, count me in," she said.

"Great! I'm so happy you're coming. Poppy and Josh always have way too much food, so don't worry about dinner."

"Sounds good. Thanks Hannah," she said.

After Hannah left, Kate looked down at her phone. Wes had sent her a picture of his own. He was in the hotel bathroom, the counter of the sink blocked the good stuff, but the mirror behind him showed his perfect ass and Kate had to clench her thighs.

Later that day, Kate texted Wes that she was thinking about him, but with the exception of the sexy photo this morning, he had been strangely quiet. She knew he was probably in his head about all of this, and she hated it. But what could she do about it from here? Now, she was sitting outside of Poppy and Josh's house, working up the courage to go in. She'd been in this house many times before. The previous owners used to host town functions here, but she hadn't been since she was a kid. It had sat empty for over a decade before they finally bought it.

As she was working up the courage to go in, Sam's truck pulled up. Perfect, she would be able to go in with Sam and Jackson and not have to deal with showing up when the hosts hadn't actually invited her. Both Sam and Hannah had invited her, and she knew Josh and Poppy well enough to know that she was more than welcome, but this was definitely outside of her comfort zone.

"Hey Kate, I'm glad you decided to come. We got thirty minutes till puck drop and with you here, Poppy won't complain about me watching the game and not playing games," he said.

"It is not that serious," Jackson said to him. He took Kate by the hand and placed it in the crook of his elbow. "Let's head in, I'm starving."

Kate walked up the stairs to this grand house. As they entered, Kate took it all in. It was as she remembered it with the high ceilings and grand staircase, but they had done lots of work. It still had the feel of a beautiful old home, but very well kept, with some modern updates.

"Kate, hi, I'm so glad you could make it. Can I take your coat?" said a smiling very pregnant Poppy.

"I'll take her coat," Sam said as he made his way to the coat closet.

"Sam, I'm just pregnant. I can still do things," she said with minor irritation in her voice. "Come on in, Kate. We have plenty of food in the kitchen."

"She's just mad because I made her stop working last week. I think she needs a little rest before she has this baby," Sam said quietly.

"I can still hear you," she called from the kitchen. "And really, I feel fine."

"And you look beautiful," Josh said as he snuck in behind her and gave her a kiss on the cheek. "Lexi and Liam are running late. They should be here soon," he said.

"Here," Poppy said as she handed Kate a plate. "Help yourself. We'll set games up in the dining room a bit later."

Kate was quiet and observing everything. She knew most of these people from living her life here in Mystic Falls, Poppy and Josh had been one year ahead of her. And although Hannah recently moved here with Graham, she knew her well enough from the bookstore. All these people were great, but the energy of all of them in this house was welcoming. They all seemed to genuinely love and care for each other. While Kate didn't feel a part of that, they still made her feel very welcome. Like someday, if she let them in, they would be like that with her. She hadn't belonged to a group of people like this since her college days. It would be amazing to be a part of a group of people like that again.

As she finished eating, Sam came over to her. "Pucks about to drop. Wanna go watch the game?"

"Are you really going to watch hockey the whole time, Sam?" Poppy complained.

"Hey, it's a big game. The Magic could clinch a spot in the playoffs. And Kate's boyfriend is playing his old team, and there is bad blood," he said.

Kate gave him a look, "Thanks for throwing me under the bus," she said, only half joking.

"Oh, I didn't know you were dating one of the Magic players? Isn't your brother on that team?"

"You know damn well her brother is on the team," Sam said to his sister.

"Yes, he is. And yes, I am dating Wes Darling," said Kate.

"Wes Darling," Poppy said. "Isn't he the hot blonde one that was here for the winter festival?"

"Yeah, that's him."

"I met him when I played at Madison Square Garden once. He seemed like a good guy," Liam chimed in.

"He is," said Kate with a smile.

"Well, I'll allow it this time," Poppy said, giving her brother a look. "But only because of Kate."

"Thanks Poppy, I appreciate that," Kate said.

"You'll have to come back another time and actually play games with us. It just might be a while," Poppy said, patting her belly.

"I'd love to come another time," Kate said, surprised by the honesty of her statement. She was enjoying her time here.

A little while later, everyone was settling down. Sam, Hannah, Liam and Kate were all in the back room watching the game while everyone else was visiting and playing games. Her and Sam talked about the game and to her surprise Hannah kept up.

"You know a lot about hockey," Kate said.

"Yeah, my dad used to take me to Rangers games all the time growing up. I've always loved the sport."

The first period was over, and it was still 0-0. Wes and Conner were both playing great, although this game was very physical. They had both taken some pretty big hits, but the defensemen were right there. Ethan was on fire. Kate liked watching him play. All goalies had their own style, and Ethan was good. He was closing in on 6 '5 so he played much differently than Kate did, but he was still fun. He liked to trash talk other players, and Kate loved to watch them get riled up because they knew the unwritten rule of hockey. Never touch the goalie. Ethan totally used that to his advantage. It was fun to watch.

Before the break, Wes was being interviewed. Kate watched it very carefully, trying to see where he was at, knowing this game was going to be very hard for him.

"How is it being here tonight, playing your old team? There have been rumors that you and Blake Kelly have some bad blood." said the reporter.

"I'm just happy to be here playing the game we all love. I'm happy being with the Magic. We're a family," he said very diplomatically.

"Good luck with the rest of the game, Wes."

"Thanks," he said, winking at the camera and heading into the locker room.

Kate loved those little winks, because she knew they were just for her.

The second period was underway, and Florida was skating with a giant chip on its shoulder. Brishnavik managed to snipe a goal from the blue line making the game 1-0 for the Magic, and Florida really started pushing. Conner took a high stick to the face and came away with a bloody mouth. Kate cringed. She hadn't seen a game quite this physical in a long time. During the power play, two giant Florida defensemen both slammed Wes in a corner while they were trying to dig out the puck. He laid on the ice for a long moment and skated over to the bench. When he was back on the ice and skating his next shift, Kate breathed a sigh of relief. That relief was even bigger when the buzzer ended for the end of the second period.

"Wow, that's a rough period. Florida is out for blood, and the refs don't seem to be calling much." Sam seethed next to her. Kate wished she was seething with anger too. That would feel better than the panic filled pit that was forming in her stomach. She wanted this hockey game over, right now she didn't even care who won as long as everyone made it out injury-free.

The game was picking back up, and whatever the coach said in the locker room had worked. The Magic came out looking to win. Within the first two minutes, Conner got the puck to Wes and he scored. It was now a tie game 2-2. A few minutes later, Wes snagged the puck for a turnover and was heading down the ice, but before he made it out of the neutral zone, Blake Kelly skated right into him. He planted himself for a hit, but then he leaned in with his shoulder as Wes hit into him. Kelly lifted his arm, flipping Wes up over his head and slammed him down on the ice. He landed hard with his head and shoulder, and his arm crumpled under him. And Kate watched in horror as Kelly raised his stick and brought it down hard in the middle of Wes's back.

Kate stood with a gasp as his helmet rolled away from him on the ice. He just laid there for what seemed like an eternity.

"Get up," she pleaded, but he didn't. He laid there still as Conner skated past him and threw down his gloves and started punching Blake Kelly. The camera didn't even watch the fight. All eyes were pinned to Wes, who was still motionless on the ice.

"Get up. Get up. Get up!" Kate was shouting at the TV.

Sam stood next to her, and she barely registered his hand on her back. All the trainers for the Magic were now out on the ice with him, and he was still motionless. They were pulling a stretcher out onto the ice when they took the camera off the ice and the commentators started breaking down the hit.

"Fuck! I knew I should've gone down for him," she said in a panic, pulling out her phone.

"Are you okay?" Sam asked.

"I have to get to Florida. He had a thing with Blake Kelly because that guy is a dick. I knew he might retaliate, but I didn't think it would be that bad. I need to get down there," she said as she pulled up the airport in Glendale on her phone searching for the fastest way to get to Florida.

"That was a hard hit. Blake Kelly is getting ejected from the game. Conner McPhee has five for fighting. They are taking a five-minute break before resuming the game. We'll be back after the commercial with an update on Wes Darling."

"Hey Lexi," Liam called out. "Feel like going to Florida tonight?"

"Sure," she answered from the other room without even looking up from the chess game she and Graham were engaged in, no idea what had just happened in here.

"That didn't look good," Sam said.

And she fucking knew that. He didn't move. His arm looked like it was broken under him the way it was laying, and he was KO'd.

"Kate, I have access to a plane in Glendale. We can get you there faster than any commercial flight can," Liam said.

"Are you serious?" she asked him, eyes wide. She should have refused such a grand gesture from someone she hardly knew, but right now, she was overtaken with the need to get to Wes as soon as possible. She knew he had a concussion and probably other injuries. And she knew he was already nervous about this game because he knew something like this could happen. The fury that he had been put in this situation was overwhelming, but not as overwhelming as her need to get to him.

"Yeah, we can leave in an hour. Do you need to go home to get anything?"

"Ummm... yeah," she said in a daze, reaching for her keys.

Liam reached for her hand and took the keys. "Hey, I'll

drive you home. Lexi can follow us, and we'll leave from there."

"Yeah, okay," she nodded numbly. She would later deal with the fact that she was about to fly in Liam James's private jet, right now she just wanted to be with Wes.

CHAPTER 23

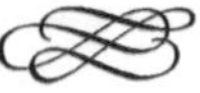

WES

es woke up in a hospital bed with a splitting headache. He looked around the dimly lit room and tried to figure out what was going on. His brain was a mess of pain and fog. Bits and pieces of the game started coming back to him, but he couldn't remember much. Looking down, he found his arm in a cast and a sling holding it close to his body. As he was starting to come to himself more, the pain was coming with it. His head was pounding, and the entire left side of his upper body was in pain.

"Mr. Darling how are you feeling?" he barely registered the woman's voice.

Turning slowly to face her, the nurse was monitoring the machines he was hooked up to. "I'm just going to take some quick vitals and I'll go get the doctor," she said as she took his blood pressure and temperature.

He still hadn't said anything. He was too out of it to really understand what was happening. After she left one of the team doctors and Conner walked into his room.

"Hey man, how you holding up?" Conner asked.

All Wes could do was nod, although he did take note of

Conner's black eye, busted lip, and the cut on the bridge of his nose. He cocked a small smile. "Don't worry man, I fucked him up real good," Conner said.

The Doctor from the hospital and Scott, the team doctor, came next to Wes and shined a light in his eyes.

"You have a grade three concussion, but that's to be expected the way your head bounced off the ice. Are you in much pain?"

Wes nodded.

"I'll see what we can get you. You have a cracked humerus bone and fractured your radius in two different places in your left arm. Your shoulder's dislocated and you have three broken ribs. Good news you should make a full recovery," said the trainer.

"Did we win?" asked Wes.

"No, we lost 4-2," Conner said.

"Fuck," Wes grumbled out.

"Don't worry man, we'll still make playoffs."

"Did you fuck up Kelly?" Wes asked.

"You know I did."

"What happened?" Wes asked Conner. The room was lit very dimly, but even this amount of light hurt his head.

"After that dirty hit, I took him out. He got ejected from the game for unsportsmanlike roughing and I got five for fighting. Once they got you off the ice there was a five-minute break and the game was a fucking mess after that," Conner said as he ran his hand through his hair. He sat down next to the bed. "The team is on their way back, but I stayed back with Scott," he said motioning to the team doctor. "And coach is here too. He is dealing with the GM and the organi-zation. Kelly will for sure get a suspension, but coach is trying to get him out of the league."

"How long am I out?" Wes asked the doctor.

"We will assess that later. Right now, you just need to

heal. You have a nasty concussion. We'll need to start concussion protocol on you. Do you have someone to stay with you?"

He looked at Conner.

"I can stay with him," Conner immediately replied.

Wes gave his head a gentle shake, then winced from the pain. "Have you talked to Kate?"

"No, do you want me to call her?"

"Yeah, I want to talk to her."

"Okay," Conner said as he dug into his pocket as another Doctor came into the room. "I'll step out and call her."

He watched as Conner stepped out of the room and the Dr started his examination.

"I just need to ask you a few questions, Mr. Darling."

After the Doctor left, he had established he had a stage three concussion, and all the other stuff the team doctor had told him about. The only new information was he would have to stay the night for observation. The brain fog was setting back in, and he was having trouble keeping his eyes open.

CHAPTER 24

KATE

"You have to let me see him. I'm his girlfriend," Kate said loudly with increasing anger to the receptionist in the hospital.

"Ma'am, I cannot let anyone in to see Mr. Darling. I am under strict orders."

"I understand that, but I am his girlfriend! I need to see him."

"Let her in," she heard a familiar voice say.

Turning around, she had never been more relieved to see Conner in her entire life.

"Fine," the receptionist said, her voice dripping with irritation. "Go on back."

"How is he?" Kate said quickly as she ran into Conner and gave him a rough hug. He winced but hugged her back. "How are you?" she asked, finally taking him in. "You almost never fight on the ice.

"Only when it's warranted, and it was fucking warranted. I'll be fine. Wes is pretty messed up. He was asking for you."

"Is he okay? Did he break his arm? It looked fucked up on the ice."

"Yeah, he broke his arm in two different places and cracked in another. He has a dislocated shoulder and grade three concussion, but he should be okay," Conner said.

"Can I see him?"

"He's with the doctors right now. I'll take you to see him when they are done. He just sent me out to call you anyway. But seriously Kate, how did you get here so fast?"

"Liam James."

"Excuse me?" Conner said, not quite following.

"You knew he moved to Mystic Falls, right?"

Conner nodded.

"I was at a game night at Poppy and Josh's and he and Lexi were there. Sam and I were watching the game and I kind of freaked out, so Liam James flew down with me in his private jet."

"Only in Mystic Falls," Conner said, shaking his head.

"Right? He said they could fly me back, but I'm hoping I can text him back and tell him they don't have to because I don't plan on leaving Wes's side. When can I see him?"

"Soon. Let's go to the room and wait there," he said, opening the door for her.

She followed him, her panic starting to ease now that she knew he wasn't seriously injured and would make a recovery with time.

"What is going to happen to Kelly?"

"He was ejected from the game, but I hope he gets kicked the fuck out of the league. Wes and I petitioned to have Kelly sit out of this game, but the organization wouldn't go for it, and look what fucking happened. He's suspended for sure, but I hope he's out of the league. He's a fucking menace."

It took a lot to piss off Conner, and he was pissed. Good. So was she. She just wanted to see Wes, but it was a small comfort to have Conner here with her.

They got to Wes's room, but the door was still closed.

"Let's have a seat. We can see him when they're done," he said, bringing her over to the bench. "So, he gets hurt and you hop on a plane?" Conner asked with raised eyebrows.

"Yeah," Kate looked, confused by his question.

"I didn't realize things were so serious between you guys. You only met him two months ago," he said.

"I know, I just needed to get to him."

"You really like him, don't you?" he asked with a soft look on his face.

She nodded slowly and looked him in the eyes. "I do. It just kind of happened and I'm so fucking scared. But yeah...I really like him, Conner." Her voice caught. She had been so fixated on getting here that she had pushed all these emotions aside, but right now they were rushing through her.

Conner wrapped his arms around her, and she cried on his shoulder. She hadn't cried on him like this since everything went down with Jason. This wasn't like that though. When that had happened, she was broken, but right now, she was just worried.

"He's really okay?" she asked, her voice muffled in Conner's shoulder.

"Yeah, KitKat, he's pretty banged up, but he'll be okay."

She took a few breaths and pulled herself back together. "Do you think he is out for the season?" She thought she knew the answer to that one herself and she knew he would be pissed.

Conner nodded. "It's not official yet, but considering we only have four weeks left of the regular season, he's out."

"Fuck," Kate sighed out.

"Yeah...I'm so pissed this happened. It shouldn't have happened," Conner said with his head between his hands and his arms propped up on his knees. "This whole situation is so fucked."

The door to Wes's room opened and out walked the doctors.

"How is he?" Conner asked.

"He'll make a full recovery in time," said the Dr. "We are going to keep him overnight, but he should be able to head home tomorrow. You can decide if he stays here for a bit or you can find a way to fly home comfortably tomorrow."

"The team jet is waiting. We'll let him decide tomorrow," said the team doctor.

"Sounds good. We'll be monitoring him tonight. Are you Kate?" the doctor asked her.

"Yeah," she quickly said.

"He's been asking for you, but he needs sleep, so keep it quick. One of you can stay with him tonight. Just let them know and we can get you set up."

Conner started to say, "I can stay –" Kate cut him off with a glare. "Or you can stay," he said with a chuckle.

"I'm gonna go find coach and give him an update on Wes. You guys head on in," said the team doctor before walking down the hallway.

Apprehension filled Kate as she walked to the door. She had fought hard to get here, and she was dying to see him, but she was nervous.

"Come on, KitKat. He's okay," Conner said as he pushed the door open.

Her eyes found Wes and her heart broke into a million pieces. She had never seen him like this before, and while she knew he would look rough, she was not prepared for this. Half of his face was bruised and swollen. He also had a cast and sling holding his shoulder in place, but the worst part was the vacant look in his eyes. Kate had seen that look before. Playing hockey, she had been around her fair share of head injuries but seeing him like this was awful.

"Kate," he said as their eyes connected and she was vaguely aware of the tears streaming down her face. "Aww, don't cry Red," he said, reaching out for her. She took his hand, and he weakly squeezed her. "Do I look that bad?"

"No, you're as handsome as ever," she said as she moved closer to his bed.

"I find that hard to believe. How did you get here so fast?"

"I was watching the game and I flew down as soon as you got hurt," she said, wiping a tear away with her free hand.

"I knew you loved me just as much as I love you," he said.

Those words. He had just said he loved her. He had never said that before. Was that just the head injury speaking? Did she love him? If she thought about it...well, she wouldn't think about that right now. She didn't have time for it. Right now, all that mattered was Wes. She was here and he would be okay.

He gave a long blink. Kate could see he was ready to sleep. It was well after midnight.

"One of us can stay with you tonight. Which McPhee do you want, Wes?" Kate asked, knowing the answer.

"Only the best one," he said, winking at her with his eye that wasn't swollen. "Sorry man, but you're just not as cute," he said to Conner.

"What the hell? I'm plenty cute. All the pictures Sasha keeps posting to the Magic's Instagram prove I'm more than cute. But you have chosen," he said with feigned offense.

Kate smiled at him. As much as she was an emotional wreck right now, it felt good to be here with Conner and Wes. They were two of the best guys she had ever known and probably two of the most important people in her life, although that wasn't a thought she was ready for quite yet.

All she wanted to do now was focus on Wes and getting him home and healed.

"I'll find a nurse to get you some extra pillows and blankets," Conner said as he patted Kate on the arm and left.

"You scared me," she said as she gently sat on the bed next to Wes.

"I'm sorry, Red. I didn't mean to scare you, but I have to tell you how glad I am to see your face." Reaching up his hand he cupped her face. She nuzzled into him. "Come here, lay with me."

"There's not enough room," she said.

"Sure there is," he said, attempting to scoot over.

"Stop, you're hurt."

"I know and feeling you next to me would help me so much. Would you really deny a wounded man?" he said, giving her a pitiful look.

She gave him a look, but then settled in next to him.

"This side of my body is good, I promise. It feels so good to have you next to me." He held out his good arm and she snuggled into him, and he put his arm around her.

"I'm so glad you're okay," she said as she melted into him.

"I'm so glad you're here," he said as he stroked her arm.

She laid there with her head on his chest. His arm had stilled, and his breathing slowed. His eyes were closed and even with a painful swollen face, he looked peaceful. She wished she could stay snuggled into his side for the rest of the night, but there wasn't room for two of them in this bed, especially with the way they would be checking on him all night. Trying to not wake him, she slid out of his grasp.

Conner came back in with a blanket and an extra pillow. "That chair reclines," he said motioning to the chair on the other side of the bed. "Are you good here tonight?"

"Yeah, I'll be okay."

"If you're sure. Coach, Dr Scott, and I are going to check

into the hotel across the street. We're taking the team plane back to Glendale tomorrow once Wes is released. You're all set to fly with us."

"Thank you, Conner," she said, giving him a hug. "Go ice your face," she said, giving him a gentle shove.

"That's exactly what coach said. If you need anything, I'm across the street," he said, pulling her in for one last hug. "Whatever this is, I'm happy for you," he said, gesturing between her and Wes.

"Thanks."

"Okay, see you tomorrow."

After he left, she got herself situated and texted Liam. The fact that she had the personal phone number of Liam James was something to unpack tomorrow as well. There was lots of stuff to unpack tomorrow, and the list just kept growing.

Kate - Thank you so much for getting me here. I cannot tell you how much I appreciate it. The team is going to fly me home tomorrow, so you guys can head back whenever you are ready.

Liam - Is he okay? How are you holding up?

Kate - He has a grade three concussion, a broken arm, and a couple broken ribs, but he'll be okay. I'm sure the team will make a statement. I'm okay, thank you again for everything. I don't know how I can repay you.

Liam - I'm happy to do it for a friend.

Holy fuck. She was friends with Liam James. Her life had taken a turn in January. She went from never talking to anyone except Bridget and occasionally her family, to having a group of friends, and a boyfriend. Now she was friends with Liam James. She didn't quite know how to come to terms with all of that.

Kate - Thank you

That was all she knew to say. She got into the chair and tried to get comfortable next to Wes.

CHAPTER 25

When Wes woke up the next morning, he was still really fucking sore, but some of the brain fog had cleared. Next to his bed Kate was curled up in the reclining chair giving little snores. He wished she could have spent the night with him in this bed, but it wasn't very big. Hopefully tonight he would be home and in his own bed with her.

The door opened and in walked the doctors.

"You seem to be doing better," said the Dr. looking over Wes's chart. "Your vitals are great. Your concussion is where we would expect it to be. No screens or harsh lights. You're on concussion protocol for fourteen days," he said.

Wes nodded. Concussion protocol was commonplace for athletes, so he knew the drill.

"How long am I out for?" he asked them.

"We'll determine that once we are home," said the team doctor.

"Am I out for the season?"

"We'll figure it out, but the important thing is a dislocated shoulder and a clean break should heal one hundred percent.

At least it wasn't a joint injury, those are much harder to come back from."

Wes knew he was right. It could have been so much worse, but that wasn't much of a consolation right now. Right now, he just wanted to get back on the ice as soon as possible. That and he wanted Kelly out of the league.

"Any news on Kelly?" Wes asked as his coach entered the room.

"The league is meeting today. He'll be suspended for sure, but we're hoping to get him kicked out of the league. We could even discuss legal ramifications when you're feeling better."

Wes nodded. He didn't know if he wanted that, but he did want him out of the league. The three men continued talking as he looked over to see Kate sitting in the chair folding the blanket she had been sleeping with. He sighed contentedly as she gave him a little smile.

"We can start getting you released, but someone has to sign saying you won't be alone for forty-eight hours because of your concussion."

"You and Ethan live in the same building. Could he stay with you?" asked Coach Wagner.

He looked over to Kate, "Will you stay with me?" he asked.

She just nodded, the coach gave her a second glance, he seemed to be piecing together who she was.

"Okay, we'll get the paperwork going," he said as he left.

As he walked out, Conner came in. "I come bearing breakfast and coffee," he said tossing Kate a bag of fast-food breakfast. "Sausage egg and cheese biscuit and a coffee so sweet with so much cream it's basically a warm milk shake," he said to Kate with a smile.

"You remembered," she said with a small chuckle.

"Some things you never forget, KitKat. How are you doing, man? Two egg McMuffins?"

"Thanks, and I've been better, but I'm at least a little more with it today. You look like shit too," Wes said.

"Ehhh, it's all good. I haven't had a good fight in years. I couldn't let Cash and Taylor have all the fun."

The coach and doctors left the room and the three of them ate breakfast and got ready for the day. He was ready to get home. He was ready to be in his bed curled up with his girl.

After a while, Conner went out to see if he could get a timeline for when they would be leaving, and that gave Kate and Wes a moment together.

"Come here," he said, reaching for her.

Taking his hand she came and sat on the edge of his bed, "Thank you so much for coming. I'm so glad you are here."

"Of course," she said.

"Kiss me," he said, pulling on her hand.

"I don't want to hurt you," she said timidly.

"You won't hurt me, come here," he said, pulling her closer.

She leaned up and gently kissed him. He wanted her to be less gentle. He wanted her to actually kiss him, but there would be time for that. Right now, she was here, and he could touch her, and that magic that danced between them whenever they kissed drowned out any pain he was feeling.

Pulling her next to him, and getting her to snuggle in, he kissed the top of her head.

"Thank you for staying with me. You're going to be much better company than Ethan," he said, laying his head on hers.

"Of course, I hate that this happened."

"Me too. I wish I could say it's part of the job, because things like this could happen in any game. Mistakes happen, but this didn't feel like a mistake."

"It wasn't a fucking mistake," she said darkly. Something inside of him smiled at her anger on his behalf. "He fucking flipped you while you were flying down the ice and then hit you with his stick. I hope you never have to play him again."

"You and me both, Red."

"When you were just lying there on the ice...I thought...well I just hated it," she growled out.

"Hey," he said, rubbing her arm. "I'm okay. I'll be back on the ice good as new soon," he said then he kissed the top of her head.

After a while, they all came back into his room and got him checked out. By the time they made it to the airport, and all got loaded into the plane, Wes was worn out. Head injuries are like that. He slept most of the way home. When they got back there was some of the team there to greet him. He was happy to see Ethan there.

"I was worried about you, man. Conner fucked him right up," Ethan said, and Conner gave him an appreciative nod.

"Good," said Wes. "I'm going to be fine, hopefully I'll be back on the ice soon."

Wes tried to ignore the faces the people around him made when he said that. The doctor said he would make a complete recovery. Hopefully he will be back by playoffs. They actually had a shot this year, but something told him not to get his hopes up.

Getting home from Florida had been exhausting. He was once again painfully loaded into an SUV to get them home. But now that he and Kate were home he was ready for some peace and quiet, but it looked like Scott was heading up to the apartment with him.

"Is this necessary?" Wes asked grimly. He was just ready to be alone and with Kate and start to move past this whole thing.

"I'll be out of your hair soon," he promised. "I just want to see where you guys are, give Kate some instructions and get you resting. I also have some painkillers for you."

"Let's get this over with," he said. He dug into his pocket with his good hand and unlocked the door. It felt good to be home, but he was exhausted and had a headache and was still in quite a bit of pain.

They walked in behind him, and Scott and Kate started going over concussion protocol. The rest was pretty straight forward. The organization was just crossing it's t's and dotting it's i's, because they were just as eager to get him back on the ice as he was. But he knew they wouldn't let him back before he was ready, not that he really wanted to be. Getting back in too soon could turn this injury that would heal into one he would have to baby his entire career.

"Alright," Scott said, "you guys are all set. On Monday come into the training center and we'll take a look at you and talk about getting you back on the ice."

"Sounds good, man."

"If you have any questions Kate, call me. I put my number on the paper with the instructions."

"Thanks," she said. "I'll call if I have any questions."

Kate walked him to the door while Wes sat on the couch.

"Is he gone yet?"

"Yes, he's gone," Kate said as she came and sat next to him.

Wes put out his arm and she snuggled right in. He was so ready to be alone with her like this. He just needed a break from it all, and it looked like he was about to get one.

"Let's get comfortable and get into bed," he said.

"Do you want to shower first?" she asked.

"You going to shower with me?" he asked with an eyebrow cocked.

"Wes, no. There will be none of that for at least forty-eight hours."

"Not even a little?" he asked, nuzzling the side of her head.

"Nope, not even a little. I'm taking care of you mister. Now let's get you in the shower and I'll get you something to eat. Then we can snuggle in bed, and you can enjoy my lovely company."

"But not your equally lovely body?"

"Wes. Don't make this harder than it is going to be," she said as she leaned over to kiss his cheek.

"Being around you for two days and not being able to do that...it's gonna be very hard, Red. If you get my drift."

"You're incorrigible," she said as she slapped his good leg. "Let's get you comfy and in bed."

Kate helped him into the shower. Once he was done, she helped to get him situated in bed and went to make him food. His phone buzzed on his bedside table, he knew screens were a no no, but he glanced long enough to see his mother was calling.

"Hi mom."

"Baby, how are you?" she said, her voice dripping with concern.

"I'm okay. I have a broken arm and a dislocated shoulder and a concussion, but I'll be okay. I will live to skate another day."

"Good, is Ethan taking care of you?"

"Ummm no." He hadn't actually told his mom he was seeing anyone, and this didn't seem like a great time, but it was what it was. "My friend Kate is staying with me."

"Your friend Kate?" he could hear the smile in her voice.

"Yeah, she's Conner McPhee's sister."

"Okay, well you sound like you need sleep. Call me later when you are feeling up to it and tell me all about your new friend Kate."

"Thanks mom, I'll call you soon."

"Okay baby, I hope you feel better."

"Love you," he said.

"Love you too."

He hung up the phone and set it back on the nightstand before closing his eyes and taking a deep breath. His head was pounding again. When he opened his eyes he caught sight of Kate standing in the doorway holding a plate.

"Thanks, Red," he said. She gave him his plate and went around the bed to have a seat.

"That was your mom?"

He nodded. "She's worried about me, but I told her I'd be fine." Wes could feel the irritation in his voice. It was a combination of feeling helpless and being in pain. It all made him feel on edge.

"Are you doing okay?" Kate asked tentatively. She seemed to pick up on that irritation, but he didn't want to talk about it.

"Should we watch a movie?" he asked instead.

"No screens," she said with a slight head shake.

"Seriously? No screens and no sex. It's like the 1800's up in here," he groaned.

"Actually, that's not a bad idea," she said, getting up off the bed.

"What's not a bad idea?" he asked as she walked over to the bookshelves.

She perused his shelves while he started to eat.

"A-ha!" she said, turning around with a copy of Pride and Prejudice in her hands. "Have you read this one yet?"

A warm glow settled deep in his chest, and the irritation he was feeling before evaporated. "Are you going to read to me?"

"I thought it might be a good way to pass the time," she said softly.

"I love it," he said, then patted the spot next to him on the bed. "Come over here and introduce me to Jane Austen."

She started reading while he finished eating. Once he was done, they both got fully into bed. She laid on his chest and read to him. It wasn't bad, but he didn't really care what she was reading. She could be reading him a cookbook and he would feel just as content. He was still pissed he had to be going through all of this because of fucking Blake Kelly, but having her here next to him, reading to him, made it better.

"Ya know, I don't think anyone has read to me since I was a kid," he said.

"That's a shame. I love to be read to and to read to people. It's relaxing."

His mouth cracked open with a yawn. "It sure is," he said. He could feel his eyelids getting heavy. The doctor said he would be tired, and he was. He tried to stay awake and listen but sleep eventually found him.

When he woke up Kate was gone and the sun was starting to sink. He must have been asleep for a couple hours. He went to get out of bed, forgetting about all of his injuries and winced, then eased himself up.

"Kate," he called.

"Yeah, I'll text you his address. I emailed mom what I need you guys to pick up from my house and the groceries we could use." She paused to listen as he rounded the couch. She smiled up and mouthed 'hi'. "Yeah, I have a spare set of keys in the drawer next to the refrigerator. Yep. Okay, I'll see you guys later."

She set her phone down on the coffee table next to a pad and paper. "How are you feeling? It's time for some pain meds."

"I could use 'em," he said, easing down next to her.

She walked over to the kitchen counter and got him a pill

and a glass of water. He picked up the notepad on the table. It was a list of things she needed and a to-do list.

"You've been busy," he said, taking the pill from her and swallowing it down.

"Yeah, I just need to take care of a few things if I'm going to be staying here for a while. My parents are driving my car here and picking me up some stuff from my house and some groceries. I still need to text Hannah and see if she will stop by Bridget's to ask her to take in any deliveries for the store. Bridget doesn't have a phone, it would be infuriating if it didn't suit her, but yeah, then I'm good to be here."

"Your parents are coming here?" he asked.

"Yeah, I think they're bringing some dinner too. My dad was worried about you. My mom was more concerned with why I was here taking care of you. I told them we had been dating since you were in Mystic Falls, and I swear my mom almost swooned. You made quite the impression," she said with a chuckle.

"Good, so your parents know now?" he asked.

"Yeah, which means everyone knows. Once my mom knows something, she likes to spread the word."

He laughed, "Yeah, I can see that," he said, relaxing back on the couch.

"They should be here in an hour or so. Do you want to spend more time with Elizabeth Bennett while we wait," she said holding up Pride and Prejudice.

"Get in here," he said, extending his arm. She snuggled right in picking up where they left off. He kicked his feet up on the extension of the sectional and Kate sat next to him. He put his arm around her and listened to the calming sound of her voice reading Jane Austen. Before long, his eyelids started to get heavy again, until he was fast asleep.

CHAPTER 26

KATE

After Wes had fallen asleep, Kate covered him with a blanket, got her phone, and went to the bedroom to call Hannah. She had already messaged Sofie that she wouldn't be at the bookstore this week. Sofie said she would cover a couple days and be there to let the groups meet that used the space. She needed to get moving on hiring Ashton. It would be good to have someone pick up the slack. There was work she could do here though, so she could start on that.

Pulling up Hannah's contact information she pushed the call button.

After two rings Hannah picked up.

"Hello," she answered.

"Hi Hannah, it's Kate. I was wondering if I could ask you to do me a favor."

"Of course, how is Wes? We were all worried about the two of you."

"He should make a full recovery, but he's pretty banged up."

"That's good, we've all been thinking about you. Is there anything you need?"

"Actually yes, can you please go over to Bridget's store and see if she can pick up any packages that get dropped off at the bookstore. I'm going to be here all week. She doesn't have a phone, or I would call her myself."

"That's no problem, I can swing by there tomorrow morning."

"I appreciate it. As soon as I get back, we can get started on your release party."

"That's fine, but please don't worry about that right now. Just take care of Wes. Is he out for the season?"

"They haven't said yet, but I think he probably will be."

"What's going to happen to the guy who hit him?"

"No word there either. The league is holding a hearing to see what will happen. Hopefully it's ruled as intent to injure."

"Okay, Kate, well, keep us posted. I'll talk to you soon. If you need anything else at all just let me know,"

"Thank you, Hannah, I really appreciate that,"

She sighed as she hung up. It felt good to have someone who she was starting to consider a friend. It had been a long time since she had let people in like this.

There was a small knock at the door. Kate had thought she would need to go down and let her parents in, but when she opened the door, to her surprise, it was Ethan.

"Hi Ethan," she said quietly as she opened the door, trying not to wake Wes.

"How is he?" he asked.

"He's sleeping right now, but he's okay."

"Is he being a little shit? I know he can be obnoxious when he's hurt," Ethan said with a friendly chuckle. "Last time he was injured, we were still playing in Minnesota. When the team had a road trip, he stayed with my family. My sister was going to kill him by the time I got back," he said in his gentle nature.

"No, he's still pretty out of it. I think the concussion and the pain meds are keeping him mellow."

"Good. Please call me if you need a break. How long does he need to be baby-sat for?"

"He can't be alone for forty-eight hours, but I'm good there. I need to figure out when he needs to go see the trainers and doctors and all that."

"I can check in on that and take him. Don't worry about that."

"So, you guys have been friends a long time right?" she asked.

"Yeah, he spent a lot of time at my house in high school. My mom and sister kind of adopted him right along with our coach's family."

"I can't imagine what it would have been like to move away from home so young."

"Yeah, it was hard for him. He's always someone who carries a lot of responsibility that isn't really his. Like he always felt like he had abandoned his mother, but now he takes care of her. I remember when he got hurt last time. It was six months before the draft. He was so scared it was going to affect things there, but he was still the first pick."

Kate nodded. There was so much about Wes that she didn't know yet, but she wanted to.

"Do you want to stay for dinner? My parents will be here with dinner soon," she said with a smile.

"Dinner with mama and papa McPhee? Count me in."

Her phone vibrated in her hand. "That's them now, I'll go get them." She turned to leave.

"Hold on, I'll just let Ernie know to send them up," he said as he pulled his phone from his pocket.

"Oh, thanks."

A few minutes later there was a knock at the door. Kate opened it, and in walked her parents carrying a few bags of groceries, her overnight bag, and a crock pot full of soup.

"Alright, Katie. Where should I plug this thing in?" her mother asked, slightly lifting the crock pot in her hands.

"This way. The kitchen is right over here."

"How's Wes?" she asked, pulling her into a hug. Kate and her mom were of a similar build, and looking at Nancy McPhee was like looking into the future. Kate had always been the spitting image of her.

"He's good."

"Ethan Yellowtail," her father said, holding his hand out to shake his. "How are you doing? I've met you a couple of times when I came to Conner's games."

"I remember, I'm doing good. I just came to check on Wes."

"Well, I brought plenty of soup," her mom said. "I just need to heat up this bread in the oven and throw together a salad. You should stay for dinner."

"That sounds wonderful."

"I don't think there have ever been this many people here before," said a sleepy voice from the couch.

"Well, I just wanted to make sure Kate didn't want to kill you yet," Ethan said, walking over and gave him a slick handshake.

"No, we're good right, Red?" he looked over to her with a small smile.

"So far, he's been a stellar patient."

"Mr. and Mrs. McPhee, nice to see you again. I really appreciate you bringing her what she needs from home," he said.

"Please, call me Nancy," she said from the kitchen. "I'm happy to do it. I can't believe this is how Katie tells me you two were seeing each other. Does Conner know? He hasn't said anything either."

"Yes, mom, Conner knows. It's only been since he was at Mystic Falls in January. Can we please drop it?" Kate groaned.

"Not another word. I hope you like chicken noodle soup. If not, I can make you something else, Wes."

"Soup is great. Thanks," he said politely.

"I saw that hit," said Gus with a shake of his head. "I hope he gets thrown out of the league. The commentators were talking about bad blood between you two. Intent to injure is nothing to mess around with," said her father officially.

"You and me both," Ethan agreed. "Blake Kelly is a menace, and I hope he's gone."

"I agree with you. And yeah, there is some bad blood there. He's clearly still pissed about it," he said, gesturing to his arm that was still in a cast and sling.

"Are you in much pain?" her mom asked, concern dripping from her voice.

"No ma'am. Kate's been taking good care of me. The headache is the worst part of it right now."

"Well, I'll finish up dinner and we'll all get out of your hair so you can get some rest. Ethan and Katie, would you mind setting the table?" she asked.

Kate smiled at the way her mom was always the mom in the room. She had played mom to many of the boys her dad had coached over the years. So, the fact that she just asked a literal millionaire, who's one of the best goalies in the world, to set the table made her chuckle. A hockey player was a hockey player to her. The only one she might have pause about asking to set the table would be the great one himself, but even Wayne Gretzky might have to set the table in the McPhee household.

"Of course," Ethan said as he walked over to the cabinet and got down the soup bowls.

"Please help him, Katie," she said.

"Yes, mom."

After they all finished eating, Nancy cleaned up while Kate got Wes situated in bed with more pain meds. He was looking tired again. The doctor said he would sleep a lot the first couple days, and to let him. It was the best thing for him.

Coming out of his bedroom, her parents were finishing packing up.

"You have leftovers in the fridge, Katie. If you need anything else, please call us," her mom said as she pulled her in for a hug. "I'm so happy to see you with someone again. He is a very nice young man."

Kate wished she didn't cringe at her mother saying that, but she did.

"See you soon, sweetheart," her dad said, going for a hug next. "Next time we go see one of Conner's games you'll have to come with us."

"Yeah, I can do that."

She shut the door behind her parents and let out a slow breath. She had just told Conner, now her parents knew, and if her parents knew, then her mom was already planning her wedding. She meant well, but she just couldn't help herself. And Kate had a funny feeling Wes would be right there planning it with her if he was up to it. It all just seemed so fast.

When he fell on the ice, the fear Kate felt was like nothing she had ever felt before. She felt like her heart was breaking. Like a piece of her was dying, and she needed to get to him. When she saw him lying in that hospital bed all broken and bruised, she would have given anything to take his pain. But now it was all sinking in. Now her carefully curated world was bumping into this new world. One that still felt unsafe.

When she was with Wes, it felt very safe. He made her feel loved and adored. It was simple when it was just them.

But they both had pasts to contend with, jobs with complications, and family and friends who cared for them. The deeper they got, and the more those lives intertwined, the harder and more complicated it got. The more Kate let him into all the parts of her life she had previously had nicely compartmentalized, the more she saw how much work she still needed. The fear of being hurt like she had been with Jason, of being treated like Jason had treated her all lived right there under the surface. The literal and figurative scars had barely healed.

No matter how many times she told herself Wes was nothing like Jason, she couldn't help her reactions sometimes. It made her even more angry at Jason. When they first got together, she had been so impressed with Jason's intelligence, which she now saw he wielded like a sword. He used it to disarm younger women so he could manipulate them. If you thought he was smarter than you, he could easily make you feel stupid. Once you questioned your own intelligence, he could then make you feel inferior. And once you felt inferior, the real torment started. The name calling, the yelling, even the occasional shove and shake because you no longer felt you were worth anything more than that. Until one day you find yourself bleeding on the floor, broken glass all around you, and wonder what on earth happened to get you to this point?

That was the moment Kate had started reclaiming herself. Her brother helped to drag her out of it, and piece by piece she started putting the pieces back together. She was getting there, but she wasn't strong enough to withstand a storm yet. She would crumble. The thought of being broken into a million pieces again terrified her. She was willing to take a chance with Wes, but all this just felt like a lot.

When she walked into his bedroom though, all that fell away. The way he smiled at her when she walked into a room settled her heart. The way he reached for her settled in her soul. And the spark that danced between them every time he put his arms around her brought her peace. The kiss he gave her left her wanting more, but she was confident there would be time for that later. And the more time she spent with him, the more confident she felt.

CHAPTER 27

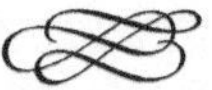

KATE

It had been over a week since the incident. Ethan had taken Wes in for another meeting with the team trainers and doctors to have him looked over and determine how long he will be out for. Kate was hoping for good news. Wes was trying to remain upbeat, but she could tell he was having a hard time. There was an edge to his voice that wasn't there usually. He would most likely be in the cast for another five weeks, which would get them well into the playoffs. Then he will still need time to do rehab once it was off, but she was just trying to be supportive. Even throughout this whole ordeal, he remained Wes. He just did what the doctor said and moved on. Though she could tell it was starting to wear on him.

She took this Wes-free time to go get some grocery shopping done. She needed to pick up some more fresh fruits and vegetables and the thought of ordering them had crossed her mind, but she always liked to pick her own produce.

As she was picking up a bag of apples, she heard it. A voice that sent a chill right through her.

"Kate? Is that you?" turning she saw Jason walking towards her.

She froze. Panic gripped her and her heart raced. She wanted to leave. She was tempted to run from him. She hoped if she stayed still enough in the produce department, maybe he would walk right past her, but he maintained eye contact and strode right up to her.

"What are you doing here?"

"Just doing a little shopping," she said, gesturing to her cart.

"I see that, it looks like you're taking care of yourself."

She felt the jab, but she moved on. "Yep, well I need to be going."

"This is the second time I've seen you here in Glendale. I think it's a sign," he said with a smile. Kate thought he was trying to be charming, but she knew he was a snake in the grass. "What have you been up to?"

"I'm just staying with a friend for a few days while they recover," she said.

"You always were so good at taking care of people," he said. What's funny was it wasn't true. Caregiving wasn't something that came easily to her. People like her mother were caregivers. They couldn't help it; it was just who they were. That was not who she was. She was taking care of Wes because she cared about him and wanted him to feel better, but also because she knew he would be doing the same for her. Because when you're in a relationship with someone, you take care of each other. All Jason ever did was think about himself. He was nothing like Wes.

"It's been nice to see you, but I must say I was quite surprised to see you with that hockey player last time. I almost thought for a minute you were together, but I know better than that. You left that part of your life behind you a long time ago."

She was too stunned to speak; she just nodded her head. She started to back up and turn around to her cart.

"I'll have to come to Mystic Falls and see your store. I'm sure you've done amazing things with it," he said. Then he put his hand on top of hers. Her heart pounded in her chest as she stared at his hand touching hers. She wanted to scream. She wanted to crawl right out of her skin, but she just stood there appearing calm while sheer panic coursed through her.

"I've been thinking about you since we ran into each other at the pub. Thinking about old times. I would really love to go out and get some drinks."

She just stared at him. What part of the past was he thinking about? Because it sure as hell wasn't the abuse that was running through her head right now.

His thumb started to rub the hand he was holding to the shopping cart. "It would be really great to reconnect with you, Kate."

"I gotta go," she said as she started to pull away from him. "I can't leave my friend alone for too long," she said.

"It was great to see you Kate," he called behind her.

She made her way to the self-checkout, her heart pounding and her breath caught in her chest. She was close to just leaving the cart, but she could do this. There were still items left on her list, but she wasn't going to have a panic attack in the middle of the grocery store. Taking a deep breath, she managed to get checked out and made her way to the car.

She turned it on, turned up the music, and tried to collect herself enough to drive home. Emotions swirled inside of her. Anger at him for being a dick, at herself for not standing up to him, shame that this all still affected her so much, confusion, sadness, all of it was there fighting for top billing in her brain.

Finally, she was calm enough to drive home. As she put distance between the store and him, she started to feel better. By the time she was in Wes's apartment putting away groceries she was feeling almost normal, but that underlying panic she felt wouldn't go away. She still felt so close to breaking, even here in Wes's condo.

She had been home for about an hour when the door opened, and Wes came sulking in. Ethan followed with a concerned look on his face.

"How'd it go?" asked Kate apprehensively.

"Not great," Ethan said, slipping past her to get water out of the fridge.

"I'm fucking out for the season," Wes grumbled dropping his bag loudly on the floor. "I can't even start physical therapy till after playoffs start."

She had never seen Wes like this before. She went over to him and put her hand on his arms, and he snatched his arm away and stomped away from her.

"I'm sorry, Wes."

"Hey man, you'll be good as new next season. It sucks, but you'll be back on the ice."

"Says the man about to leave to go to practice," he said, glaring at him.

"Good luck," Ethan said, shooting Kate a pitiful look as he opened the door. "I'll stop by later," he said as he left.

This was not the kind of energy Kate was used to, and she was still on edge from running into Jason. She took a moment to remind herself Wes isn't Jason. Wes had never hurt her, yelled at her, or even been angry at her. This was not the same.

"Hey," she said gently, walking over to him. "It's gonna be okay."

"Looks like Blake Kelly got his fucking way."

"Wes," she said, her hand resting on his back.

"You don't understand. If I don't have hockey, then I have nothing to offer. Hockey is all I have. I never went to college or prepared for anything else. It's all I've ever done since I was a kid. He fucking knew that. He was trying to punish me," he said darkly.

Kate could feel that old panicky feeling sinking in. Wes wasn't Jason. She tried for a deep breath that wouldn't come.

"Wes, he's going to get suspended. Probably even tossed out of the league," she said, rubbing his back.

He turned abruptly facing her and yelled "I don't fucking care what happens to him, Kate! He did this, and now I'm fucking out for the season. Our shot at the cup is fucking gone. We have all been working our asses off and for what?!"

He twisted away from her, pulled back, and threw his phone across the room. It hit the bowl that held the keys with a loud burst as glass shattered hitting the floor.

At that moment adrenaline pulsed through her body. It was like she was there with Jason that day she fell through the table. She cowered down protecting her head. The phone had come nowhere near her, but the full body flinch she did was on instinct alone.

Only then did Wes seem to pull out of whatever he was going through and really look at her. All the anger gone from his face, now it was replaced by confusion and concern.

"Hey, I'm sorry. I wasn't going to throw that at you. I was just mad," he said gently as he reached for her.

She twisted out of his loose grip. "I need to go to the bathroom," she said as she quickly walked into the bathroom, shutting the door behind her. She turned on the sink and splashed the water on her face. Tears were already streaming down her face. She couldn't do this. She couldn't let other people affect her like this. She refused to let someone else have that much power over her.

There was a gentle knock at the door. "Kate, are you okay?"

"Yep, I'm fine. I just need a minute," she called out trying to sound casual. "I'll be right out."

"Can I come in?"

"I'll be out in just a second," she said. She took a breath and sat on the toilet with her head between her hands. What was she even doing? She wasn't ready for this. She wasn't ready to be in another relationship. She was going to get hurt, and it would be just like before. She couldn't do that again. But right now, she would go out there and make some lunch.

Standing up she looked in the mirror. Her eyes were a bit red rimmed, but she would be okay. She smoothed her hair back into a bun and took a final breath.

As she walked into the living room, she saw Wes by the door sweeping up the broken glass. He stood up and emptied the dustpan into the trash. The look on his face gutted her.

"I'm so sorry. Are you okay?" he asked.

"Yep. I'm good. I'm gonna start on some lunch. Chicken taco salad sound ok?" she said quickly walking into the kitchen.

"Kate, stop for a second," he said, following her out into the kitchen. "What happened? I'm so sorry I scared you. The way you flinched..."

"It just startled me, no biggie," she said as she started getting ready to prep food.

"Kate, look at me."

She stilled; her back was still to him.

"Look at me."

Slowly she turned to face him. She wished she could wipe the look of concern on his face away. That he would drop this and let her pretend like nothing had happened, but he clearly wasn't going to do that.

"I would never hurt you. You know that don't you?"

She nodded.

"Does this have anything to do with your ex? Because if he ever touched you. I swear to god, I'll fucking kill him."

"Wes, stop."

"Kate, I'm serious. I'm so sorry that my outburst scared you. It was so fucking stupid. I was just mad at the situation."

"I know that. I know you would never hurt me, and I know you were angry at the situation. Can we please just drop it so I can make lunch?"

He held her in place with a stare.

"Please, can we just let it go? For now?"

He gave a small nod. "For now. But I think we need to talk about this, Kate. Please trust me."

She took a deep breath and bit her bottom lip. Wes walked around the counter and put his arm around her. This time she didn't brush him away. She let him hold her and she wished she didn't like it as much as she did. But something had changed, something inside of her had shifted. The walls she had been slowly breaking down with Wes were all back up. He held her close and kissed the top of her head and breathed her in.

"Do you need any help?" he asked.

"Nope, I got it. Why don't you go get some rest? I'll get you when it's ready."

"Okay, I'm here if you need me," he said as he rubbed her arm.

"Thank you, I appreciate that," she said looking up into his eyes still full of concern. "I really do."

He nodded. "Okay, I have some game videos to watch. I'll go do that, but call me if you need anything."

He leaned in for a kiss, but she knew if he kissed her, the thin string that was holding her together would snap completely apart. She turned her head, and he kissed her cheek. Then she turned her back to him completely. He stood there for another moment watching her. Then without a word, he turned slowly and went into his bedroom. Only after Kate heard him rummaging around in his bag and pulling out his tablet, and game sounds played over it did she relax completely.

What the fuck just happened?

CHAPTER 28

WES

Yesterday had been the worst day of this whole fucking ordeal. He had been so angry when they told him he was out for the season. He expected it, but that didn't help when the news was delivered. He had yelled at Ethan about it the whole way home because Ethan knew he was just blowing off steam, but when he got home his day went from bad to worse.

He wished he would have calmed down when Kate had tried to console him. Instead, he yelled at her and threw his phone across the room like a toddler throwing a temper tantrum. Only he wasn't a toddler, he was a grown man. The way she flinched kept replaying in his head. She had covered her head and hunched over, leaving the room in tears. And from that moment on she had been here, but not really here.

He had tried to go to the bathroom to help her, but she had already shut him out. He had tried to hold her, but she was stiff in his arms. When she turned away from his kiss, he knew something was wrong. Well, he knew something was wrong from the moment it happened, but that sealed it for him.

He had remembered the first night together when they had run into her ex at the bar. The panicked look in her eyes when she searched for him. The way she had warned him Conner was there, but most importantly, the way she had buried her face in his chest and told him that he needed to be patient with her because her ex had done a number on her. He did this. Wes was sure of that. He had seen this before, and the fact that he was seeing this again in the woman he loved had him seeing red. But he would be calm and patient with her, like she had asked him to on the first night she came back to his place.

So, this morning when he woke up and she was clear on the other side of the bed, his heart was just about to break. This was the first morning he woke and didn't find her in his arms, her mess of red curls all over both of their pillows. She was on her side on the edge of the bed curled up. He ached to reach over and snuggle in behind her, but his fucking arm was still pinned to his chest.

He got out of bed and decided to do the next best thing. He could make eggs one-handed right? At least it was his right hand. He got out the bacon and eggs and managed to put together a quick breakfast.

As he was plating it up, she came out wiping the sleep from her eyes. Her eyes looked puffy, and he wagered it was from all the crying she had done yesterday and tried to hide from him. He was at a loss about what to do.

"You made breakfast? You didn't have to do that. I could've done it."

"I'm getting better. I can make bacon and eggs one handed. Sadly, I could not butter the toast, but besides that."

"Thank you, Wes," she said, stepping into the kitchen to butter both of their pieces of toast.

"Shall we?" she said, carrying both plates to the table.

"Ethan is picking me up. The team doctor is looking at

my shoulder today. Hopefully I can stop wearing this," he said, pointing to the sling he wore to stabilize his shoulder after being dislocated. "I'm also meeting with the team's therapist."

"That'll be good. I'm going to try and get some work done while you're gone," she said like his words didn't even really filter in.

"Sounds good," he said.

And after that they ate in silence. Things still weren't right. He wanted to fix it, but he had a feeling that if he pushed, he would end up pushing her away, and he did not want to do that.

He got ready and headed down to meet Ethan in the lobby.

"Hey man, you look rough. Are you still mad about not being able to play?"

"Of course I am, but shit kind of took a weird turn last night. I'm kinda messed up about the whole thing?"

"Yeah?"

"Okay, so I was pissed when you left right?"

"Yeah."

"I may have yelled at Kate. Not at her, but still yelled and threw my phone across the room," he said.

"Dick," Ethan muttered. "What would Anna say about that?"

Wes knew what Anna would say about it. He knew he had been raised better than to pull shit like that. His own mother and the women of Ethan's family made sure of it.

"I fucking know. But then Kate flinched. Like covered her head and ducked. I didn't even throw my phone in her direction."

"What?" Ethan looked over at him with raised eyebrows.

"I know. She told me when we first got together that she had an asshole ex. We ran into him that night when she first came out with us. I didn't think too much of it. But looking back, she had this look of panic on her face when we ran into him. She told him he should leave before Conner saw him. I think he might have...." The words wouldn't even come out. The thought alone made bile rise in his throat. The idea of a man laying his hands on Kate made him sick with fury. He wanted to tear that fucking guy apart.

"You think so?" Ethan was with him without him having to say those words out loud.

"Yeah, the way she flinched...."

"Hey, Wes, maybe control your temper, but I think there's more to her reaction than you losing your temper."

"I get that," he said as he raked his hands through his hair. "But the thing is now, she won't even talk to me about it. She won't kiss me. She hardly even looks at me. It's like she's not even there."

"Damn, maybe just give her some space. It sounds like you really triggered her."

"I know, I'm trying. I just hate seeing her like that."

"Yeah, that sucks. This whole situation is messed up."

"Yeah... I just feel so bad. I wish I could take it back. I don't know why I did that."

"Look, losing your temper like that is never good. I know you were pissed and deep in your own shit. Just give it some time."

Wes nodded as they got out of his truck and made their way into the Magic center.

After Wes finished up with the doctor, he was waiting for his therapy session. Conner was walking out of Sasha's office.

"Hey man, I heard you're our for the season. That sucks. There goes out shot at the cup," Conner said sitting down next to him.

"I know, I'm so fucking pissed."

"I think coach is looking for you though, I shouldn't be the one to tell you this. So, act surprised, but Kelly's out of the league."

"Seriously?"

"Yeah. There was a hearing today. They said he played with obvious intent to injure and caused immense suffering. I think they are leaving it up to you and the Magic as an organization to go after him legally."

"Well, that's something. It sucks that I have to be out for the season because of it, but at least I'll make a full recovery and we can kick ass together next year." Wes fist bumped Conner. He was searching for that silver lining, because it was hard to find for the past week.

"Can I ask you a question?" Wes asked.

"Shoot."

"Kate's ex. What do you know about him?" he asked.

"He's a pompous douchebag."

"Anything else?"

"Look man, I'm okay with you dating my sister, but I draw the line at giving you relationship advice."

"You're right. Sorry, it won't happen again."

"Conner," Sasha Maloof's voice called from her office.

"I gotta go," Conner said as he stood up and walked quickly down the hallway.

"Chicken," Wes called after him.

Conner raised his middle finger without looking back and moved quickly down the hallway into the locker room.

"Wes, are you ready?" asked Denise, a petite black woman with locks falling down her back.

"Yep," he said, stepping into her office. He sat on the couch as she sat in the chair across from him.

"When we met last week, you were still healing, but they wanted me to do a follow up with you now that we have a timeline for your injury. How are you feeling?"

"Like shit. Put me down for weekly sessions," he said, shaking his head.

"That bad huh?" she said with a weak laugh.

"Yeah. There's some other stuff going on too. You helped me so much when I signed on, I think I could use it again."

"That's what I'm here for. What would you like to talk about?"

And he let it all out. She already knew his past with his mom and Florida, now he just had to fill her in on everything else. He would need his full hour this time, plus many more to come.

An hour later, Wes was finally home. He was hoping Kate would talk and they would be able to patch things up, but when he walked in his house, he knew he was wrong. Things were even more fucked up than he had known. There sitting on the couch with her bags packed was Kate. She looked like she had been crying.

"What's going on, Kate?" he asked nervously.

"I can't do this, Wes. I thought I could, but I can't."

"Can't do what?" he asked as calmly as he could, although his heart was starting to race.

"I thought I was ready to be in a relationship, but I'm not. And I'm not sure if I ever will be."

"Kate," he said as his legs somehow managed to carry him over to the couch. He felt like he was about to pass out. "You can do this. I'll give you space if you need it, but this isn't the end. This can't be the end. We're meant to be together."

"I'm so sorry, Wes," she said as tears started to stream down her face. "If there was anyone I would be able to be with it would be you, but I just can't."

"I'm so sorry. I never should have lost my temper like that. It won't happen again."

"Wes, don't make this any harder. You've been amazing. You are amazing. You'll find someone who is deserving of you and all the warmth and love you have to give. I know that. I just can't be that person."

"Why? I don't want anyone else, Kate. I want you. Only you."

"I'm so sorry," she looked down at her hands and tears dropped onto them.

Wes turned her face to him, ignoring the tears that were streaming down his own face. "Kate, please, let me fix this. It won't happen again, I promise."

"Wes, it's okay. You were angry. Next time don't ruin your phone about it, but someone who wasn't as messed up as I am would know you were just blowing off steam. I thought I was better, but I'm not. I wish it could be different, but it's not."

"Please don't do this. We can work through this. I want to be better."

"You don't have to be better. You're perfect. I just can't."

She looked at him, eyes brimming with tears.

"Please, just talk to me," he pleaded.

"Wes. You don't think it kills me that I'm so broken I can't even let the person who's my ideal match in every way love me? This is tearing me apart, but I can't. I had to rebuild myself once, and you only get one do over like that in your life. I can't do it again. I wouldn't survive."

"Kate, I will never break you. Your heart is safe with me," he said, taking her hands, pleading with her.

"Please don't make this harder than it is. I need to get back to the bookstore. I need to get back to Mystic Falls."

She stood to leave and picked up her back.

"Kate, please, I'm begging you. We can work this out. I'll do whatever I can to prove you are safe with me."

"No one is ever truly safe, Wes. I trust you would never intentionally hurt me, but this is for the best," she said as she pulled her hands out of his and walked out of the door.

The deafening sound of the click of the door closing behind her had him collapsing on the couch, sobbing. How on earth had he fucked things up this badly? How had he not known? He should have known. He had to make this right.

KATE

The next day Kate opened the bookstore. The numbness she felt was a welcome change from the pain she felt before. Walking away from Wes had been one of the hardest things she had ever done, next to putting herself together after Jason broke her. He had left her quite literally battered and bleeding. Those five days at Conner's alone, she had just laid in his guest bed. Just laid there figuring out if life was even worth living anymore. Jason had stripped away everything she loved, everything that she was, and replaced it with someone she didn't know. Someone who didn't stand up for herself, someone who felt like they deserved the abuse. Somehow, in all that darkness, she found the spark inside of her. That spark that said she was worthy. That spark that said her life was worth living.

She pushed away everything else and protected that spark. Slowly she fed the spark. She kept the things that scared her away, in fear that the next thing might douse it out entirely. As she fed the spark, she built the walls around it higher and higher. It was still so fragile that a gust of wind would make it go out. She needed it to be stronger so she could stand on her own. Only once she was able to fully depend on herself did she feel safe. The walls had done their job, she was going to be okay.

It took her a long time to get to that point. She fought hard to get to that point. But it seemed that every person she had started to let in had slowly broken down those walls. Wes ripped them down. He saw her. When she was with him, her flame burned bright. Sadly, that also gave him the power to step on that flame and put it out. She knew he would never do it on purpose, but if he did, even on accident, she wouldn't survive it.

After she got the coffee started, she looked around at her little bookstore. This place had saved her. This place had given her purpose when she was drowning, and she felt better being in its comforting walls again.

The bell sounded over the door and Bridget's wild red hair came around the corner.

"I didn't expect ye to be back until next week, lass. Why are ye home so soon?"

She just looked at Bridget and swallowed hard.

"I just needed to get back to get some things done," she said.

"What happened, my dear?" she asked as she took her hand.

"Nothing," Kate said quickly.

"I don't buy that for a second. Did something happen with that handsome hockey player of yers?" she asked, eyes brimming with concern and kindness.

"We just decided that it wasn't working," Kate said, hoping in vain Bridget would drop it.

"Is that right? Ye both decided that?"

"Bridget, I'm sorry. I'm just not in the mood for this right now. I have a lot of work I'm behind on."

"Alright lass, I'll leave ye to it. But what would ye think

about stopping by my shop when ye finish up work for the day. Sometimes, a tarot card reading can be just what ye need to help figure things out when yer head is all muddled up."

"I'll think about it," she said.

"I'll see ye later, my dear."

Watching Bridget leave the store, Kate couldn't help but think about Wes and the reading he had been given. That had been part of why he was so sure about her. That was one thing she loved about Wes, he never wavered. He was all in, no matter what he was doing. He had been all in with her from the moment he asked her to skate. She had tried so many times to push him away that weekend, but he was there in his gentle, persistent way. And really, that was a gift. She knew without a doubt he would take no for an answer about anything, but he was also going to be right there when she changed her mind, which she inevitably did. Part of her yearned to reach out and find out if that was the case now. If she were to text him, would he text back? She knew he would, and he wouldn't even be mad that she had walked out on him.

She wished this could be different, she wished she could be stronger. She picked up her phone and looked at the text message he had sent her last night.

Wes - Kate, I'm not sure exactly what you are going through, but please know that I am here. I know you need space, and I am going to give that to you, but don't take that as a sign that I'm not committed. I am going to text you once every day, if that's okay with you. If you don't want me to, say the word and I won't. But if you still have feelings for me, just give us a chance. So, this is me, saying I'm here. I can help you through whatever you're going through, or I can simply wait until you're ready. I meant what I said, you're it for me, Red. I'm not going anywhere.

But she pushed that aside and went about taking pictures of their new release to put up in the online shop before she put them in the store.

It was time to close shop for the day. Kate was turning the key to lock up as she noticed the light from Bridget's store next door was still on. It was a cold night in March, and the store looked like it was glowing with warmth. Maybe a reading would be what she needed to figure stuff out. At this point, things were so messed up that it couldn't hurt.

Walking a few steps next door, she could almost feel the warmth from inside. She opened the door as the bell tinkled overhead. Kate had been in the store a few times before. But those had been just in and out trips in the light of day. Here, in the evening hours, there was something truly magical about it. There was none of the harsh overhead lighting. She had lamps and candles burning. Everything about it had this warm, inviting glow that seemed to beckon her in. It smelled like jasmine and sandalwood, but there was something else. Something cool and refreshing. Something that reminded her of the ice. Something that reminded her of Wes, but it didn't make her heart sad like most memories of him did, it just made her feel as content as she always did when it was just the two of them.

"Hello? Bridget?"

Bridget appeared from the back corner looking other-worldly. There was something about her that always felt magical. Kate wasn't one to believe in that stuff, but if anyone had an ounce of true magic, it was Bridget.

"Kate," she said with a kind smile. "I'm so glad ye decided to come. Is it a reading ye would like?"

She just nodded and shook off the part of her that felt silly.

"Alright lass, why don't ye join me here at the table?" She gestured to a small two-person table covered in a purple tablecloth with celestial patterns in gold.

Bridget sat down and began shuffling her well-worn deck of cards. Setting them down in front of Kate, she told her to cut the deck. As she cut the deck, a warm feeling spread through her, and some of the stress she was carrying lifted. Her shoulders relaxed.

"Alright, let's see what the cards have to say," she said as she laid out the first card.

The first card Bridget flipped over was the Eight of Swords. The card depicted a woman bound and surrounded by eight swords. "Oh, my dear," Bridget said with a voice that contained so much empathy. "Ye have certainly been through it. There has been someone in your past who has not treated ye properly and it has caused ye immense suffering. But this card is in the past," Bridget said as she reached out and took her hand. "I think it is best that we leave this card and the cause of the suffering there."

Kate nodded. If only it were that easy. She would love to leave it all in the past, but she just couldn't seem to shake it.

"The next card I flip will be pertaining to your present situation." She flipped over the card to reveal the Six of swords. "Another swords card I see. This one is more of a transition card. It can be a card of healing, but it can also be a card of running away. Running away can be an act of great bravery and self-preservation, but only if we are running away from something for the right reasons."

Kate gave her a raised eyebrow. Bridget knew her current situation. She knew that Kate was running away. When she ran from Jason, it had been an act of bravery. This time it wasn't. She knew that and so did Bridget.

"Now, let's see what the future holds for you." Bridget turned over the third and final card. It was the World. "Oh, my dear, the world is at yere feet. If ye can navigate your present circumstances and try to find the bravery to take what ye want, you will have all of yere wildest dreams. You can have it all, love, career, family, anything you want is yeres to take if you can navigate yere current circumstances."

Kate just nodded. Navigate her current circumstances. That sounded easy enough, but her head was always so muddled with shadows of the past. It was too full of things she didn't know how to properly deal with, that she chose to hide from.

"It is all in the cards, my dear. You can do this. I know things seem insurmountable at times, but I know that lad loves ye, and ye love him."

"I do..." she said barely above a whisper.

"Then the choice is yours."

Kate took a deep breath and looked at the cards. She wanted the future Bridget had talked about. The vision of her and Wes living a happy life of joy and love surrounded by family would be amazing. She wanted that so much, but Bridget was right, the vulnerability it would take to reach out and grab it seemed insurmountable. She just wasn't sure she was capable of it.

"Thank you, Bridget," she said.

"What do ye think, Kate? Do ye have any questions?"

"I don't know. I want those things, but I'm just not sure if I'm strong enough to take them. Bad things happen, even when no one means them too."

"Ye're right Kate. Life is full of suffering, that is just the facts. Ye cannot know a full life without suffering, but ye also can't know a full life without joy. Despair is always there, but so is love. The key is to find someone who ye trust to help celebrate the good times and hold ye through the bad times. Sometimes people who have been hurt pull away from the things that bring them joy because they have known immense pain, and the thought of that loss again is too much to bear."

Kate knew that sentiment all too well. The idea of self-preservation at all costs. It had served her well before, but did it still serve her?

"I think the important question to ask isn't what happens if I get hurt again, but rather what could happen if I chose to be brave. I understand that not everyone is worth the risk and cost of bravery, but some people are."

The words she was speaking were like a balm to her soul. She knew that Wes was safe. It was no guarantee there wouldn't be pain, but maybe he was worth the risk. If anyone was, it was him.

"Here I have something that might help. I can see that you're still a bit foggy on the path before you." Bridget stood up from the table and moved behind the counter. She climbed up on a stool and got down a glass jar filled with loose leaf tea. "I call this clari-tea. Drink this when you need help making a decision, and this will help you to find the answers you seek," she said, scooping out a few scoops into a little plastic pouch, then handing it to her.

"Thank you, Bridget. What do I owe you?" she asked, reaching for her purse.

"Ye owe me nothing. I just hope I've been able to help."

"It's definitely given me a lot to think about," she said.

"Well, when you are thinking about it, drink that."

"Will do, thanks."

By the time Kate made it home, she was exhausted. She had hardly slept at all last night, and it was catching up to her. She popped a pizza in the oven and took a quick shower. Then she ate it in bed, watching reruns and trying to forget everything, until her phone dinged.

> Wes - No text telling me to stop, I'll take that as a good sign. I thought about finishing Pride and Prejudice, but I decided to wait on that. I decided to go with a re-read of the hobbit instead. How did you feel about the hobbit movies? We never talked about those. I miss you, Kate. And I am here.

Her heart ached to text him back, but she was just so scared.

THE WEEK WENT ON, and everything was the same. It all still sucked. She missed Wes, but she couldn't bring herself to call him. She was working on autopilot, not taking any real enjoyment out of her work like she used to. The only thing that even made her smile was her nightly text from Wes.

> Wes - So today I may have searched for clips of you playing hockey. I found some of you playing in college. You were amazing. I can't wait to see you on the ice again someday. I know I will. As always, I miss you and I am still here.

> Wes - finished the hobbit today. Thought about watching the movies but decided against it. Lord of the Rings is a much better adaptation. Please let me know if you think I'm wrong. Maybe I should start making inflammatory statements to entice you to respond. Like the 80's adaptation of the Stand was better than the book. Nope, I can't even type that without feeling wrong about it... I miss you, red. I'm here.

> Wes - It's been a week since I have been sending you these nightly texts. The fact that you are reading them tells me there is still hope, Kate. I'm here.

She just didn't know what to do. She wanted to be with Wes more than anything. What was keeping her away? She looked over at her purse and saw the corner of the tea Bridget had given her a couple of nights ago. Talking with Bridget was the closest she had come to any form of clarity, what could it hurt?

Digging the little pouch with the tea out of her purse, she was thinking about what she was hoping to figure out. She wanted to be able to move on from everything with Jason and be in a real relationship with Wes. The tea smelled like cinnamon and orange with traces of something minty. Spearmint? Peppermint? She wasn't sure, but when she took a drink, it was the best tea she had ever had. She blew on it and took another sip. While she didn't magically figure anything out, it was delicious.

She curled up with her cup of tea and turned on an old movie. She was about thirty minutes into the movie when there was a knock at her door. She got up to see who it was. When she answered the door, she saw her dad standing there with a brown bag of food.

"Chili dogs?" he asked.

She smiled and then collapsed into his arms in tears.

"Katie." He quickly set the bag down and pulled her into his arms. "What's the matter, sweetheart?" he said as he stroked her hair.

"Everything is messed up, Daddy. I don't know what to do."

She had never done this before. Even when she broke up with Jason, she didn't do this around people.

"My sweet girl, what is going on?"

"I don't even know where to begin," she said as she wiped her tears and walked over to the couch and got a tissue and blew her nose.

"The beginning sounds as good a place as any," her dad said as he sat down on the couch.

"I mean I would have to go back really far, like all the way back to Indiana," she said sitting next to him.

"Well, I have been wondering what happened there, so that sounds like a good place to start."

And so, she did. She started back in Indiana. It all came flowing out of her. She told him about why she left hockey and how hard it had been when Conner won the championship and went on to the Magic. She waited for him to say something, but he just patiently waited for her to continue. Leaving hockey was the easy part.

The Jason part was the hard part. And while she did leave out key elements about just how bad the abuse had gotten, she told him most of it. From the way he separated her from everyone to the cheating. It actually felt good to tell him. She glanced over at him, his lips were tight, and his brow was furrowed, but he let her finish.

"When I finally left, I stayed with Conner for a while until I moved home. After that, you're pretty much up to speed."

He still didn't say anything, he just pulled her into his arms and hugged her. When she heard him sniffle in her ear, she finally pulled out of the hug to look at him. There were tears in his eyes, and he reached for a tissue from the box she was holding.

"I owe you an apology, Katie."

"No, you don't. I never told you."

"You never told me, but I'm your dad. I should've known. I should've recognized what was happening when you were pulling away when Conner was getting drafted. I thought you just needed space."

"I did need space. And honestly, nothing you could've said would've changed things."

"Maybe not, but at least you wouldn't have been alone." He wiped his nose. "As for Jason…did Conner know?"

"Some of it."

"Well, at least you had him. I never did like him, but I had no idea."

"No one did. I hid it from you."

He just nodded, taking it all in.

"What brought all this back up? And why are you back early from helping Wes?"

She looked away as another tear ran down her cheek.

"I left him," she said on a shaky breath.

"Did he hurt you?" he asked quietly.

"No, Daddy, he would never. Wes… he would never do that," she sputtered out as the tears started again.

He pulled her into his arms for another hug and this time she really let herself feel it. She hadn't had a hug that felt like this from her dad in years.

"Then what happened?" he said, rubbing her back.

She sat up and took another sip of the tea from Bridget. "I was just scared. He was really mad when he found out he was out for the season and was yelling and I kind of freaked out."

"Was he yelling at you?"

"No. He would never hurt me or even yell at me. But I just

don't know if I can be in a relationship. I think I might be too broken."

"Sweetheart," he said, cupping her face. "That is not true. You are not broken. You may have been knocked down, but you're not broken. I still see you."

She just shook her head.

"I mean it, Katie. I still see you. I see that eight-year-old girl who could out skate any guy on the team. I see the fourteen-year-old girl that punched Derek Fipp in the mouth for talking about her. I see that seventeen-year-old who fiercely defended her baby brother when he came out to his team and a couple of them ran their mouths. I see the adult woman who was strong enough to put herself back together all on her own. You are one of the strongest people I have ever known, Katie. I mean that."

She just closed her eyes as tears streamed down her face and shook her head. "I don't see her anymore."

"Well, it's a good thing you're not alone in it this time. I'll remind you of her anytime you need. You are fierce and you always have been."

She just nodded and sniffled.

"As for Wes, that boy loves you, Katie."

"I know he does. I'm just so scared."

"Well, then this is me reminding you that you are strong and brave, and you can do hard things," he said with a wink.

She gave a weepy laugh. Her mom had said those words to her every morning before she left the house. She had so easily believed them for so many years. Maybe she could believe them again. "Thank you, Dad. I think I needed to be reminded of that."

They sat in silence for a moment both starting to process the conversation they had just had.

"I think I might need to talk to someone..." she said quietly.

"I think that's a good idea. Talking it out with someone removed from the situation can be helpful."

She just nodded and sat there for another moment.

"Did you say something about chili dogs?" she said quietly.

"I did," he said with a small smile. "When I saw your car in your driveway, I went to Twistees and picked them up. Do you want them?"

She nodded and blew her nose.

"How about this, I'll go get us some plates and we can eat some chili dogs and find a game to watch?"

"That sounds wonderful."

And that's just what they did. They ate and watched a game and it felt normal. She still had a long way to go, but she could do this. She could fix everything. This was a big step, it was a hard step, but she was glad she had finally decided to do.

That night before she went to bed her phone buzzed.

Wes – I miss you. I'm sitting here looking at Pride and Prejudice trying to decide if I should finish it or wait for you.

She looked at it. He had texted her once a day like he said he would, but that was it. She missed him. So, she took a deep breath and picked up her phone. She could be brave because Wes was worth it.

Kate – Wait for me.

The dots started dancing immediately.

Wes – Always. I'm here, Kate.

Kate – I miss you.

Wes – I miss you too. I've missed you every day.

Kate – Me too. Thank you for not giving up on me.

Wes – Never. You're it for me Red. I know I've said it before, and it is as true as it ever was.

Kate – Thank you. I think I'm going to go to bed.

Wes – Goodnight.

Kate – Goodnight.

CHAPTER 30

KATE

It had been a week since she left Glendale. Almost three weeks since that terrible night in Florida. Everything was still such a mess. Kate was getting the meeting room set up for the cookbook club tomorrow. That was one of Kate's favorite days of the month since they all usually brought a dish to share from the book, and it was usually delicious. The bell in the store sounded and she stepped out to see who had come, only to have her heart drop out from her chest when she saw him standing there.

Jason. He was in her bookstore.

"What are you doing here?"

"I told you I was going to come see your bookstore," he said with a calm smile.

"You drove all the way here to see the bookstore?"

"Well, not just to see your store. To see you as well, Kate," he said walking closer to her, reaching for her hand.

She quickly stepped back out of her reach.

"Well, I think you wasted a trip. Please leave," she said as calmly as she was able to.

"Kate," he said, stepping closer. "Please, can we just talk?"

Her butt hit the counter, and he was still moving closer. He reached out and took her hand, but at that moment something inside of her shifted. She was able to see him for what he was in a way that she couldn't before. Before, he had been this big bad monster who had broken her and ruined her life, but she had given him too much power, and it was time she took it back.

"No, we can't talk. You need to leave," she said, finding a certainty she hadn't felt in years.

"Kate, come on. We were good together."

"Are you fucking kidding me right now?" She yelled as she pulled her hand out of his and pushed him away. "I blocked you for a reason. I don't want you in my life anymore. Period."

"Kate, come one. I love you. I never stopped, and I know deep down you love me too."

"I do not! And you never loved me, you loved the idea of me. You loved that I let you control me and mold me into who you thought I should be. Well, fuck that and fuck you too, Jason."

Damn, that felt good. That felt really good.

"Kate, I'm surprised at the vulgarity. And I do love you. I know I haven't always been good in the past, but I'm putting all that behind me. I'm ready to be a better man, please let me show you."

"Are you still fucking your TA?"

"Are you still fucking that hockey player?" he said letting his mask slip a little, but Kate could see through all of it. She could see him for what he was, and she was not about to let him push her around in her own bookstore.

"Yeah, I am. I'm in a relationship with him, and he is a better man than you ever could be."

He scoffed. "I highly doubt that."

"Jason, when I left you, I was literally bleeding and broken," she said.

"Kate, you know I never meant to hurt you like that," he said, advancing to her again. She held a hand up to stop him.

"You may have never intended for me to fall through that glass table, leaving marks and permanent scars, but you definitely meant to hurt me. You meant to hurt me each time you made me feel stupid. Each time you made me feel like I was less than. Each time you pushed me or grabbed me. Those were all intended to hurt me and control me. Those days are over Jason. Over."

A look of shock fell over his face. She had never stood up to him like this before, and it felt good. She had just left and blocked him, she never really dealt with him. Maybe this closure is what she needed.

"I am with someone else now. He is smart and he treats me better than anyone has ever treated me before. He encourages me and loves me just as I am. And he's better in bed than you could ever dream of being."

He stepped back sputtering.

"Because of him, I know I have the strength to say get the fuck out of my life. You have done enough harm. Don't ever come near me again. You are not allowed in my life anymore. If you see me in Glendale...no you don't, keep moving. And don't you dare think about stepping foot in Mystic Falls again."

She started walking towards him.

"I should've done this a long time ago. I've spent the past year and half in a fog from the damage you caused, but not anymore. I'm in love with someone who has shown me more love and kindness in the past few months than you ever did in the years we were together. Leave now. I never want to see your fucking face again," she said giving his chest a shove towards the door.

He stopped because he had bumped into something. Someone to be precise. Kate's mouth fell open when she saw Wes standing there glaring at him. Jason turned around and a brief look of terror crossed his face.

"You heard the lady. Leave. And if you even think about talking to her ever again, I will fucking tear you apart..." he growled out. "That is if she doesn't first," he said looking at Kate with an adoring smile.

Jason turned to leave the store, but neither of them cared about him at that moment.

"You're here," she said as she ran into his arms.

"I'm here," he said as he held her close.

"How are you here?"

"I just had a feeling. I told you I trust my gut, and my gut told me to get to you today."

She was still pressed tight against him, listening to his heartbeat, which again, matched up with her own.

"I'm so glad you're here," she said, tears catching in her throat. "How did you get here?"

"I ubered," he said as he ran his hand up and down her back. "It was either that or wait for your brother or Ethan to drive me, and they are both out on a road trip."

She pulled back to look at him. There he was smiling down at her, with his blue eyes sparkling, and blonde hair framing his face.

"How long were you there?" she asked, wondering how much of all that he had heard.

"I came in at 'are you still fucking that hockey player', and I tell ya, it took every ounce of my control not to jump in and kick his ass right then. But then you started to let him have it, and it was a fucking masterpiece. I'm so proud of you," he said, kissing her forehead.

Kate surged up on her toes and kissed him. She had missed him, missed this connection that existed between them. She needed him right now. Her lips parted and his tongue swept into her mouth. She couldn't wait anymore.

He pulled her back up and traced his finger along her jaw. "Don't ever leave me again, Red. I'm not sure I can live without you."

"Never. I'm so sorry."

"You don't have to apologize," he said as he caressed her face. "I'm sorry. I never should have lost my shit like that. And correct me if I'm wrong, but I do believe you told him you love me," he said cupping her face with one hand. "Because you have to know, I love you too. I love you so much."

"I do love you," she said, reaching up on her toes to kiss him. "I'm so sorry I left like that. I should never have done that."

"That is all behind us. We're here now and that is all that matters."

"We still have some stuff to figure out. If this is going to work, I need to be here at the store more, and you are still in Glendale."

"Red, baby, that's the easy stuff." He bent his head down and kissed again. This time, the kiss registered deep inside of her, the way his kisses so often did.

"When do you need to get back to Glendale?"

"Not till Monday," he said as he picked up the bag he had next to him.

"You packed a bag? Feeling pretty hopeful I see," she said grinning up at him.

"I told you. I had a gut feeling. Are you done with work for the day?"

"Yeah, let's go home," she said, kissing him one last time.

"Let's go home."

CHAPTER 31

WES

es wasn't sure what had made him so certain that he needed to get to her today, he just knew he needed to. It may have seemed crazy that he packed a bag and paid an uber to drive him an hour away, but he was so glad he did. When he entered the bookstore and saw her ex there, he was about to barge right in and fuck him up, especially after he asked her if she was still fucking that hockey player. But then she just seemed to come to life and told him to fuck right off. He had never been prouder of anything in his whole life.

Now, he was on his way home with her, and it seemed like forever since he'd been able to kiss her and be with her. The energy dancing between the two of them was electric. They did have some things to figure out, but that could wait for another day, because the restraint he was showing as he respectfully waited for her to unlock her door was impressive. All he wanted to do was turn her around, rip off her clothes, and fuck her right here against the door. But it was too cold, and he wouldn't want to embarrass her in front of her neighbors. But he could not wait to get into that house and have her all to himself.

Once they were in, she hung her coat up in the closet, his eyes caught on the sway of her hips.

"Can I take your coat?" she asked.

He shrugged it off and handed it to her.

"This is your first time in my house, isn't it?" she asked.

"I've seen the entry way before, but that's it." Their eyes connected with a heat he had never experienced.

"Do you want a tour?" she asked breathlessly, unable to stop looking at him.

"Yeah, a tour would be great," he rasped out, his cock already starting to twitch to life in his pants.

"Well, this is the living room, over there's the dining room, and upstairs there's a bathroom. But let's go ahead and start the tour in my bedroom," she said with a playful grin as she ran to the stairs.

"I like the way you think," he said following her, joy filling his every movement.

He had always enjoyed their sex. It was great sex, but now they would be having make-up and I love you sex all in one. His heart was fit to burst out of his chest. The only thing wrong with this moment was his arm was still in a fucking cast, but he was not about to let that stop him.

Once at the top of the stairs, he gave her ass a little spank, "Okay Red, which door? Or I will fuck you right here in the hallway."

Her breath caught and she looked back at him, her cheeks already pink with heat. Turning to the door on the left, she opened it and they walked into her bedroom. They were all over each other, pulling at clothes and kissing each other deeply. Her clothes were gone in seconds, he took a bit longer with the cast to contend with.

Once they were both naked, he stopped to look at her.

"Damn, I've really fucking missed you," he said, then he bent down and kissed her with such passion it almost took his breath away. Her hands roamed his body and when she wrapped her hand around his cock, he was in danger of coming right then. He needed to take a moment.

He gently pushed her down on the bed and kneeled before her. Kissing her, he ran his hand all over her soft body. He could really have done this better with two hands, but he would still make her come. He massaged her breast and thumbed the nipple while their mouths were still connected. Whatever magic it was that danced between them felt electric. He was on fire with passion for her. Moving his hand lower, he grazed over her soft belly until he slipped it between her legs and squeezed the mound of her sex.

The moan that escaped her lips had him nearly mad with need. He kissed down her neck and chest. He drew her nipple into his mouth as he dipped his fingers into her core. She was already slick and swollen and everything he had been missing. He moved his finger and circled her clit. She moaned again and spread her legs further for him. The way she opened for him spurred him lower. He kissed down her belly and stopped, gazing at her spread open before him like this.

He blew a small breath over her clit and her entire body shivered. Then he licked it as he slid his finger inside.

"Oh my god, Wes. I've missed you," she said, grabbing a handful of hair as her hips started to grind against him. He licked her clit with a little more pressure, working his fingers inside her. Words couldn't do justice to how much he had missed her, so he would show her, and if she would allow him, he would show her again and again tonight. He moved his fingers with a bit more intensity and sucked her clit into his mouth, then she broke pulling his hair and calling out his name, and his heart was about to burst.

When she came back to herself, he was sitting there between her legs smiling contently at her.

"I missed that," he said with a wicked look, rubbing her legs. She beamed down at him running her hands through his hair.

She reached into the bedside table next to him and pulled out a condom. "Get on the bed," she said.

And he did, she climbed between his legs and wrapped her hand around his cock, stroking him as he bucked into her hands. She looked up at him with a smoldering gaze and swept her hair to the side. She lowered her head down and sucked him into her mouth.

"Fuck," he hissed out, grabbing at the sheets.

She pulled back and ripped open the foil packet and rolled the condom down his length, climbing over him. "I've missed you so much. I'm so sorry," she said as she leaned forward and kissed him. This kiss was sweet and filled with so much passion, it felt like he was about to burst wide open.

He cupped her face and pushed his forehead to hers, "There is no need to apologize. I love you, Kate." He kissed her again. While they were kissing, she lined his shaft up with her core. Then she sat down, lowering herself down onto him slowly until he was fully sheathed inside of her.

"I love you too, Wes," she said as she began to slowly rock her hips. She felt so fucking good. His thumb found her clit and began to make circles. She moaned and put her hands on his chest and began to ride him with a little more force.

He was in heaven. The sight of the woman he loved riding his cock, her tits bouncing right in front of his face, and a look of passion that was just about to take over her clearly written on her face. He added a little pressure with his thumb, and she went back to ride his cock a little bit faster and harder. He was just about to come when she cried out and the hands that had been planted flat on his chest fisted and her pussy began to squeeze his cock in rhythmic pulses. He grabbed her hip and bucked into her hard until he finally slammed her down on his cock while he lost himself to the pleasure.

She rested her forehead against his. They were both panting and sweaty, but it felt so fucking good.

"Never leave me again," he said as he sweetly kissed her mouth.

"Never," she replied and sealed that solemn promise with a kiss.

CHAPTER 32

KATE

The next day Kate needed to go into the store for a bit. Wes came with her to help set up the room and keep her company. He went next door to visit Bridget. Kate didn't know why that made her smile, but it did. Her clari-tea seemed to have worked, she thought with a small chuckle. They went over to Smokey's for lunch. It was perfect, like no time had passed. She was glad he was here for a couple days, because she was not ready to be apart from him yet. She knew they needed to discuss what their future looked like.

She wanted this to work more than she ever had. The fear that had been stopping her from fully committing to a life with him was gone. She knew she was deeply in love with him, even if it had only been a few months. And she had known he loved her too, and probably had for a while now. He said as much when they were in Florida.

So, later that night when they were snuggled up on her couch eating pizza watching the Hobbit movie, which was not as good as the book, she decided they should talk about some of the things she was too scared to bring up before.

"So, I've been thinking," she said, sitting up and looking at him. "We are doing this right. In it for the long haul and all that, right?"

"One hundred percent. You have me until I'm old and wrinkly," he said with the quintessential Wes cocky grin.

"But what does that look like now? You live an hour away. And as much as I love you, I kind of want to stay here and run the bookstore."

"I want that too; I think we can work it out. I've been thinking about it," he said, pausing the movie.

"You have?" she asked.

"Don't sound so surprised. I think about our future all the time. What if we did a split the time thing? Off season, I live here in Mystic Falls with you. I can commute an hour for the training I need to do then since it's not every day. During the season, you stay in Glendale when I'm in town and you can commute then. When I'm on road trips, you can stay here in Mystic Falls. It's not perfect but I think it's a start."

She thought about it. That could work. The drive to Glendale wasn't terrible. People from Mystic Falls made that drive all the time because it was the closest city. It was a pretty good compromise.

"I think that'll work. I like that we'll be in Mystic Falls some of the time. It's a great place to live," she said.

"I agree," he said as he raised her hand and kissed it. "I've always had a good time here. All three of those do have a cute redhead involved, but I like it here, nonetheless."

"I think you would like Sam. I've been watching your games with him."

"Yeah, and I hear you are a personal friend of Liam James," he said.

"Well, Wes, I am a pretty big deal," she said with a wide grin spread across her face.

He moved to tickle her, only to be reminded he was still only working with one hand.

"How much longer until that thing is off?" she asked.

"Three more long weeks," he groaned.

"Another thing I've been thinking about," she said. This one made her more nervous to talk about. Wes could sense that, and he kissed her hand, holding it tighter. "I feel a lot better after finally telling Jason off, but I know I still have a long way to go," she fiddled with the blanket they were snuggling under. He waited patiently holding her hand for her to continue, just like he always did. She took a deep breath. "I think I may need to go to therapy to work through some of the baggage I have from all of that."

"I think that's a great idea, Kate. I went to therapy when I moved to Glendale. I had a lot of stuff I needed to unpack from my time in Florida, and from some of the stuff that happened to me growing up. Therapy is good for everyone. I've actually been seeing my therapist again after everything that went down in Florida and everything that went down between us," he said.

"I'm sorry I made you go back into therapy," she said, feeling guilty that she'd hurt him.

"Hey, Kate," he said as he turned her face back to his. "I'm back in therapy for my own mental health. It has nothing to do with you. Playing Blake Kelly, being injured and out for the season, and everything that went down between us, I just needed someone to talk to. There is no shame in that."

"You're right. I'm still sorry though."

"And I'm sorry I threw a temper tantrum and scared you. I'll be more careful in the future."

They sat there in the silence of the moment, both facing each other in honesty and strengthening their relationship.

"It's okay, Wes. I overreacted."

"No, you didn't. I should never have yelled like that,

period. I'm very sorry you went through what that asshole put you through. I will do my best to be mindful of this in the future because you deserve a safe space, and I want to be that for you. I'll do my best to deal with my anger before it comes out in bursts like that, but I'm not perfect. I'll mess up from time to time, please just know I would never hurt you. If you need space, I'll gladly give it, but please just stay in it with me and don't walk out like that."

"I promise. I'll do my best to get the help I need to heal from all of this, but even when I need space, I'll take it in the next room, or maybe a night out with friends. Deal?"

"Deal," he said and then leaned over and kissed her.

"I love you, Wes. I really fucking do."

"Right back atcha, Red. I've loved you from the moment I saw you on the ice. When I saw you take off your helmet, I thought to myself, 'I'm going to marry that girl', and I still think that."

And at that they snuggled back in and turned the movie on, both just happy to be there in each other's arms.

EPILOGUE

One year later

Wes

It was hard to believe all that had gone down in the past year. Once Kate and Wes got back together, they were both in it. Wes had never been happier in his entire life. He had been able to rehab and train over the summer and hit the ice in the fall with Conner without missing a beat. The Magic dominated the ice that year, and Wes couldn't help but think it was partly because of his good luck charm that was in the stands for every home game.

He and Kate had settled into a nice rhythm. They split their time, and Wes loved the time he got to spend in Mystic Falls. It was a wonderful little town. He actually considered Mystic Falls to be his home, even though he still spent a great deal of time in Glendale. Kate was able to spend that time with him. She had hired Ashton at the bookstore, and since then, she's been able to focus more on the internet store and social media presence, which she did in the office they had set up for her in the condo's guest room.

And while Wes was still in his own hockey season, he was enjoying a rare day off in Mystic Falls, taking in a hockey game he wasn't playing in. He was sitting in the stands with Gus and Nancy McPhee who were both beyond thrilled to be cheering on Kate.

In the fall, Kate had taken the leap and joined the recreation team in Mystic Falls. Wes loved watching her on ice. The fire inside of her still drew him in. She was a quick goalie and moved across the ice fast, blocking pucks. This was only the second game he had been able to catch, and it was a damn shame, he wished he was able to see all of them.

When the game was over, the teams went back to change.

"Are you guys still coming over for dinner tonight?" Nancy asked.

"That's the plan," he said.

"Good, I have a roast in the crockpot."

"That sounds delicious."

The three of them visited until Kate came out and joined them.

"I still love seeing you out there on the ice, Katie," said Gus pulling her into a hug. "You played great out there."

"Thanks, dad."

"I'll see you later this evening, right?" Nancy asked.

"We'll be over later," Kate agreed.

Once they were alone, Wes pulled her into a deep hug. "I have to say Red, watching you play is still one of my favorite things. I only wish I got to see it more."

Later that night, they were home cuddling on Kate's couch. They'd had a lovely dinner with her parents. Wes had been accepted into the McPhee family seamlessly, but that's just how the McPhee's worked. They were warm and welcoming. Wes loved it. He had taken Kate to Detroit to meet his mom over the summer. It was a nice visit.

But tonight, he had some other plans. The past year had been amazing, and he was anxious to make this permanent. They had talked about getting married before, and he wasn't going to push because he knew Kate had a lot of healing to do when they had gotten back together last year. She had been doing it though. She had been in therapy since then, and she was in this, and she had been since. Of course, there were hard times, but she had stayed in it, and he had given her the space she needed. But those moments were few and far between, mostly they were just happy.

And much to Wes's surprise, Kate brought up the idea of getting married. He knew he had wanted to marry her from the moment he saw her on the ice over a year ago, he never wavered on that. He just had to wait until she was ready too.

So, after she'd brought it up, he enlisted the help of her friend Frankie, who had become a fixture in their lives as well, to help pick out a ring. He knew she would like it, and he knew she would say yes, but he still found himself nervous. He was calm and cool on the ice, and they were a favorite for the cup this year, but asking his girlfriend, who he had already talked about wedding stuff with, to marry him had his heart racing.

They settled into her couch to watch Lord of the Rings together and his heart smiled, remembering the first time they watched these movies together. He was sure even then this day would come, but it was finally here. The ring was in his pocket and the girl was in his arms.

He wiped his sweaty palms on his pants and dug deep for courage. Why was he so nervous? He knew she would say yes, and he knew he loved her more than anything in the world. Okay, it was time to get this over with.

"Kate," he said in a voice that was surprisingly shaky.

She turned to him with a small smile. "What's up?" she said her eyebrows pinched together as she took in his face.

"I love you," he said, but that's all that would come out.

"Oh, I love you too, baby," she said, and then turned back to the movie.

Okay, it was now or never. He took his arm from around her and she looked at him again with a quizzical expression. Then he reached into his pocket and dropped to his knee.

"Kate," he said, taking a breath. Her hands flew to her mouth, and she took a deep breath, her eyes wide with surprise.

She gasped, and just looked at him, tears starting to gather in her eyes.

"I've known I wanted to marry you from the moment I saw you on the ice. I have been sure of that every day since, and I will be sure of it every day for the rest of our lives. Please marry me."

"Yes!" she yelled and threw her arms around his neck. They both tumbled to the floor, and he couldn't help but laugh. But then her lips found his and he was no longer laughing. He pulled back and slid the ring onto her finger.

"Oh Wes, it's beautiful!" She looked at the ring on her hand. "I can't wait to marry you!"

"Right back atcha, Red," he said, and then he kissed her. He kissed her and she kissed him right back. He would never get tired of the fire from this woman in his arms, and now he had her for life. And even that didn't seem like quite enough time to love this woman.

IF YOU OR anyone you know needs help please call the National Domestic Abuse Hotline at 800-799-7233 or visit https://www.thehotline.org/

RECLAIMING KATE PLAYLIST

Spotify playlist

Where You Lead - Carol King
Me - Kelly Clarkson
First Day of My Life - Bright Eyes
The Best - Tina Turner
Everything has Changed - Taylor Swift, Ed Sheeran
Do You Believe in Magic? - The Lovin' Spoonful
Sky is the Limit - Mark Ambor
Nothing - Bruno Major
Little Things - One Direction
What Was I Made For? - Billie Eilish
If You Love Her - Forest Blakk, Meghan Trainor
In Love with Your Soul - The Collection
Lover - Taylor Swift
Love Like This - Ben Rector
Intrusive Thoughts - Natalie Jane
Love in the Dark - Adele
Before You Go - Lewis Capaldi
I Am Falling in Love - Isak Danielson

I Won't Give Up - Jason Mraz
Your Hand Is Safe in Mine - Blush
Abcdefu (angrier) - GAYLE
I'll Stand by You - Jake Wesley Rogers
You & Me - James TW
Grow as We Go - Ben Platt

ALSO BY MARY WARREN

Mystic Falls

A Highlander for Hannah

Spotlight on Poppy

Lexi Lets Go

Magic in the Mountains

Glendale Magic Hockey

Conner

Never Miss an update or special offer by subscribing to my newsletter!!

ABOUT THE AUTHOR

Mary Warren lives in Illinois with her family. When she's not writing stories of fat women, she's reading them and advocating for better fat representation. Mary founded Fat Girls in Fiction, pointing out positive fat representation for women, femmes, and non-binary people in books. This project became a community and is something she is immensely proud of and happy to be working on.